Winner of the Historical Association Young Quills Award
for Historical Fiction 2017

This historical tale is steeped in intrigue, mystery and danger.
BOOKTRUST

*. . . a wonderfully explosive adventure . . . I loved reading about
(and rooting for) Tom, though I have to admit developing
a rival soft spot for his mouse.*
JULIA GOLDING

*It's a lively, entertaining and exciting read and
will be of great interest to all children . . .*
BERLIE DOHERTY

The writing is lively and the pace never flags.
HISTORICAL NOVEL SOCIETY

The action is non-stop and exciting . . .
THE SCHOOL LIBRARIAN

PRAISE FOR *THE BURIED CROWN*

. . . a stunning historical story, embroiled in magic, myth and legend.
THE PHOENIX

*This fast-paced adventure zips along, with chapters
that often end on exciting cliffhangers.*
BOOKTRUST

*History, runes, ravens, and lost treasures abound as this
skilfully woven tale of reality and fiction ultimately
delivers a very satisfying conclusion.*
HISTORICAL NOVEL SOCIETY

Definitely pick it up.
TEACH SECONDARY

A MESSAGE FROM CHICKEN HOUSE

Don't you love the forgotten parts of history, the bits you only see in a blink amongst the intrigues of kings and queens? Clever Ally Sherrick has found a girl court fool in a famous historical portrait and imagined her tale. The story is set in a time when people with learning difficulties were treated with varying degrees of respect and disdain, but Ally shows how wisdom, music and beauty thrive in this girl's heart. Her journey is wrapped up in the real threats to the throne and the crown – can Cat's direct take on life, her love for her sister and her brilliant way with music save the day?

BARRY CUNNINGHAM
Publisher
Chicken House

THE QUEEN'S FOOL

Chicken House

2 Palmer Street, Frome, Somerset BA11 1DS
www.chickenhousebooks.com

ALLY SHERRICK

Text © Ally Sherrick 2021
Illustration © Georgie McAusland 2021

First published in Great Britain in 2021
Chicken House
2 Palmer Street
Frome, Somerset BA11 1DS
United Kingdom
www.chickenhousebooks.com

"may my heart always be open to little". Copyright 1938, © 1966, 1991
by the Trustees for the E. E. Cummings Trust, from COMPLETE POEMS: 1904-1962
by E. E. Cummings, edited by George J. Firmage.
Used by permission of Liveright Publishing Corporation.

Cover design and interior design by Helen Crawford-White
Typeset by Dorchester Typesetting Group Ltd
Printed and bound in Great Britain by CPI Group (UK) Ltd, Croydon, CR0 4YY

The paper used in this Chicken House book is made
from wood grown in sustainable forests.

1 3 5 7 9 10 8 6 4 2

British Library Cataloguing in Publication data available.

ISBN 978-1-912626-15-1
eISBN 978-1-913322-25-0

In loving memory of my lovely brother-in-law, Paul Clark,
and for Elisabeth, Jo, and sisters everywhere.

'may my heart always be open to little
birds who are the secrets of living'
E. E. Cummings

Also by Ally Sherrick

Black Powder
The Buried Crown

PROLOGUE

I sit tall in my saddle and peer into the trees, through the tangle of brambles and moss-covered branches.

'*Papa*? Are you there?'

The only reply is a rustle of dead leaves and the harsh cries of the rooks circling high above. Reluctantly, I lift the reins and urge Jongleur forwards, into the shadow-filled depths beyond.

He can't have gone far . . . He was only a little way in front. I spy a sudden movement in the shadows ahead. A hooded man is crouched behind the trunk of a fallen tree, his frozen breath hanging in white clouds above his head. He's partly hidden by a thorn bush, but I can see the bow and quiverful of arrows strapped to his back. A poacher? It's hard to tell . . .

Using the bush for cover, I slide down from the saddle and creep closer, pulling my cloak tight about me as I go.

The man's on his feet now and nocking an arrow in his bow. He swivels sideways, raises the bow and takes aim into a small, frost-covered clearing beyond the trees. I peer past him searching for the target, then start. It's not a boar or a deer his arrow is trained on – it's a man.

But he hasn't spotted the danger yet – he's too

busy tying the reins of his horse to a tree. My chest tightens. I dart my eyes back to the bowman. His bowstring's pulled taut – he's preparing to shoot. I have to stop him. I go to shout a warning, but the word sticks like a burr in my throat. And then—

Then it's too late.

I watch in horror as the man in the clearing slumps sideways and falls to the ground with a strangled cry. Panicked, his horse rears up, breaks free and gallops off into the trees.

The bowman slings his bow over his shoulder, but as he goes to step forwards, Jongleur snorts out a sudden breath behind me. The bowman starts and turns his head to listen. I drop to the ground. He hesitates, then mutters something under his breath and crunches off in the direction of the clearing. His footsteps jerk to a halt. There's a heart-stopping silence before they start up again and hurry away into the distance.

I wait for as long as I can bear, then slip out from my hiding place and race towards the clearing, stomach gripped with a growing sense of dread.

I'm halfway to where the man's lying when I spot his horse trotting back towards me from out of the trees. My heart shrinks up inside me. *No! Please!* I dash forwards, but I know already who it will be.

• CHAPTER 1 •

England, May 1520

Cat

We are busy in the herb garden singing and getting eggs from the chooks when the horses come. You don't hear them, Meg. But I do. They start a long way off – *pit-pat*, *pit-pat*, like the rain when it falls on the Great Church windows.

I stop the song and strain my ears.

'What is it, Catty? Did you hear something?' You come and stand with me and put your fingers in through mine.

I frown my face then stand on my toe-tips and listen some more. The pitter-pattering turns into thrumming and drumming and then you hear it too.

'Horses?'

I nod my head. You shine me a smile. 'If only I had ears half as sharp as yours. It will be travellers passing on the road outside.' Your eyes go all far-off and dreamy. 'Don't you wish you could go with them?'

I shake my head. I like it here with you and Nonny Sweet-Bee, singing and spinning and looking after the chooks and the herbs.

But the travellers are not going past. They are coming here. Because now the noise has gone from thrumming and drumming to thundery-loud and there are men's voices coming from over the top of the wall shouting, 'This is the place!' and, 'Whoa!'

You look at me, your eyes all owly-wide. 'I wonder who it could be?'

I am going to tell you I don't know, but then the door in the wall creaks open and a nonny comes bustling in. 'Where's the Sparrow maid? The Holy Mother wants to see her – at once!'

I go all shivery and hold on to your skirts. I don't like Holy Mother Sharp-Tongue. She is always clacking and squawking at me and saying it is my fault for things when it is not.

You put down the egg basket and squeeze hold of my other hand. 'It is all right, Cat. I will go.' You pull me close and hug me tight, then you pick up your kirtle-skirts and follow off after the nonny.

My heart jumps and pangs. I don't want Holy Mother Sharp-Tongue to clack and squawk at you too.

'I want to come with you.' I stumble-run behind.

'No, Cat. Stay here. I'll be back soon, I promise.' You flutter me another smile and do the criss-cross sign on your heart.

I hang down my head and scuff the dirt with my shoes. The door creaks shut, and then you are gone.

But you don't come back soon, even though I wait and wait. I plop down in the dust and listen for your feet, but the only sounds are from the chooks rootling and scratching in their pen and the birds in the 'H is for Hollybush' chit-chattering fit-to-burst.

The sun beats on my bonnet hot-as-hot and my head is going all in a spin. I reach in my apron for my birdy-flute, but then there's a click-clack of shoes. The door opens and Nonny Sweet-Bee is coming through it with her face all pink and flustered.

I jump up and stumble-run to her. 'Where is Meggy?'

She closes the door shut and puts her hand over my shoulder. 'Your sister is speaking with Holy Mother Agnes.'

'Is she telling her about the horses?'

Her face frowns. 'The horses? No, not them, but about our visitors, yes.'

'You mean the men doing the shouting?'

She bites on her lip and nods, then she pulls me close. 'Come now, Cat. Let us do some more letter learning.' She takes me to sit on the bench by the wall and picks a stalk from the pile in her basket. She holds it out. 'What is this one?'

But I don't want to do my letters. I want to go and be with you, Meg.

'Cat?'

I stare at the blue flowers and puff a sigh. 'L is for Lavender.'

'Very good.' She gets a stick and traces an 'L' shape on the ground.

'And this?' She holds out a white-and-yellow flower.

'D is for Daisy.'

'Excellent. Now, you.' She gives me the stick and watches me wobble the shape of a 'D'. She pulls out a piece of 'T is for Thyme', but then a voice calls out. It is faint and faraway, but it sounds like you. I put the stick down and strain to hear.

Nonny Sweet-Bee scrunches her face. 'What is it, Catkin?'

I am going to tell her, but then there's a hee-hawing like the noise Stewer Boneyface's horse makes when he whips it and it isn't happy, and a man's voice, all hard and gratey, shouts a curse-word.

I poke my fingers in my ears to stop it, but then your voice swoops over the wall again, all scared and high:

'No, please. You're hurting me!'

'Meg!' I jump from the bench and fly myself out through the door. Big puffy dust-clouds prick at my face. I wipe them off and blink my eyes shut and open.

And then I see you.

You are on top of a big, brown horse with your eyes wide and scared and your face all paley-white. But you aren't on your own. There's a man too and he's holding you tightly-fast. The horse gallops past and you see me and call my name. But the man puts his hand on your mouth and makes the horse keep on going along the track that leads to the Outside World.

'Wait for me, Meggy!' I snatch my skirts and run after, but then my ears fill with a new sound.

Kerthump! Kerthump! Kerthump!

The ground shakes and bounces against my feet. I look round behind and see another man on the back of a thundery-black horse riding towards me.

I wave at him to stop, but he keeps on coming. Coming and coming and coming. Then the horse gives a high laughing noise and goes up on its back legs.

'Gah!' The man drags the horse down and turns it round and round. His black cloak swooshes and swirls out and more dust flies up so all I can see is the glittery sparkle thing on his hat. The dust goes back down to show his face and I give out a gasp. One eye flashes back green and gold, but the other is covered over with a black patch. There's a snaky red line poking out from it and joining up with the black beard on his chin.

'What are you doing, fool? Get away!' He jabs his horse-stick at me.

My ears are paining me from all the noise and my heart is bumping hard-as-hard, but I stay standing where I am. 'I am going to be with Meggy-Peg.'

'What?'

'Meggy-Peg. I have to go with her, she's my—'

The man's red lips curl into his beard and his eye goes pointy-sharp as a knife. 'Stop wasting my time or I'll give you a beating you won't forget!' He lifts the stick above his head.

'No!' Nonny Sweet-Bee rushes over with her arms in the air and her skirts flapping. 'Please, sir! She is only a child.' She grabs my hand and drags me back so the man can't reach.

'And an idiot one at that!' The man makes a growling noise and kicks the sides of the horse with his boots. It gives another high laugh then pounds off and away, its hooves all thundery-loud on the stones.

I pull on Nonny Sweet-Bee's sleeve. 'They are taking Meg. I want to go too.' I point to the gate-arch, but you have gone. Then the man on the thundery-black horse clatters through it and goes away too.

I try to run after again, but a hand holds me fast. 'Be still, girl!'

I turn round. Holy Mother Sharp-Tongue is there with two more nonnies, her face all frowning and angry.

'But I want to be with Meg.' I try to wriggle free, but the other two nonnies catch me and pull me tight.

Nonny Sweet-Bee squeezes her hands together. 'Please, Holy Mother. Cat has done nothing wrong. She—'

'Silence.' Holy Mother Sharp-Tongue spits out the word like a hissy-cross cat. 'Take the girl inside and lock her in the Infirmary cell. She may come out tomorrow when she has calmed down. As for you, Sister Beatrice.' She snaps her eyes on Nonny Sweet-Bee. 'I am sure you have plenty of weeding to do.'

Nonny Sweet-Bee bows her head. 'Yes, Holy Mother.' She gives me a soft, sad look then click-clacks away.

'But when is Meg coming back?'

Holy Mother Sharp-Tongue's eyes go black and pointy and her mouth pulls pinchy-tight. 'Understand this, Cat Sparrow. Your sister has gone for good. Now stop asking about her or it will go the worse for you.'

My heart bumps and pangs even harder. Whatever 'going the worse' means, it does not sound like a good thing. I wish Holy Mother Hildy was still here. She would try and help. But she is dead and gone and Holy Mother Sharp-Tongue is the one in charge now.

She clicks her fingers at the other two nonnies. They heave me up and drag me away but my heart is so full of aches and pains I don't do anything to stop them.

And now I am here all alone in the pitchy-black. I have tried to go to sleep, but my head is brimmy-full of sounds. The skitty-skat of rats' claws on the stony-cold floor. The snuffles and snores of the night-nonny and the other orphlings in the Infirmy beds outside. And over it all, the bumpety-thud of my own heart which is squeezing and panging fit-to-burst.

I pull the scratchy blanket over my head and grip my birdy-flute tight-as-tight. I want to blow it and sing you back, Meg, but Holy Mother Sharp-Tongue will get in a fury, so I speak your name instead.

Mouse-quiet at first.

'Meg. Meggy. Meggy-Peg.'

Then loud.

'Meg!'

And more loud.

'Meggy!'

And louder even than that.

'MEHHHG!'

The walls bang and bounce the sound all around. One of the orphlings outside screeches and wails and the night-nonny rackets her stick against the door and tells me the same thing as Holy Mother Sharp-Tongue. That you have gone and I will never see you again and the best thing I can do is to say my prayers-to-God and ask him to watch over you in your new life.

'What new life?' I say. She makes a puffing noise through the peephole and tells me in a warmer voice to 'hush-and-go-to-sleep.'

I want to tell her that I can't do that without you being here, but she shuffles off, so I hug my own arms round me instead. Then I curl myself small in the straw bed and sing our sleeping song, soft-as-soft.

'Hush! Hush! Little Catty Sparrow
Sleep your sleep until the morrow
Still and quiet, in my arms
I will keep you safe from harm.'

But it is no good. I can't make it work on my own. Those men need to bring you back so you can sing it with me. Then we can hug each other tight and make everything like it used to be.

· CHAPTER 2 ·

Cat

It is morning now and Blackbird is warbling his wake-up song from the 'H is for Hollybush' in the outside. The window-hole is too high to see, but his voice is there, loud and clear. It makes me all warm and happy because it is like the morning song we sing:

> *Blackbird trill*
> *Robin shrill*
> *Sparrow chirrup*
> *Throstle toot.*
> *Trill, shrill, chirrup, toot,*
> *Bang your drum and pipe your flute.*
> *Pipe your flute and bang your drum,*
> *Morning's come! Morning's come!*

And then I remember about the men on the horses and the warm feeling shrinks to a scrapey-cold stone in my middle. I have to try and call you home, Meg – before it is too late.

I pull my birdy-flute out from the blanket and get up. I rattle the pea inside and point it to the window. Then I cover my fingers on the holes and blow.

Peep. Peep. Peep-peep! Like the robin chicklings on their nest in Nonny Sweet-Bee's herb store.

The blackbird rustles and gives a *chook-chook*. He is scared, but I can't help it – I have to make you hear me. I try again. *PEEP. PEEP. PEEP-PEEP!*

Sriiiii! The blackbird clatters away.

Footsteps click-clack to the door. I take another breath. Quick – before they come.

PEEEEEEP!

The lock scrapes and the door creaks open. A voice shrills into my ears. 'What is all this? How dare you interrupt our holy offices with your caterwauling?' Holy Mother Sharp-Tongue comes swishing inside the room, her eyes all pointy-black and full of angry fire.

PEEP. PEEP-A-PEEP. PEEP. PEEP!

'Stop that now!' She snatches at the birdy-flute.

'No!' I pull away, but my feet get tangled in my skirts. I slip-tumble down and bang my head against the ground. 'Aarghhhh!'

'Don't be silly, girl.' Holy Mother Sharp-Tongue tries to drag me up, but I push her off.

'I hate you!' I hug my arms close and go to-and-fro, fro-and-to.

A warm dribble runs over my cheek and a drip of

red splashes down on the floor. Another drip falls beside it. My chest goes spiky-tight. 'No! No! No!' I scrunch my eyes shut and go to-and-fro again in time.

Holy Mother Sharp-Tongue shakes me and squawk-screeches like an angry crow.

More red drips from my head. My insides go all squirmy-sour and water comes in my mouth. I make a groan and drop into my skirts. Then my eyes shut and it all goes black-as-black.

Soft whisperings brush my ears. Someone is saying their prayers-to-God. I keep my eyes tight shut and listen.

Dear Lord,

I humbly beg you to watch over your daughter, Cat Sparrow, and keep her safe from harm. She has an honest and open heart as you who made her know. Some, like me, love her for it, but there are others who see it as a weakness, a chance to scold and taunt her, or worse . . .

I flutter my eyes open and sit up. It is Nonny Sweet-Bee. I put my arms round her and press my face in her gown. 'I love you too, Nonny Sweet-Bee!'

She strokes my hair, then she holds me back and looks at me with crinkled-up eyes. 'You should not have said those bad things to the Holy Mother, Cat.'

'But she hurt me. And she was going to take my birdy-flute.'

'She didn't mean to. It was an accident.' She squeezes my arm to tell me it's true.

But it isn't. Holy Mother Sharp-Tongue did mean to take it, I know she did. I puff a sigh and look round-and-about. We are in the orphling room in the Infirmy. All the beds are empty and there is only me in mine. I feel my head with my fingertips. A strip of cloth is wrapped over where The Blood came out. It hurts to touch. I press my lips together and pull my hand back down.

The door to the outside is open and filled full of bright sunbeams. I peer through it, but I can't see you yet. 'Did Meg hear me? Has she come back?'

Nonny Sweet-Bee puts my chin in her fingers. They smell of my best smell of all – 'R is for Rosemary' – but her eyes are all wet and sad. 'No, my Catkin. She is too far away.'

My heart shrinks small. 'But she will be back soon?'

Nonny Sweet-Bee drops her fingers. She makes a deep-breathing noise in her nose, then shakes her head. 'She has gone to work in a grand house for a very rich and important man.'

'The man on the thundery-black horse?'

Her eyes fill up with dark clouds, like the sky when it is going to rain. 'Not him, no. He is the man's servant.'

'Is the grand house near?'

'It is in a big town called London.'

'Can we go?'

She shakes her head again. 'I'm afraid not.'

'Afraid?'

'I mean, no.'

'But I want to see her.' I grip the blanket and go to-and-fro on the bed. 'I want to. I want to. I want—'

'Hush, Cat. Here, look – Meg left something for you.'

She reaches into the pouch-bag tied round her middle and pulls out a stick wound-about with tufty-white wool. It is Meg's special spindle – the one with the bead at the end, round and yellow as the sun.

Nonny Sweet-Bee hands it to me. 'She wanted you to have it.' Her teeth chew on her lip. 'She . . . she says you must look after it for her and be good. Will you promise to do that?'

I run my fingers over the wispy-soft thread and nod.

'Good.' She puffs another breath. 'Now it nears the hour of noon, and I must join Holy Mother Agnes and the others in the church for prayers. But I will bring you some bread and cheese after.'

She gives me a sip of honey-water and hugs me close, then she turns and hurries through the door.

I lift the spindle and stroke the wool against my cheek. It is soft and warm and smells of sheep. I take the end of the thread and unwhirl it, then twist it back around the stick. It is not so neat now, but it doesn't matter. If I close my eyes tight shut, I can see you there spinning round with your arms stretched wide, smiling and smiling and singing out my name.

My heart goes all fluttery and I sing back. 'Meg. Meg. My Meggy-Peg!'

But when I open my eyes, you have gone again.

Nonny Sweet-Bee was right. You must be too far away to hear. But if I go to London it will be different.

So, that is what I will do.

· CHAPTER 3 ·

Cat

I scrunch my hair into my bonnet and wriggle my feet down in my shoes. I try to put my apron over my kirtle-skirts, but I can't do the ties and I pull it off again. My cloak has ties too, but the sun is still shining bright through the door so I leave it behind on my bed.

Your spindle must come though, Meg – I promised to Nonny Sweet-Bee to keep it safe for you. My birdy-flute too. I put them in the bag you sewed for my eleven years' birthday and poke my head through the strap.

The bell of the Great Church clangs to tell the nonnies to stop and hurry inside to do their wailing-and-groaning and say their prayers-to-God. The nonnies do a lot of wailing-and-groaning. Praising-Our-Lord, Holy Mother Sharp-Tongue says. If they sang at me like that, I would tell them to stop. It is sore on the ears and makes my heart feel achy-sad. Happy songs are best, like the ones the birds sing to wake up the morning.

I feel in the bag for my birdy-flute and your spindle, just to be sure, then I go out through the door. The yard is empty apart from a big black shadow where the Great Church tower is blocking out the sun. The bell is still clanging though. I put my fingers in my ears and hurry off. When I get to the herb-garden wall, I breathe in a breath and sniff in all the smells: the 'L is for Lavender', the 'R is for Rosemary', the dusty-flustery chooks. I am heavy in my chest about leaving, but I want to be with you again *so* much . . .

I puff a breath, then turn and walk fast-as-fast down the track that leads to the gate-arch.

The gate is shut, but there is no one keeping watch. I pull on the bolt. It stays shut. I use my other hand too. The bolt gives a rat-squeak and jumps loose. The bell has stopped clanging and the nonnies start off with their wailing-and-groaning. I look round-and-about, but there is still no one. I turn back to the gate and pull it open. My heart is bumping hard and fast. I peep into the Outside World. I am scared, but it is where London is so I have to go. I say a quick prayer-to-God and go through it.

A track runs off between two hedges. It is rocky hard with ruts. As I go along, my feet knock into the lumps and bumps and I fall down. My kirtle gets all dirty with mud and sticks, which Holy Mother Sharp-Tongue would not be pleased about.

The sun stings on my face and neck and my mouth goes dusty-dry. My stomach is grumbling too. I look round-and-about, but it is not time yet for the 'A is for Apples' and 'H is for Hazelnuts' and there is no sound of any water. Nonny Sweet-Bee said she would bring some bread and cheese. It might be there in the Infirmy now. But I have been walking and walking a long while and I must be nearly at London, so I will keep going on.

I pass more hedges and fields without seeing another person, but I don't feel so on my own now because the birds are all singing their evening songs: the pidgies *coo-cooing*, the throstle *chee-chee-ing* and the blackbird fluting fit-to-burst.

The sun is halfway to the ground when a banging noise starts up. There is screechy laughing too. I hurry round the bend then open my eyes wide-as-wide. Instead of fields, there is a barn and a row of small houses with straw on their tops, like the one Stewer Boneyface lives in. Smoke is coming out from the chimney of one, and two children – a boy and a girl – are playing outside the door with a ball. I wave with my arms and trip-stumble over.

They stand and stare with owly-wide eyes. Then the boy drops the ball and walks up closer. When he gets there, he stops and gapes with his mouth.

'What d'you want?'

'Have I come into London yet?'

His eyebrows pull high into his curly brown hair.

He gives a pig-snort and turns round to the girl. 'D'you hear that, sister? She thinks this is London.'

The girl pinches her mouth shut. She peers at me stony-hard like the man on the thundery-black horse did – but with two eyes, not one.

My insides turn all squeezy-tight but I make my mouth go in a smile. 'Hello. My name is Cat Sparrow and I am eleven winters old. What are you called?'

The girl's eyes shrink into slits. 'Keep back.' She swishes up a bunch of stones and skitters them at my legs and feet.

She is not being very friendly. I will have to say some more. 'Do you know my sister Meg? She was taken by a man on a thundery-black horse.'

The boy gives another pig-snort. 'You're wrong in the head, you are.' He rolls his eyes and flaps his tongue.

The girl gives a loud goose-honk. She swishes up more stones and throws them again, but higher. Some spike me on my head and shoulders. I cry out and go backwards.

The boy snatches off my bonnet and throws it in the air.

'No!' I jump and bump against him.

'Get off me, idiot!' He pushes me back at the girl.

She pushes me too, but only a bit because then there's a loud shout: 'Dick and Mary! What are you doing?'

I look round. A woman comes hustle-bustling out through the door. She grabs Dick-and-Mary by their necks and pulls them away. Maybe she will help instead.

I step forwards. 'Hello. I am Cat Sparrow. Do you know if Meg came here?'

The children snort and honk again. The woman turns round and stares. She shakes her head and makes a Holy-Cross sign on her chest like the nonnies do when they say their prayers-to-God, then she clicks with her tongue at Dick-and-Mary. 'Come in for your supper and leave the poor creature alone.' She drags them off into the inside and bangs the door.

My eyes go all blurry. I don't understand. Why didn't they want to be my friends? I put my arms round me and crouch down. My bag is there in my lap. I reach inside and stroke the soft wool round your spindle so I feel better. Then I stretch out and pick up my bonnet, but my hair is all in a tangle and I can't make it go on properly. I wipe my eyes with my skirts. Then I stand up and look round-and-about.

'Meg? Meggy?'

There is more laughing from inside the house and a window slams, but still you don't come. I drop down my head and puff a breath. This can't be London yet. I have to keep going. I walk away quickly in case Dick-and-Mary come out with their snorts and stones again.

When the houses stop there are trees. The wind rustles and shakes their leaves and black shadows creep over the track. It is dark and cold without the sun. I shiver and hug my arms tight. I want my cloak, but it is no use because I left it on the bed in the Infirmy.

Suddenly, there is a loud swooshing noise. An owl hoots across me into the trees. I cry out and curl up small.

My heart is bump-thudding so loud I don't hear the voices. Then the wind pushes them into my ears and I do. I stand up and listen some more. They are coming from a track leading off inside the woods. There is a fire crackling too, all warm and glowy, and a smell much better than gruel-water. Better even than the bit of roasted chook you took for us last Yuletide when Cook was too busy boxing another orphling's ears for not turning hard enough on the spit.

I stumble towards it, crick-cracking on sticks and getting snatched by thorns and twigs. I am nearly there, but then a black spider-thing swings out and digs into my head. I scream and try to get free, but it shrieks and screeches and holds on tightly-fast. I shriek back and trip on a tree and fall down in a pile of leaves.

'*Lâche-le*, Pépin!'

There's a clattering of sticks and the spider-thing

is ripped off me. It gives another shriek-screech and goes quiet.

I blink and stare up into the dark. A paley-white face is hanging there, its eyes all big and shining. The eyes look over me and get even bigger. '*Sainte Vierge!*'

A man's voice calls out from where the glowy light is. 'What is it, Frenchie-boy – you ain't made yourself useful at last and caught us a hog for our supper?' He lets out a hooting laugh. Others laugh with him.

The face stares some more then speaks breathy-quiet in words I don't understand.

'*Pas un cochon mais une fille.*'

· CHAPTER 4 ·

Jacques

At least, I think it's a girl, but not like any I've ever seen before. Her kirtle is stuck with twigs and leaves and her bonnet is on back to front, her hair springing out from beneath like a mass of uncarded wool. As for her face, it's hard to see properly in this light, but with those small, bright eyes and turned-up nose and that wide mouth and narrow pointed chin – she looks more fairy than human.

A sudden shiver runs through me. What if she is – a fairy, I mean? I know from the songs the minstrels sing at home how fairy-folk can turn a person to stone for the smallest slight. Why would it be any different here?

She scrambles up on her feet. I shiver again and take a step back. 'Please, I am sorry, I—'

'I'm Cat Sparrow. What is that big spider-thing doing by your ear?' Eyes wide and startled-looking, she points a finger to where Pépin sits chattering angrily on my left shoulder.

Spider? My throat tightens. What if she's worked her magic on him instead? I lick my lips and dart a quick look, but he's still the same monkey-shape he was before. I curse my foolishness. *Papa* wouldn't have let this scrap of a creature scare him. The familiar ache starts up in my chest again, but I do my best to push it back down. I can't think about him – not now.

Planting my hands on my hips, I throw back my shoulders and stand tall. 'He is a monkey, not a spider.'

'Mun-kee?' The girl says the word in her strange sing-song voice as though trying out the sound. The same way I did when *Maman* first taught me how to say it in English.

'Can I stroke it – the munkee?' She springs forwards suddenly, hand outstretched. Pépin gives a warning *chee-chee*.

'Pssht!' I pull him down to my chest and shield him with my cloak. 'I . . . I think it will be better if you leave him alone.'

The girl's mouth turns down. But rather than doing as I say, she snatches hold of Pépin's long grey tail instead. With a loud screech he scrabbles free and clambers on to my head, arching it well out of reach.

The girl gives a cry of fright and shies away, jamming her fingers into her ears.

I glance over at the camp, but Gobbo and the

others are too busy drinking and telling each other loud jokes to have heard. Lifting Pépin down again, I hold him close and make soft chirruping noises until he stops shivering and starts to relax. I frown at the girl. She stares back at us, pulling hard on her bonnet flaps and looking as if any moment she might burst into tears.

A twist of guilt curls up inside me. 'It is all right. He will not hurt you. He is frightened, that is all.' I stroke Pépin's head. He turns his bright amber eyes on her, then buries his face in the soft leather of my jerkin.

The girl blinks and rummages in the patched bag hanging down at her side. She tugs out a stick wrapped round with what looks like a tangle of woollen thread, presses it to her cheek and closes her eyes. It's a spindle – I can see that now. Perhaps she's a cottager's daughter who's strayed from home and got lost in the woods?

I'm about to ask when her eyes flutter back open. 'What is your name?'

I hesitate and take a quick breath before answering. 'Jacques. Jacques Bonhomme.'

The girl puts her head on one side. 'Jack-Bon?'

I can't help smiling. 'Almost. But Jack will do.'

She smiles back, showing two rows of small, gappy teeth. 'You sound funny. Do you live here, Jack-Bon?'

'No, I am staying here tonight in the camp with

my—' I frown. What should I tell her they are? I look back towards the glow of the fire. Gobbo is strutting about on his skinny legs, doing what he always does when he's had too much ale – boasting what a great actor he is and daring anyone to disagree. Meanwhile, the rest of them are nodding and draining their battered tankards, or sitting with their heads slumped on their chests pretending to be asleep.

I turn back to the girl and heave a sigh. 'With my friends.'

It's easier to call them that, though it's not true. The only one who has shown me any kindness since I joined them is the master – *Maître* Tarleton – but he must have gone off to pass water or else fetch something from one of the carts because there's no sign of him.

The girl peers in the direction of the campfire then tugs on my jerkin. 'Can I see them?'

I shake my head. 'It will be better if I speak to them first. They are not very—'

Before I can finish my sentence, she turns and sets off at an uneven trot through the trees.

'*Arrête!* I mean, stop!' Holding on tight to Pépin, I dash after her. She's so unsteady on her feet, I'm certain to catch her. But then, as I'm closing in, the toe of my boot catches on a log and launches me into the air. As I throw out my hands to break my fall, Pépin bounds free and scampers up a nearby tree.

I lie there for a moment, all the breath knocked out of me. As I haul myself to my feet, a chittering noise sounds above me. I look up to see Pépin perched on a tree branch just out of reach.

'*Reste là!*' I wag a finger at him, daring him to move, then throw a hurried look towards the camp. But I'm too late. The girl is already there, clutching at her grimy skirts and swaying from side to side, her mass of curly red-orange hair shining gold in the firelight. By the time I reach her, she's in full flow.

'So I went through the gate-arch into the Outside World and now I am going to London to find my sister, Meg. Nonny Sweet-Bee says the man on the thundery-black horse took her there.' She takes a breath, then wrinkles her nose and points at the cauldron of rabbit stew bubbling over the fire. 'That smells good. Can I have some?'

The men stare at her, their mouths hanging down wider than a row of open drawbridges. Gobbo is the first to act. He swipes a flaming stick from the fire and jabs it at her. 'Gah! Get away from here, hell-hob!'

The girl gives a small cry and stumbles backwards. As Gobbo advances, Bardolf and the others lurch drunkenly to their feet, cheering him on. A bitter taste floods my mouth. I can't let him do this. I push my way in between them and snatch hold of Gobbo's ale-stained sleeve. 'Leave her alone!'

'Get off me, you dirty Frenchie!' He shoves me back and swings the stick up, sending a shower of orange sparks into the cold night air.

'Stop calling me that!' I ball my fingers into fists and make to run at him.

A voice booms out halting me in my tracks. 'What mischief is afoot here?' A tall, bearded figure storms into the circle. It is the master, *Maître* Tarleton. His eyes flash as they light on Gobbo, stick raised and ready to strike. 'William Gobbo! I might have guessed.'

'What? I ain't done nothing. It's this hobgoblin-girl here, trying to cast spells on us and make off with our vittles.' Gobbo lowers the stick and jabs it at the girl again, then turns his mean, lizard-eyes on Bardolf's ale-flushed face. 'Ain't that right, Ben Bardolf?'

'Oh . . . Er . . . I s'pose so, aye.' Bardolf blinks and peers about him as if he's not sure what Gobbo is talking about.

I clench my jaw. 'But . . . but that is not true. She is not a "obgoblin", or whatever Gobbo called her.'

Gobbo puts his hands on his scrawny hips and puffs out his chest. '*Master* Gobbo to you, Frenchie-boy! And how would you know when you can't even say the word right?'

'Quiet, all of you!' *Maître* Tarleton fixes his gaze on me, his forehead scrunched in an angry-looking frown. 'Who is she then, boy?'

I shrug up my shoulders. 'I am not sure, *Maître* Tarleton. *Pardonnez-moi*, I mean, master.' I glance at the girl who is stood there wide-eyed and staring. 'She told me her name is Cat Sparrow. She—'

'Yes! Yes! I am Cat Sparrow, but you can call me Cat if you like.' The girl beams at *Maître* Tarleton and dips into a wobbly curtsey.

He arches an eyebrow. Gobbo gives a jeering laugh. Bardolf and one or two of the others join in.

I frown. She's making things worse. Why doesn't she keep quiet? I grab her hand and shake my head, but it's clear from the puzzled look on her face she hasn't understood. As she opens her mouth to speak again, I jump in.

'I think that perhaps she is lost, master.'

Gobbo snorts and spits out the mouthful of ale he's just taken. 'She's lost all right.' He circles a bony finger above his ear and makes a sound like a cock crowing.

The girl shakes her head. 'That is wrong. It is like this. *Cock-a-doodle! Cock-a-doodle!*'

Gobbo snarls at her. 'And how would *you* know what's right from what's wrong?'

'Because I look after the nonnies' chooks.'

There's more rough laughter. Instead of joining in, Gobbo glares at the girl and bangs the stick on the top of his boot. Anger flares up inside me. I want to tell him – all of them – exactly what I think of their bullying ways, but I need their protection, at least until we get to London. I bite down on my lip and dig my nails into my palms.

The girl makes a shivery noise and creeps closer to the fire. *Maître* Tarleton's look softens. He strokes his bushy brown beard and frowns. 'What are we to do with you eh, maid?'

Before anyone can answer, the girl reaches into her bag. She pulls out a small clay object, puts it to her ear and shakes it. There's a faint rattling sound. She nods her head as if satisfied, then presses it to her mouth and blows a single clear note.

'A magic whistle. She's using it to weave another spell. Quick, stop her!' Gobbo snatches the thing from her hand.

The girl's eyes fill with panic. 'My birdy-flute. Give it back!' She sways unsteadily towards him and tries to grab it back, but he swings it high above her head. Her face crumples. 'But I need it to call for Meg so she can hear me in London.'

Gobbo puts it to his scabby lips and blows a harsh, ear-piercing note, then calls out in a mock high voice. 'Meg! Oh, Meg! Can you hear me, Meg?' He cups his hand to his ear and flutters his eyes as if pretending to be a maid.

Bardolf explodes in a whinnying laugh, but the rest shift about uneasily and look down at the ground.

The girl's eyes light up. She turns and peers back into the trees. 'Meg? Are you here, Meg?'

My stomach lurches. I plant myself in front of Gobbo. 'Stop it, *grande brute*!'

He thrusts the glowing stick to my face. 'What did you call me?'

'Enough, man!' *Maître* Tarleton grabs the stick and throws it back on the fire. 'Give the poor maid back her whistle, and let the boy be.'

Gobbo scowls at me. He makes a big show of polishing the mouth of the flute on the seat of his grubby breeches then hands it back to the girl with a mock bow. She snatches it from him, cradling it against her chest and hiccupping softly.

Maître Tarleton gives a loud sigh and shakes his head. 'I don't know where she's come from, but she can't stay with us. Not unless she can earn her keep. And though it pains me to agree with *Master* Gobbo here' – he casts him a quick sideways look – 'I don't see how that's possible with nothing but tangled wool for brains.'

Maman never taught me that expression, but I understand its meaning well enough. I grip him by the arm. 'But, master—'

'Silence, boy! My mind is made up. The maid can stay with us tonight. But come the morning, we will give her into the local priest's care and be on our way without further delay. If we are to get a place at the court revels, we *must* make London tomorrow and Greenwich by eventide. Now make yourself useful and help us all to some coney stew.'

I keep a lookout for Pépin while we're eating, but he doesn't reappear. After we've finished, the *maître* and the others get up and make their way to the carts leaving me and the girl to sleep by the fire. I mound up some leaves and drape a blanket over them.

'Here, this is for you.' I look up, but the girl is peering back out into the trees again.

'What are you doing?'

'Waiting for Meg.'

My heart jolts. 'Listen.' I take hold of her hand. 'Gobbo, he did not mean it. Your sister . . . she . . . she is not coming.'

She twists round to face me. 'She isn't coming now?'

'No.'

'But tomorrow?' Her bottom lip is quivering.

I give a sigh. She can't have understood what the *maître* said earlier, but I don't have the heart to tell her now. 'Perhaps. Now you must lie down and get some sleep.' I pat the blanket.

She drops down on top of it and curls into a ball, hugging her bag tight against her. She murmurs her sister's name again and the person she calls Nonnysweetbee, then her eyelids flutter shut and she falls still.

I lay my own blanket across her and slide down beside her, doing my best to ignore the twigs spiking my legs through my woollen hose. I turn and stare at her sleeping face – the fine gold-coloured eyebrows and lashes, and the scattering of pale orange freckles on her nose and slightly flushed cheeks.

Maître Tarleton said she had wool for brains, but I don't think he's right about that. She might speak in a strange way and not know when it's best to keep quiet, but she's full of questions and her eyes are as bright as a bird's. Her mother – Nonnysweet-bee? – must be worried about her.

A picture of *Maman* flickers in front of me. Her blue, almond-shaped eyes; her long, chestnut-brown hair; the dimple in her left cheek when she smiles, which she did a lot once, but hardly ever does now. My throat tightens. I miss her. But I can't go home. Not until I've done what I came here to do. What I swore to my father on my life I would . . .

I reach inside my jerkin and fish out the small leather pouch which hangs from a cord around my neck. Taking a deep breath, I undo the strings and pull the piece of torn kerchief free. In spite of the dirt that's ground into it, it's still possible to make out part of the strange rope design embroidered into it in fine gold thread. I trace a finger over the loops and curls wishing for the hundredth time I'd been able to find the rest of it. Who does it belong to? Discover that and I will be a step closer to keeping my vow. As I stare down at it, the air around me darkens and I'm back there with *Papa*, riding . . . Riding from day into night.

A ripple of fear snakes along my spine. I grit my teeth. I can't let myself go there. I have to look to the future instead. Bundling the cloth up, I thrust it back inside the pouch.

A furry, grey shape comes pitter-pattering towards me from out of the trees.

Pépin! I knew he'd come back to me. With a mix of relief and gratitude, I lift him on to my lap and chuck him under his small, black chin. 'Are you hungry, *mon ami*?'

He chirrups and nips at my fingers. I reach for a piece of leftover bread. As I hand it to him, a sharp crack of twigs sounds behind us and a sweaty hand clamps over my mouth. Pépin leaps clear with a loud *chee-chee* and runs chattering beneath a nearby bush. Heart beating wildly, I claw at the hand trying desperately to break free, but it only grips tighter.

'Stop your squirming, Frenchie-boy!'

Gobbo! My heart beats faster still as he squats next to me and yanks me back by the hair.

'My old grandad was right. You Frenchies fight worse than girls.' He strokes a rough finger over my cheek. I shiver and turn my head away. 'What's wrong? Frog got your tongue?' Gobbo closes his hand round my throat and slides his face close to mine. My stomach heaves at the sour-ale stink of his breath. 'Now, listen.' His eyes narrow to two gleaming slits. 'If you cross me again, you and that gibbering monkey of yours will wish you'd never been born, understood?' He slips his hand down to the blade at his belt.

I swallow hard and give a quick nod.

'Good. And be sure to keep that idiot-friend of yours out of my way too.' He throws the girl a sneering look, then spits into the fire's dying embers and stomps back off towards the carts.

I shudder as I watch him go. He's my mortal enemy, I know it now for sure. We should get away from him, Pépin and I, but with so many thieves and cut-throats on the road, it's too dangerous to travel alone. Besides – I glance over at the girl again – it would mean leaving her to his mercy and I couldn't do that; it wouldn't be right.

· CHAPTER 5 ·

Cat

A throstle whistles me sharp awake. I blink my eyes open and look round-and-about. Instead of a wood roof and stone walls, there are creaking branches and rustling leaves. Another sound screeches close by. I press my bonnet flaps in my ears and jump up quick-as-quick. It is the munkee-spider again. He is bouncing on a log by the burnt-up fire and chattering at me with his teeth. My chest squeezes tight because he scared me, but now I have scared him too.

'Here, munkee.' I reach out my finger and wiggle it. He stares at me with his honey-glow eyes, then he slinks over and sniffs it. I do my best to go still-as-stone and wait. The munkee turns his head on one side, then he lifts his black furry fingers and curls them round my pink one.

Footsteps crunch on the leaves behind. It is my new friend, Jack-Bon, huffing and puffing a bucket with both hands. He splashes the bucket down with a groan and frowns his face at us.

'What are you doing?'

'Saying hello to the munkee-spider.'

'His name is Pépin.'

I sound the word in my head, then try saying it out loud. 'Pippo.'

Pippo looks at me and gives a birdy-chirp. I let out a giggle. Jack-Bon rolls his eyes, but he flickers me a smile too. 'He belonged to my *Papa*.'

Jack-Bon opens his mouth to say more, but then other feet come crunching behind.

'Look sharp, boy! This is no time to be idling.' It is the tall man with the booming-big voice and the even bigger belly – the one called Master Tarley.

Jack-Bon's face goes flushy-pink – like yours, Meg, when you are cross. 'I am not idling, master. I am bringing the water for Hotspur.'

Master Tarley makes a growling noise. 'Well, be quick about it. You heard what I said last night – we need to make good progress today, and we've got a stop to make I didn't bargain for.' His eyes shrink small and stare at me the same as Holy Mother Sharp-Tongue's when I have done a wrong thing.

'Yes, master.' Jack-Bon heaves the bucket and sploshes it forwards. Pippo makes a *cheep-cheep* sound and spring-leaps on his shoulder.

I feel inside my bag for your spindle and my birdy-flute. Still there! I pull my head through the strap and run after Jack-Bon and Pippo so I can't hear all the rest of Master Tarley's huffs and mutters.

There are two snorting horses with carts in the trees. Each cart has a cloth roof pulled over its top. Clatters and bangs are coming from inside one and a voice shouts out all scratchy-sharp, 'Watch out, Bardolf, you clodpoll. You nearly had my eye out!'

It sounds like the one with the pinchy face and darty-quick eyes called Gobble. I don't like him and you wouldn't too, Meggy-Peg. He doesn't want to be my friend – or Jack-Bon's. If the one called Hosper is in there, I don't want to go near.

But Jack-Bon walks past that cart and goes to the other one instead. There are rufflings and snufflings coming from inside, and a bad smell too. It is like the dead hedgyhog Nonny Sweet-Bee and me found in the wood-pile by the chooks' house, but worse. I push my nose in my arm and press my mouth tight shut.

Jack-Bon hangs down his head and sighs a breath. *'Le pauvre.'*

'What does *lepoor* mean?'

'It means that he does not deserve to live like this. In this . . . this prison.' He slops down the bucket and drags a bowl from beside the cartwheel. 'Down, Pépin.' He pulls the munkee off his shoulder and puts him on the ground.

I blink and peep into the dingy-dark. There is a giant basket inside. But instead of sticks of 'W is for

Willow', it has got iron ones, thick as Master Tarley's fingers. When the light comes back in my eyes, I see a hairy brown mound in the back.

'Is that him?'

'Yes,' says Jack-Bon in a sad-soft voice. 'Here, Hotspur, I have brought you some water.' He pushes the bowl through a space between the iron sticks.

The hairy mound lifts his head and sniff-snuffles the air. He gives a low grumble, then gets on his shaggy legs and shuffles to the better light with a rusty chain chinking behind.

I hold my breath tight in my mouth. 'I have never seen a Hosper before.'

Jack-Bon gives me a sharp look, but then his face changes back to being sad. 'Hotspur is his name. He is *un ours* . . .'

'He doesn't look like one.'

'What?'

'A horse.'

Jack-Bon frowns. 'Not a horse, *un ours* – a bear.'

'A bear?'

Jack-Bon nods. We both stand still and watch Hosper's black nose dip in the water and slurp a drink. There are pink baldy patches on his legs and chest. One of his eyes is milky-white and the other one isn't there at all. A thought flutters in about the man on the thundery-black horse. He had one eye too, but his was green and glittery-sharp. I give a shiver and look back at Hosper.

41

'He looks sad.'

Jack-Bon puffs a breath. 'The men who owned him before *Maître* Tarleton used to make him fight with fierce dogs. They put his eyes out so it was more difficult for him to win. They pulled out his claws and most of his teeth too.' He shakes his head and wipes his sleeve over his eyes.

I come closer to the iron basket and wiggle my hand inside. 'Poor Hosper.' The bear pushes his head up close to my fingers. He sniffs at it, then he closes his milky-white eye and makes soft growl-ings inside his throat.

'Why is he here?'

'Because *Maître* Tarleton and the others use him to make people laugh when they perform their plays.'

'People play with him?'

Jack-Bon sighs another breath and shakes his head again. 'They make fun of him and call him names. It is not the same.'

My stomach flip-flops inside me. 'Like Dick-and-Mary yesterday?'

'Who?'

'Dick-and-Mary. They took my bonnet and said the same word some of the orphlings say when the nonnies aren't looking. *Iddy-at.* The man on the thundery-black horse who took Meg said it too.'

Jack-Bon's eyebrows push together. 'Why did he take her?'

'Nonny Sweet-Bee says it was to work in a grand-house-in-London. But I am going to find her and take her back to be with me and the nonnies.'

'And who are the nonnies?'

'The ladies who look after us and all the other orphlings. They spend their time saying prayers-to-God. Like this.' I press my fingers together and make a wailing-and-groaning noise the same as the nonnies do.

Jack-Bon's eyes flicker wider. 'So, you live with the holy sisters – the nuns?'

'The nonnies, yes. I don't like Holy Mother Sharp-Tongue, but most of the others are kind, and Nonny Sweet-Bee is best of all. She is teaching me my letters. "A is for Apple", "B is for Birch", "C is for—"'

'What are you doing, boy?' Master Tarley's voice booms at us from on top of the other cart. 'This is no time for teaching the maid her letters! Gobbo, you take the cart with the beast. Everyone else, follow behind.'

Gobble jumps off the back of the other cart and marches round to Master Tarley. He thumps his hands on his hips and stares at him with his face all red and full of the furies. 'Why's it always me that gets to pull that stinking great pile of—?'

But I don't find out what the pile is made of because then Master Tarley shouts down at him. 'Because *I* am the master of this company, and if you don't like it, you know what you can do!' He flips his whip on the horse's back.

The cart rumbles off with the rest of the other men walking behind. Gobble stands and stares after with flaring eyes.

'Who does he think he is? The King of England?' He speaks a string of curse-words I don't want to hear, then he turns and walks back to our cart. He climbs on the seat and takes his stick and looks back round at me. His face pulls even tighter. 'What're *you* staring at, half-wit?'

I don't know what "halfwit" means, but it does not sound good. I open my mouth to ask, but Jack-Bon shakes my arm and says in a loud hissy whisper, 'No. Do not cross him. He is dangerous.' He splashes more water in Hosper's bowl and loads the bucket in the cart.

'Gah!' Gobble smacks the horse with his stick. The cart groans forwards and makes Hosper's head bang against the iron sticks. He gives a hurt-sounding growl.

Jack-Bon furrows his face. 'It is all right, *cher ami*.' He reaches in and pats his fur, then he calls for Pippo to jump on his shoulder.

I tip my head to one side. I like him. He is kind. Pippo is too. They will help me, I am sure. I pull on Jack-Bon's sleeve. 'Are we going to London to find Meg now?'

His eyes flit away into the trees. He blows a long

sigh, then he looks back and holds out his hand.

He hasn't said, but it must mean yes. I shine him my biggest smile, then I push my fingers inside his and follow with him and Pippo after the cart.

· CHAPTER 6 ·

Cat

We climb out from the woods and on to the road with the cartwheels rattling and creaking up the dust. The sun shines down from the sky, hotter-than-hot and my throat is parchy-dry. Jack-Bon gives me some water from the bucket, but I'm hungry too. Master Tarley said there was no time for eating, but at the nonnies' we get up with the light, and there is always time for breakfast. I will have it when we have found you, Meg – when everything is all right again.

A swoosh of swallows swoops over our heads. They are the birds you like the most. I call out to Jack-Bon and point. He looks after and whispers a mouse-quiet word, all to himself.

'*Une hirondelle.*'

'What does that mean?'

'It is the name for a swallow in my language. *Papa* – my father – he called me it too.' He keeps on looking after, even though the swallows have all gone.

'Hi-ron-delle?'

Jack-Bon turns and flickers me a smile. 'Yes.'

'Your *papa*, is he in London?'

'No.' Jack-Bon's smile shrinks away. 'He . . . he is in France – where I used to live.' He coughs and stares at the ground.

'Our pa is dead and gone,' I say. 'And our ma. That is why we live with the nonnies and the other orphlings, Meg and me. She likes swallows, but I like blackbirds best of all. Shall I play you one?' He doesn't say but I pull out my birdy-flute anyway. I rattle the pea inside and blow Blackbird's wake-up call.

Jack-Bon's smile comes back a bit. 'It is pretty. The flute too. Where did you get it?'

I stroke my finger over the holes. 'Nonny Sweet-Bee. She said it was my ma's.' I lick my tongue over my lips and whistle Robin's evening song.

Jack-Bon's smile grows bigger and sparkles into his eyes. 'What else can you play?'

I do the *chip-chip* of Wren, but then Master Tarley calls back from the other cart that we are coming to a village and are going to stop at the church. We trundle past some houses with straw on their tops. My stomach flitter-flutters like a chickling's wings. I don't want to see Dick-and-Mary again. I hide my birdy-flute back in my bag and hold on to my spindle tightly-fast.

A tower appears in front, stony-grey against the

sky. A crow croaks and flaps off the top. Master Tarley thuds down from his cart and goes stomping to the wooden door. He creaks it open and goes into the inside.

When he is gone, Gobble and the others go and sit by the wall and throw stones in the dust and shout things like, 'I win!' and, 'Throw again!' and, 'Cheat!'

I want to go and look, but Jack-Bon tells me to keep safe with him behind Hosper's cart. We wait and wait. I lie down next to Pippo and shut my eyes. I am nearly falling asleep, but then the door creaks open and Master Tarley comes out again. Gobble and the others stop throwing and shouting and get up on their feet.

'Well?' says Gobble.

Master Tarley makes a grunting noise. 'The priest didn't want her. We'll have to try somewhere else.'

Gobble gives a pig-snort. 'What if the same thing happens again? You said it yourself, we ain't got time for this. I say let's leave her anyway, eh, lads?' He turns his darty eyes on the others.

'Yes!' shouts Badulf.

The others nod their heads and make grumbling sounds.

'No, master. You cannot!' Jack-Bon pushes through them, his voice all pitchy-high.

'What did I tell you, Frenchie?' Gobble snatch-grabs him round the middle and presses his fist on Jack-Bon's chin.

Jack-Bon's face goes paley-white.

I push through them too. 'Stop. You are hurting him!'

'Shut yer racket!' Gobble drops hold of Jack-Bon and shakes his fist at me instead.

Master Tarley shouts out at Gobble and blocks the way with his big belly, but I am too busy pulling on my bonnet flaps and going to-and-fro, fro-and-to to hear the rest.

And then our safe-together song comes inside my head. It is the same one you sang after I dropped all the eggs and Holy Mother Sharp-Tongue – who wasn't in charge of things then – shouted and gave me a stick-whipping.

I start to sing it, quiet at first, then louder and louder to block out all the squawks and cries.

'The rain doth rain
The wind doth blow
The ice doth freeze
The snow doth snow
But when I think of you, sweet bird
The sun shines bright and I'm not alone.'

I sing it over and over and then, all the squawk-ing stops still and the only sound is the cheep-tweet of the birdies in the hedge and the shush-shush of wind dancing through the tops of the trees.

I blink and look round-and-about. Gobble has dropped his hands down and is gaping with his mouth. Master Tarley and the others too.

'Heaven's angels!' Master Tarley lifts his hat and swipes at his forehead. 'And do you know any other tunes, maid?'

I blink my eyes and let go of my bonnet flaps. 'Lots. Meggy taught me.'

Jack-Bon hurries to stand side-by-side with me. 'She can make the song of the birds with her flute too. Show him.' He elbow-pokes me and gives a nod.

I pull the birdy-flute from my bag. Jack-Bon slides me a smile and does another nod. I breathe in a breath and play the wake-up calls of Blackbird and Robin and the flying call of Lark.

After I have finished, Master Tarley whistles through his lips. 'She may have her uses after all. How would you like to play before the King, maid?'

The nonnies talk about The King. Nonny Sweet-Bee told me he is in charge of everyone in the whole wide land.

I look up at Master Tarley. 'Won't he be too busy with his work to play?'

Gobble makes another snorting noise, but Jack-Bon squeezes his hand over mine.

'She would, master, I know it!'

'Very well,' Master Tarley says. 'Then she can

come with us. But it will be down to you to look after her, boy. Is that clear?' He turns round to the others. 'There's money in this, lads. You mark my words. Now back to the carts. We cannot afford to lose any more of the day.'

Jack-Bon pulls me with him to Hosper's cart. He helps me climb on the back next to Pippo, but then Gobble slams over and whispers something in his ear, soft-as-soft. He thinks I can't hear, but I can.

'I warned you, Frenchie, and now I'm going to make you pay.' He pushes Jack-Bon so he nearly falls down, then he slams back to the front. When he's on top of the cart-seat again, he cracks his stick on the horse's back. It shrieks out a whinny and makes the wheels rattle forwards.

Jack-Bon hurries after and climbs inside, then makes a shivery noise.

I look at him and frown. 'Why doesn't Gobble want to be friends with us?'

'Because we are smaller than him and he thinks weaker too.'

'Are we?'

His eyes flicker and go all far away, then a spark comes in them. He puffs a breath and grips his fingers tight-as-tight. 'Only if we let him think so.'

· CHAPTER 7 ·

Jacques

As the cart lurches off down the road, the girl – Cat – fidgets about for a while, turning round to look back at Hotspur, tickling Pépin, or playing stray notes on her flute. But then, lulled by the swaying of the cart, her eyelids close and she slumps against me. I slide the flute from between her fingers and slip it into her bag then lay her down gently on my cloak.

The holy sisters must have missed her by now. Shielding my eyes against the sun, I squint back up the track, half hoping a nunnery servant will ride into view and claim her – but it remains empty.

I look down at her again. How old is she? It's hard to tell, but from the way she speaks about her sister, Meg, the other girl sounds older. My chest tightens at the thought of what it must have felt like to be parted from her so cruelly. Digging my travelling sack from its hiding place beneath a pile of straw, I reach inside and pull out my bow and quiver. The smooth touch of the bow's wood and the jewel-bright colours of the arrow feathers bring me comfort. After Pépin, they are my most precious possessions.

Papa brought them back with him from court last autumn as a fourteenth birthday gift. They were crafted by King François's own bow-maker. The bow is beautiful – made of the finest ash-wood, pale and sleek with a strong, taut string and a grip that fits my fingers perfectly. But more special still is the silver plaque fixed to the stave. I trace my fingertip over the small image engraved on to it – a swallow perched on a heart. An exact copy of the one on our family crest.

'It is one of a kind, Hirondelle,' *Papa* had said when he gave it me. 'Just like you,' and the look in his eyes had filled me full of proud fire.

But now that fire has been put out and there is nothing but cold ash in its place.

A sudden jolt of the cart's wheels bounces me out of my thoughts. Next to me, Cat gives a small groan, then snuggles back down into sleep.

I glance to where Pépin is sitting at the back of the cart, reaching through the cage and combing his fingers through the sleeping bear's fur. It's thanks to him, and the bow skills *Papa* taught me, that *Maître* Tarleton allowed me to join his troupe. We're the 'crowd-teaser' as he calls it – 'The Bow-Boy and his Imp'. We lure people in for the main perform-ance – a play about Noah and the Flood. Our act is simple – a game Pépin and I learnt to play soon after the King gifted him to *Papa* and he came to live with us at Château de Beauregard. He pretends to steal a walnut hidden under my cap then runs up the nearest tree and balances it on a branch. I take aim with my bow and shoot the nut down, then Pépin fetches it back in return for two nuts as a reward.

As I watch him pop the fleas he's picked from Hotspur's back into his small pink mouth, my belly grumbles. I'm hungry too, but I doubt *Maître* Tarleton will make another stop before Greenwich – though I'll be parting company with them before then.

To have the chance to perform in front of the King and Queen of England is a great honour. But it's of no interest to me. London is where I am bound, though how I'll ever find the one I am hunting with only a piece of torn cloth to aid me, I confess I haven't yet worked out. At least I'll be leaving that spiteful bully, Gobbo, and his friends behind. But what about Cat? My stomach knots as I look down at her again, nestled there like a small bird, fast asleep in my cloak.

I shake my head. I'll worry about it later, after we've got to London. I stroke my fingers along the bow stave one last time, then slide it and the quiver back inside the sack. Tying Pépin to the cage with a length of thin rope, I sink down in the straw at Cat's feet and close my eyes. With the rocking of the cart, it doesn't take long before I'm drifting into sleep too.

A rough hand shakes me awake.

'Master Tarleton said to give you somethin' to eat.'

It's Bardolf. He thrusts a slab of greasy-looking pie at me. 'And feed these bones to Old Growler there.' He flings a grubby sack down beside me and jerks his head at Hotspur's cage.

I sit up, rubbing the sleep from my eyes.

Cat wriggles alongside me, blinking. 'Are we in London yet?'

Bardolf raises a straggly eyebrow. 'London's been and gone. We'll be at King Henery's grand palace soon.'

My heart drops like a stone. Stupid! How could I let myself sleep for so long?

I push up on to my knees and look back along the rut-filled road. 'How far is it?'

'Master Tarleton says we'll be there by nightfall, but I'm not so sure.' He frowns and casts a glance at the orange glow in the sky behind him.

'No. I mean, how far is London?'

Bardolf scratches his pimply chin. 'Seven miles back at least. Maybe more. Why?' His eyes narrow suddenly.

'I . . . er . . . nothing.' I busy myself with opening

the sack and pushing the greasy bones through the bars of Hotspur's cage.

Bardolf mutters what sounds like, 'Daft Frenchie' under his breath, then turns and plods off up to the front of the cart.

Cat tugs at my sleeve. 'Are we going to find Meg?'

I heave a breath. 'Not now. In the morning maybe.' As I speak the words, I feel another squeeze of guilt. I know already that when I set off back to London tomorrow, I'll have no choice but to leave her behind.

I break off a chunk of pie for her. She snatches it up and pushes past me, plopping down in the straw at the other end of the cart with a loud sigh. She stays there for a long while, playing low, sad-sounding notes on her flute and feeding pieces of pastry to Pépin while Hotspur sits in the cage beside them gnawing hungrily on the bones.

I hunker down against the cage bars and take a mouthful of pie. The meat is tough and stringy – nothing like the delicious beef and venison pies our cook, Madame Fournier, bakes at home. But it's better than nothing.

As we roll along the track, I catch glimpses through the clouds of churned-up dust of low marshy fields and a great, brown river snaking between them. Its waters are dotted with high-masted merchant ships, like the one I stowed away on to cross from Calais to England all those weeks ago. A sudden breeze blows in, laced with the smells of the river – mud and the stink of dead, rotting things mixed with the salty-sharp whiff of seaweed. I press my nose to my sleeve doing my best to keep the pie down. It's only as the track winds away from the marshes and heads through fields and orchards that I dare to breathe more freely.

The sun has almost set when Maître Tarleton's voice echoes back to us over the plod of hooves and the creak of cartwheels.

'There it is, lads! The King's favourite palace. A sight for sore eyes, eh?'

In spite of myself, a wave of excitement ripples through me. I've never seen a royal palace before. I'm pricked by the sudden memory of *Papa*'s promise to take me to King François's court at Yuletide – a promise that because of my own cowardliness, he can never keep . . .

My stomach knots and my eyes fill with bitter tears. I blink them back, then swallow hard and call out to Cat. 'Would you like to see where the King and Queen live?'

She scrambles to her feet, her eyes bright and starry. 'They are here?'

'Not far, yes.'

'Where? I want to see!' She pushes alongside me and gripping hold of the cage door, stands on tiptoes craning her neck.

The cart is lumbering along at slower than

walking pace. Untying Pépin, I hook him on to my shoulder then jump down, helping Cat after me. We scale up the bank at the side of the road and gaze at the hillside opposite. Its grassy, tree-dotted slopes remind me of the parkland we have at home, though it's clearly many times bigger. A brick tower with a small spire stands on a small grassy knoll at the top, silhouetted against the fading light.

I frown. Why is the *maître* making such a fuss? This building looks more like a hunting lodge than a palace. But then, as the carts dip down around the bend, I realize my mistake. For there, just a short way ahead, behind a great curving wall and bordering the river, is the most magnificent building I have ever seen. Its rose-pink walls are studded with windows which glitter as if glazed with thousands of rubies and diamonds, while its battlemented towers are dotted with small gold flags which dance and flicker like the tongues of a hundred tiny, fire-breathing dragons.

I draw in a quick breath. *'Comme c'est beau!'*

'Comsebo!' Cat echoes beside me.

'Beautiful, yes.' I look down at her and smile. She blinks and slides her hand shyly into mine.

We stand there for a moment longer – Cat holding my hand, Pépin perched on my shoulder – then I help her back down to the road and we set off again, hurrying to catch up with the carts.

· CHAPTER 8 ·

Cat

We didn't meet The King, Meg. He was too busy eating-and-drinking-and-making-merry to see us. That's what Gobble says. But he must have work to do too, or why is he The King?

Now the morning has come and Master Tarley has gone to see if he will let us play the play for him; the one about Noah and the animals sailing around on the deep waters. I didn't say to him, but I like that story. Nonny Sweet-Bee tells it when we are in the garden doing our digging and hoeing. Noah and his wife-and-children, and all the birds that fly in the air and the creatures that walk or crawl on the ground, are locked inside a big boat. They are looking for land, but they can't find it because it's been covered by all the rain. Forty days and nights go by and the rain stops and the dove flies off in the sky and brings a twig-leaf to Noah and the boat floats to a high hill and they are saved.

Jack-Bon hasn't taken me to find you like he said yet. But it's not his fault because when Master

Tarley went off to see The King, Gobble sent Jack-Bon to get water in a bucket. Then he gave me the clothes the dove wears and told me to go in the other cart with all the Noah things and put myself in them because he had something he calls 'A Plan'. I asked him what 'A Plan' is, but his face went all pucker-red and he shouted to me to get on with it.

I am doing my best. I have stuffed all my hair in my bonnet and put on the birdy-hat and beak, but my fingers can't to do all the coat-ties. Pippo is here, but he's too busy picking in the straw for beetles and other crawling things to eat.

In the day outside, the water from the big, brown river slip-slaps the stones and all the white birds fly about and shriek and scream like a bunch of cross, hungry orphlings. But now there's a clatter-banging too. I look out from the side of Noah's boat. Gobble has got Hosper's iron basket open and he is making Badulf and the others drag him down on the road that leads in front of The King's palace. But Hosper doesn't want to go. He is making angry growling noises and pulling on the chain tied round his neck.

Gobble gets a stick and pokes his side. Hosper growls again and swings round-and-about, but Badulf and the others pull him back.

My heart squeezes. When Noah led the animals on his boat, he was helping them. But Gobble is not helping Hosper – not one bit. I push out past the boat and climb down from the cart.

Gobble turns and snorts a laugh. 'Ah, here's our bird right on cue! Sing us a tune and let's see if old Harry Hotspur here will dance for his dinner.' He smacks his stick on Hosper's nose and makes him cry out.

My heart squeezes sharper. 'Don't!' I flap my arms and stumble-run at Gobble.

He grabs my wings and pushes his darty eyes in my face. 'Do as I say or your moth-eaten friend here will suffer.' He jabs Hosper's side again and drops me back down.

I twist my neck and look for Jack-Bon. People have come and are standing watching, but he isn't anywhere I can see.

'Come on, bird-maid,' a man shouts. 'Give us a song!'

Then a girl bats her hands and does clucking noises like a chook laying an egg. A boy runs and chases after Pippo. He gives a shriek and pitter-pats up the side of a tree.

More people are coming now. Some point and laugh. Others hoot and screech so loud it pains my ears. It was much more quiet at the nonnies' house – even though they did wailing-and-groaning and Holy Mother Sharp-Tongue was always clacking and squawking. I wish we were back there together, Meg, or you were here to make everyone go away. But you are not, so I will have to do what Gobble wants and sing.

I will sing the same song I sang yesterday – our safe-together song for if you are sad and want to make things better. But when I try, I can't make the notes come out. I breathe in and try again.

Still no sound.

I close my eyes tight-shut and feel your arms wrapped warm around my middle. And then the notes do come, but everyone is making such a rattle-clatter they don't hear.

Then Hosper stands high on his legs and gives a piercey-loud roar. Everyone shrinks back quiet-as-quiet. My own heart is thumping and banging, but still I make myself sing the words. And this time, when the people's mouths open, they are the ones who cannot make a sound.

I finish the song. The people do lots of blinking, but no one moves. I go to Hosper and bury my fingers deep and down in his patched fur and whisper the song in his raggedy ear just for him. He makes a soft rumble in his throat and presses his nose in my dove-coat. I hug him close and squash my birdy-beak against him and breathe in his dusty bear smell.

I want us to keep staying there, but sharp fingers dig into my arms and snatch me off and away. Gobble twists me round and shakes me about. 'You've had your moment, half-wit. Now it's time for some real sport. Bardolf, bring them in!'

I hear the dogs first. One, two, three – all snarling

and barking fit-to-burst. Then the people pull apart and I see them too. There is a big black one with yellow eyes and two brown ones, with Badulf dragging along behind. My stomach flip-flops. Are they going to do what Jack-Bon told me and make Hosper fight?

They jump forwards, their teeth clashing and gnashing.

I try to get free, but Gobble is holding me hard-and-fast.

Then Badulf lets the ropes go. The big black dog leaps on Hosper's back. The others dance and prance about and snatch his fur with their red angry mouths. Hosper roars and shakes his head. He bats the smaller dogs with his paws, but his claws are gone and his eyes can't see and he is only one.

My ears are full of people's shouts and screams and my chest is tighter-than-tight. But Hosper is my friend. I have to help. I push my birdy-beak up and bite into Gobble's hand. He shrieks a yell. I get free and lift my dove-coat skirts and run. I am nearly with Hosper, but then a brown dog snarls out at me.

Pippo screeches and shakes the tree-branch. I shut my eyes and scream.

There's a giant roar then squeals and thuds and loud gaspings. I flick open my eyes. The two brown dogs are lying still on the ground, their heads flopped to the side. Hosper has broken off his chain and is standing high on his legs and smashing and crashing at the big black dog with his paws.

A voice sounds out loud from behind. 'Stand away, Cat!'

I twirl about. Jack-Bon is there with his hands gripping on a bow, like the one Stewer Boneyface uses for his archree practice. I blink and stumble back. The big black dog snarls and springs. Hosper roars and bounds. Then something flies over me and hits him and he groans and crashes to the ground.

'Hosper!' I tumble-run towards him.

The big black dog's paws are poking from under him, all limp and still. There is an arrow in Hosper's chest going in and out with his breathing. His fur is all wet around it. I touch it and my fingers drip with red, but I don't care. I shush at him and rub his head and nose. He groans again, then his eye blinks shut and he goes still too.

'Hosper!' I shake him, but he stays asleep. 'HOSPER, WAKE UP!'

Footsteps hurry up behind. A hand falls on my shoulder. 'Hush, Cat, and come away.'

It is Jack-Bon. I peer round. Pippo is there too. I look at Jack-Bon's fingers still gripping the bow, then back at the arrow in Hosper's chest.

'Will he be all right?'

Jack-Bon's face has gone all white and quivery. He sucks in a breath and puffs it out then shakes his head.

My eyes prick and fill full with water. 'But he is our friend.'

'I know. I am sorry, I did not mean—'

But Jack-Bon doesn't finish because then a woman's voice sounds out from behind. 'Bring them here!'

There are more gasping noises. All of the people bow down low. Two men dressed in green-and-white stripes with big shining axes on poles arrive. They pull us away from Gobble and Badulf. Away from Hosper too.

I wiggle and squirm. Jack-Bon does the same, but the men make him drop his bow-and-arrows and it is no use because they have got us both tightly-fast. The men growl and look fierce. They pull us over to the arch where Master Tarley went to go and ask about playing for The King. A bunch of ladies in shining gowns are standing there and looking out with owly-wide eyes.

I want to go and be with Hosper, but the men won't let me. Then the ladies rustle back to leave one in a black dress with gold sparkles standing on her own.

The men bow, then they push our heads down and one barks loud in my ear.

'Kneel before your Queen!'

· CHAPTER 9 ·

Jacques

Heart hammering, I snatch off my cap and drop quickly down on one knee. I glance over at Cat, but instead of doing the same, she twists round sobbing and calls Hotspur's name.

'Silence!' The guard holding her gives her a shake, but her sobs only grow louder.

'Hush, Cat!' I try to throw her a reassuring look, but she pulls the ridiculous bird-hat she's wearing down over her eyes and turns away. My stomach clenches. She blames me for what's just happened, I know, but I was aiming for the dog. If the shot had only been clearer . . . I ball my fingers into fists. This is all that vile lizard, Gobbo's fault. It's him and his stupid friend Bardolf the guards should have arrested, not us.

My head is in such a whirl, I don't hear the swish of skirts until the last moment. I blink and look up. The small plump woman we've been made to bow to has come to a stop in front of us. She is dressed in a black-and-gold silk gown and a pair of matching slippers. A magnificent jewel-studded hood frames her high forehead and pale pink cheeks, and a ruby and gold crucifix hangs from her neck by a rope of creamy white pearls.

As the woman's grey eyes light on us, my heart does a quick somersault. If this is truly Queen Katherine, what can she possibly want with us? Before I have the chance to think anything else, Cat springs forwards and snatches at the woman's skirts.

'Can you help make Hosper better?'

The air fills with gasps and shocked cries. A stern-faced matron darts between Cat and the Queen, shielding her mistress with outstretched arms. 'Look to Her Grace!' She shoots a furious look at the guards while doing her best to keep Cat at bay.

The guard at my side jumps to life and seizes hold of Cat, pinning her arms behind her. Throwing his companion an angry glance, he gives a loud cough and bows down again before the Queen. 'I beg your forgiveness, Your Majesty. She's a proper wild-cat, this one.' As if to prove him right, Cat aims a sharp kick at his shins. 'Why you little—' He makes to strike her, but Queen Katherine raises her hand.

'Be still, all of you!' Her voice is low and heavily accented, but it rings out clear as a bell.

Everyone freezes, even Cat.

'Release the prisoners and let us see what they have to say for themselves.'

The guards bow again. Keeping the blades of their halberds trained firmly on us, they take a step back.

The Queen's gaze sweeps over me and settles back on Cat. 'Is it you, child, who was singing out here beneath my chamber window just now?'

Cat jumps forwards again. I leap to my feet to hold her back, but she pushes me off. 'I was singing to Hosper.' She turns and points at the dark humped shape lying on the ground behind us. 'He is my friend, but he's got an arrow in him and he can't get up.' She throws a hurt look at me, then hugs her arms and hangs down her head.

There are more flurries of shocked whispers and cries. Another of the Queen's ladies – a dark-haired girl in a red velvet dress – glides over to Cat and takes her gently by the arm. 'You must curtsey and say "Your Grace" when you speak to *la reina* Catalina.' She dips down in her skirts to show Cat how.

Cat blinks. 'Catty?' She pushes her bird-hat higher up her forehead and stares up at the Queen. 'I am called Catty too, but only by my sister, Meg. Most people call me Cat Sparrow.'

The girl's eyes widen, but before she can say anything, the stern-faced matron steps forwards again. 'Enough of your insolence, maid . . . bird . . . whatever you are.'

Queen Katherine lifts a hand to stay her. 'She

68

means nothing by it, Lady Boleyn, do you, child?'

Cat frowns, unsure of what to say, then fumbles beneath the open ties of her coat and pulls out her bag. 'I can play my birdy-flute if you like?'

Before the Queen has time to reply, she slides the flute free and swoops it up and down in front of her. 'It was my ma's. I can make songs from all the birds with it. This one is Robin.' She shakes the flute to loosen the pea inside, then puts it to her lips and blows a string of sweet piping notes. 'And this is Wren.' She wipes her mouth on one of the feather wings attached to her coat-sleeves and blows a harsh *chip-chip*. The Queen's eyebrows arch in surprise.

'And this is the best of all.' Cat closes her eyes and makes the throaty warbling call I recognize by now as her beloved blackbird. She drops the flute to her side and throws the Queen a beaming smile. 'Can you guess?'

More murmurs from the Queen's ladies and mutterings from the rest of the crowd, but the Queen herself is smiling. She gives a mock frown and shakes her head. 'Play it again.'

Cat repeats the call. When she's finished, the Queen signals to her ladies. They huddle around her and exchange whispered guesses until she waves them away. She looks back at Cat and clears her throat.

'We think it is the blackbird.'

Cat flaps her arms up and down. 'Yes, yes – you are right!'

The Queen's smile broadens. 'Well, you have a talent for music, Cat Sparrow, that much is sure.'

'I can sing some more too.' Cat puts her head on one side but as she opens her mouth, a familiar pit-pattering sounds behind us. My heart misses a beat. Pépin. I jerk round to see him springing up the back of Cat's bird-coat and on to her shoulders.

'Pippo!' She presses her face in his fur, her song forgotten. The Queen's ladies cry out and clutch each other as if fearing for their lives. Only the Queen and the one called Lady Boleyn remain calm.

I dip into a hurried bow. 'I am sorry, Your Grace. My monkey, he is . . .' I search for the word in English but can't find it, so I use the French instead. '*Malin.*'

The Queen reaches out and tickles Pépin behind the ears. I flinch, expecting the worst, but instead of biting her, he gives a small *chee-chee* and nuzzles his head against the back of her hand.

As I heave a quick sigh, the Queen's eyes take on a distant, faraway look. 'It reminds me of the monkey my dear mother, *la reina* Isabella, gave to me when I was a young girl back in Spain.'

I start at the mention of the name. Her gaze sharpens. 'How did you come by this creature? It is not usual for poor boys such as yourself to own one.'

'I . . . I found him, Your Grace – on the ship that brought me here from France.'

Her expression hardens. 'So, you are French then?'

My throat grows tight. I know from *Papa* that Queen Katherine's nephew, the King of Spain and now Holy Roman Emperor too, is the deadly rival of King François. And of course, it was only a few short years ago that her husband, King Henry rode into battle against the French too.

'Well?'

The best thing will be to tell her the truth. 'Yes, but—' There's a sudden low hissing behind me and a voice that sounds like Gobbo's shouts, 'Dirty Frenchie!'

Doing my best to ignore the taunts, I pull back my shoulders and give the rest of my answer. 'But my mother, she is English.'

'Hmmm.' The Queen's look softens a little. 'Well, I will forgive the French part then. But why did you shoot the bear?'

My heart sinks. Fumbling my hat in my hands, I throw a quick glance at Cat, but she's too busy chattering to Pépin and smoothing his fur to hear. 'I was aiming for the dog, but the bear and my friend' – I nod at Cat – 'they got in the way and . . . well . . . the arrow hit Hotspur instead.'

'And was this . . . this sport with the creature a part of your entertainment?'

I stumble back, shocked that she could think such a thing. 'No! It was a cruel joke thought up by two others while our master went to the palace to seek permission to put on his play. They sent me off to fetch water to get me out of the way, then they made Cat dress up and set the dogs on her and the bear.'

The Queen's frown deepens. 'I see. And where are these two knaves now?'

I hesitate.

'Come, boy. Answer me.'

I turn and scan the faces of the crowd. At first I don't see Gobbo and Bardolf, but then I do. Shoulders hunched, heads down and doing their best to slide away without being seen.

'There.' I raise my hand and point.

The Queen nods, then turns and motions at the guards. 'Arrest them!'

As they spring into action, Gobbo and Bardolf set off at a run. But the crowd closes in on them, blocking their way. Gobbo raises his fists, but then one of the guards jabs him with his halberd and he gives himself up like the coward he is. Thrusting their hands behind their backs, the guards spin them round and march them up to face the Queen. Bardolf falls to the ground and begs for mercy, but Gobbo sticks out his bony chest, refusing to bow until one of the guards forces him down on his knees.

The Queen skims her eyes over them, then gives a loud sniff and bats them away with the back of her hand. 'Have them whipped and sent on their way.'

The guards bow and drag the two men to their feet. As they march them beneath the gatehouse arch, Gobbo turns and shoots me a look colder and more deadly than any arrow-tip. I shudder and turn away. When I look again, he has gone.

Cat tugs at the Queen's sleeve. 'Will the whipping hurt?'

The Queen raises her eyebrows. 'What a strange question, child! Of course it will, but the punishment is no more than they deserve. Now, tell me, where is your home and I will have one of my servants escort you there?'

Cat pushes back her bird-hat again. 'I live with the nonnies, but I cannot go home yet. I've got to find Meg.'

The Queen's eyebrows raise even higher. 'The nonnies?'

I step forwards with another bow. '*Pardonnez-moi*, Your Grace. It is best if I explain.'

The Queen inclines her head and gestures for me to go on. So, drawing in a breath, I tell her the little I know of Cat's life and of how we met.

As she listens, the Queen's face takes on a sadder look. 'Then she is an orphan child?'

'Yes, except for her sister, Meg.'

I look at Cat, plumped down in her skirts on the

ground and singing softly to Pépin, who is lying curled in her arms. The Queen looks at her too. Her brow wrinkles again.

'I remember how it was for me when I had to leave my beloved family and come to England to be married. I was but a girl then too. To be lonely and far from those who love you is a sad thing indeed.'

My throat tightens as she speaks the words. She gives a low sigh, then bends and tilts Cat's chin with her finger.

'Cat Sparrow, how would you like to stay here in my household until your sister can be found?'

Cat's eyes grow wide and round. 'With you, Queen Catty?'

The Queen laughs. 'Yes, with me and my ladies. You will be fed and clothed and can sing and play your flute as much as you wish.'

Cat rubs her cheek against Pépin's fur. 'Can Pippo stay too?'

'If you wish, though perhaps you should ask your friend first.' She tips her head to me.

Cat gathers Pépin to her chest and jumps to her feet. 'Jack-Bon is *not* my friend. He shot Hosper with his arrow and now he is dead and gone.' She scowls at me, then bursts into sudden tears.

'Hush! Let us go inside and Lady Marjorie will show you where you will stay.' Queen Katherine signals to the girl in the red dress. She dips into a curtsey, then hurries forwards and takes Cat by the hand.

I swallow. 'But—'

The Queen holds up a hand. 'We will be sure to look after her. And your monkey too. In the meantime, if you are in need of some employment, my guards will show you to Master Gibson's office. He is our Serjeant of Revels and is hard at work making final preparations for the grand meeting between my beloved husband, King Henry, and your own King François to celebrate the recently agreed peace between our country and yours. Your experience as a player will be most useful to him, I am sure.' She smiles, though it's clear from her tone when she mentions the peace that she doesn't approve.

Before I have a chance to reply, she motions to one of the guards, picks up her skirts and sweeps off beneath the gatehouse arch with her ladies following close behind. I call out to Cat, but she's talking to Lady Marjorie and neither she nor Pépin look back.

My stomach clenches. I should be in London – doing what I came here to do. I was going to slip away in the night, but I felt guilty about deserting Cat. I could go now though. She won't miss me – that much is clear. And though I don't want to leave him, it will be better for Pépin to stay here with her than draw attention to me on the streets. If I could just get my bow back . . .

I glance at the guards. They're busy mopping the

sweat from their faces and exchanging muttered whispers. Now's my chance. I dart over to where it's lying, but as I reach for it, a hand seizes hold of my arm and jerks me backwards.

'Leave that, boy! You heard what Her Grace said – you're coming with us.'

· CHAPTER 10 ·

Cat

I have not seen Jack-Bon for a day and two nights. Lady Marjoree in the shimmery-red dress says he has gone to work for the Master-of-the-Rebels. She says he is in The King's palace and not far, but I can't see from my window, and I am as high as the birds.

My heart is panging for Hosper. He was my friend. Jack-Bon's too. I *do* miss Jack-Bon, even if it was his fault for making Hosper die. But I miss *you* most of all, Meggy-Peg.

Queen Catty said I can stay with her while they find you, but I don't know when that is going to be. I have blown with my birdy-flute out through my window. Over the gardens brimmy-full of flowers and trees. Across the brown river too. I strain and strain with my ears, but still I cannot hear you answer.

Once, a long, golden boat full of men splashed past on the river and a big red-and-gold man standing in the middle blew on his own silvery-coloured flute. *Peep! Peeep! Peeeep!* I called out to see if he was searching for you too, but he couldn't hear with all the other men's sticks splashing and the white birds shrieking in the sky above.

This is a strange place with all the hurrying around and the bowing and curtseying people must do to Queen Catty. They are like chooks running after her for seed and pecking each other out of the way. But I do like her. She is pink and pretty and she has soft grey eyes, the same colour as the turtle-doves that live in the nonnies' bell tower. But her voice is deeper – more like a pidgie's, and when she moves, her skirts swish together and her Holy-Cross necklace jingles and clicks on the sparkles on her dress.

I would like it best if it was only her and me, but her ladies-who-wait are always there too. They do so much yacketing it puts my head in a dizzy-spin.

For the first night and day, Lady Marjoree looked after me. She is kind like Queen Catty. But now Mistress Bristles has come in Lady Marjoree's place, and she is not. She is tall and pokey with sharp crow-eyes and spikes of black hair sticking from her chin. When she gets close, she puffs soury-milk and 'O is for Onion' smells out all over.

Her voice is all wheedling-high with Lady Marjoree and the other ladies-who-wait, but when it is just us, she clitter-clats like a maggie-pie or else hisses like an angry goose. She doesn't like Pippo too. She has fastened him in a basket and put him on a shelf so I can't see. He screeched a lot when she did it, but now he must be asleep because the basket is still and the only sounds coming from it are pipey-small whistles and sighs.

Mistress Bristles is not here now. She has gone away to fetch new clothes to put me in. When I asked her why she said that if I was to serve Her Grace the Queen, I must dress accordingly.

'What is a caw-dingly?' I asked. Her eyes pulled into two darty slits and she said I would find out soon enough.

The sun in the outside is shining down bright-as-bright, but it is stony-cold in here and I can't go out because Mistress Bristles has locked the door with her big iron key. I still have your spindle though, Meg. I pull it out and stroke my fingers over the yellow sun-bead, then I dangle the spindle by the thread and spin it round and round. When it comes to the end, I twine the thread and start again.

It's halfway down, but now there's a flip-flapping in the passage outside. The flip-flapping stops and something rattles in the door-lock. The door creaks open and Mistress Bristles swirls in with a mound of clothes and throws them on the table. 'There!' She clatters a pair of shears down after and faces back round to me. Her beady-sharp eyes catch on the spindle.

'What is that?' She snatches hold with her spiky nails and peers over it in the window-light.

My chest goes knotty-tight, the same as it did when Gobble poked his stick in Hosper's side. 'It is my spindle from Meg. Give it back!'

There's a loud chitter-chatter from above and Pippo's basket bounces on the shelf. But Mistress Bristles doesn't look. She frowns her face at me instead. 'Impudent wench. How dare you speak to me like that!'

'But it is mine. I have to keep it safe for her – Nonny Sweet-Bee said.' I try to take the spindle back, but Mistress Bristles flicks it round behind her skirts and gives me a hard, black stare.

'Maids should be meek and mild and know their place. You seem to think you are special because Her Grace has given you a roof over your head and these fine clothes to wear.' She jabs her finger at the clothes' pile. 'But remember this. When she has had her fill of your whistling and caterwauling and all your nonsense talk, it is back here to your cage you will come. And if you don't behave, then this' – she takes the spindle and cracks it in two bits – 'is what will become of you.'

'Noooo!' I swipe for the spindle, but it is too late because it is all in pieces. The pain in my chest is so sharp it makes me cry out.

Pippo leaps about in his basket. It falls to the floor and breaks open. He jumps out and grabs on to Mistress Bristles' skirts. She shrieks and shakes him off and switches the whippy-stick from her waist.

'I am warning you, girl. And that devil of an ape too.' She cracks the stick at Pippo. He screeches and shows his teeth to her, then he hops into a corner behind a big brown chest.

'He is not an ape, he is a munkee.'

She swipes the stick at me. 'Whisht! Now take off that ridiculous costume and put these on.' She jabs at the new clothes again.

It is Mistress Bristles who is the Devil, not Pippo. Just like the red angry one poking his stick at the souls on the wall of the nonnies' church – but I don't want to tell her in case she uses her one on me. I fumble the dove-coat off and let her bustle me into the white thing she calls a petticoat. There is a kirtle too – soft and green like 'M is for Moss' – and then a gown – the same green as the kirtle, but with shimmery-white stripes and gold stars. It is much heavier than my old kirtle which I left behind in the back of Master Tarley's cart. He will not be pleased when he finds out all that has happened, because how can he do the Noah and his boat play for The King now?

'Stand up straight!' Mistress Bristles forces my arms back and tugs my skirts in tight-as-tight.

When all the ties are tied and I am pinned in good and proper, she makes me take off my bonnet. My curls spring out and about and her eyes go owly-wide. She rustles through them with her pokey fingers.

'Well, I will give you this, girl, the good Lord has seen fit to bless you with a head of fine-looking hair, if not with much to put inside it.' Her face crinkles and she puffs a soury-onion breath. ''Tis a shame it will all have to come off.'

'Come off?'

'Yes. You are the Queen's Fool now and must wear your head shaved as a mark of your new station.'

I tip my head and puzzle over what she has said. The man on the thundery-black horse called me 'fool'. From the look of his face it was not a good thing. But to be the Queen's Fool sounds different – like I am special. I want to ask, but then Mistress Bristles swipes the shears from the table.

My heart bumps hard in my chest. 'What are you doing?'

'I told you. Cutting off your hair.'

'But . . . but I don't want you to.'

Mistress Bristles snorts a laugh. 'It doesn't matter what *you* want. The sooner you learn that, my maid, the better it will go for you. Now, come here.' She snatches at me. I go back and away, but she is quicker. She drags me to the stool with her pinchy hands and pushes me down. I put my arms round me and try to go to-and-fro, fro-and-to, but she pulls me straight again.

'Sit still!' She flashes the shears in my face, then she tugs out a curl and snip-snaps it off with the scratchy blades. She tugs another and snaps that off too.

I chew hard on my lip. The snip-snapping is paining me more than a stick-whipping, more even than breaking the spindle in two, but I'm not going to let her see. I take my bag with my birdy-flute and hide it in my new skirts. Then I close my eyes and sing an inside song so Mistress Bristles cannot hear.

It is the one Nonny Sweet-Bee taught me to help spell my name.

C is for Cowslip that nods in the breeze
A is for Ash and Asparagus green
T is for Thyme that smells so sweet
S is for Sage and Sycamore Tree
P is for Parsley and also for Pea
A is for Ash and Asparagus green
R is for Rosemary, Rose and Rue
R is for Rosemary, Rose and Rue
O is for Oak, so sturdy and true
W is for Willow and . . .
May God bless you!

I sing it over and over. When the tugging and snip-snapping stops, I blink my eyes open. A pile of orange-red hair is lying all around on the floor. *My* hair. I reach my hands to my head. It was all soft and long, but now it is spiky-short. A small gulp comes in my throat and water leaks from my eyes and goes down over my cheeks.

Mistress Bristles pushes my chin round to the light. Her glittery crow-eyes go a bit softer. She shakes her head and sucks in a breath.

'There. You are a proper fool now and no mistaking it.' She mops at my face, then hooks a green-and-white cap from the table. She pulls it down over my head and ties it tight under my chin. 'Now put these on.' She pushes a pair of green shoes at me. 'And quick about it. Her Grace has requested your presence in her chambers.'

I blink. 'But I don't have any presents.'

She puffs a muttery onion breath. 'Saints preserve us, must I spell everything out?'

'I can spell too.' I sniff and wipe my nose on my sleeve.

'Stop that. You'll ruin your gown before you've even had a chance to wear it!'

But I don't want to listen to her clitter-clatter, so I begin my letters, loud-as-loud. 'A is for Ash, B is for Birch, C is for—'

Mistress Bristles' face goes devil red. 'Enough of your cheek, wench!' She shoves the shoes on my feet, then snatches my arm and opens wide the door.

A loud *chee-chee* sounds. I twist free. Pippo is out from behind the chest and bouncing over the floor with his tail curled high. I drop down and bundle him into my arms.

Mistress Bristles swipes out her stick. 'No you don't. That creature stays here.'

I press Pippo close. I don't want to leave my friend all alone. 'Queen Catty said I can bring Pippo when I want. She likes munkees. She had one when she was a girl-back-in-Spain.'

Mistress Bristles tips her head and stares at me like a chook eyeing a too-big worm. 'Very well.' Her nose wrinkles. 'But keep the foul thing away from me. Now make haste. The Queen is waiting!'

She swings me back round towards the door, past the pile of my hair, all red and glowing in the light. To see it makes me feel sad. But happy too. Because now I am more than Cat Sparrow – I am Cat Sparrow the Queen's Fool.

· CHAPTER 11 ·

Cat

We go along a passage and down into the windy-dark staircase, then along another passage to a door with two green-and-white guard-men. One of the guard-men tells Mistress Bristles that Queen Catty is not there, so we have to go in and wait.

We step inside and the room is so golden and bright it makes my heart want to leap and dance. Green cloths hang down from the walls. They are covered in fruits and flowers and jumping white deer and big growling cats with yellow fur and pointy claws. The roof up above is blue-as-blue and full of stars. There is a golden flower too. It is marked with an 'H is for Holly' and a 'K', which Nonny Sweet-Bee says is for 'Knotty-grass' even if it doesn't sound like it. There are dry grass-stalks and 'L is for Lavender' spread all across the floor. The smell tickles at my nose and makes it want to crinkle and sneeze.

Then a bird peeps, which cannot be right,

because birds only live in the outside. But it must be true because then it peeps again. I look round-and-about. There it is, in the window, swinging in a box made out of criss-crossed silver sticks. I let Pippo down and crunch over the floor to see it better.

'Come back this instant, Cat Sparrow!' Mistress Bristles' voice clatters out loud, but then it shrinks down to a gratey croak. 'Oh! Forgive me, Your Grace. The girl, she—'

'Thank you, Mistress Bristol. You may leave us.'

I spin about. Queen Catty is standing inside the door with her lips all thin and pursey. Lady Marjoree and some of the other ladies-who-wait are there too.

'But she is half-wild, Your Grace. And as for that creature . . .' Mistress Bristles points to where Pippo is sitting inside a blue-and-white bowl with nuts and round orange things in. He gives a loud chatter, then picks up an 'H is for Hazelnut' and throws it over by her feet.

A laugh wriggles out of me.

Mistress Bristles' face goes boiling red. 'Insolent girl, how dare you behave so in front of your Queen!'

'I *said* that will be all, Mistress Bristol.' Queen Catty's voice is louder now. She does not sound pleased.

Mistress Bristles drops down low in her skirts. 'Yes, Your Grace.' She lifts back up and slides off between the guard-men who bow and bang the door shut behind.

Queen Catty swooshes past Pippo who is crunching on a 'W is for Walnut'. She comes and stands with me. 'Well, child, and what do you think of your new clothes?'

'I like these.' I pick at the gold stars on my skirts. 'But Mistress Bristles took off all my hair.' I poke a finger inside my cap and feel the prickle of what is left.

Queen Catty tips her head and her eyes go all sad and sorry. 'It is hard for you to understand, I think, but . . . Well, it is a sign of how special you are. And it means that while you live here with me, no one will hurt you.'

'Not Gobble and Badulf?'

'No. They will not trouble you again. They have received just punishment for what they did and been sent far away.'

'Not even Mistress Bristles too?'

Queen Catty's eyebrows go high. 'Mistress Bristol is your Keeper. She is here to care for you. She might need to be strict with you sometimes, but it is for your own good.'

I want to tell Queen Catty about the whippy-stick and about Mistress Bristles breaking your spindle, Meg, but then the bird in the silver box peeps out again. I *have* to see it. I hurry over and press my nose to the cold sticks all around. The bird is small and brown with a milky-grey chest. It hops across its perch and shines its glittery black eye on me.

There's a rustle-swoosh behind and Queen Catty is side-by-side with me again, her fingers chinking on the glittery beads round her neck. She smells of the spicy-warm buns Cook baked when Holy Mother Hildy was in charge of the nonnies and grand-and-important people came in from the Outside World to see her. I close my eyes to taste them better.

Queen Catty taps her nails on the silver sticks and makes a high whistling noise. It is not as good as my birdy-flute, but I don't say.

'It is a nightingale – a gift from my husband, the King. Have you seen one before?'

I shake my head. 'Why is it in the box?'

'To keep it from flying away.'

I scrunch my face. 'But what if it wants to?'

Queen Catty gives a small puff and sigh. 'We cannot always do what we want – even a queen.' She puts her hand down and stares through the open window, then she looks back and flickers me a smile. 'Besides, if it flew away, we would not be able to hear its lovely song, would we?'

I tip my head. 'But it might sing more loud and lovely if it was up and flying in the sky.'

Queen Catty frowns her face as if I have spoken something wrong, but then it goes back to normal and she laughs a small laugh. 'You may be right,

Cat Sparrow, though I do not think it would please the King if I let it go free.'

Footsteps sound from outside in the passage. I look behind in case it is Mistress Bristles coming back. The footsteps get louder and then Queen Catty hears them too.

She glides round. The guard-men slice back their axe-poles. A grand man in a silvery-grey coat all covered with curly gold knots bangs into the room. Lady Marjoree and the other ladies-who-wait do curtseying and 'my-lording', but he barges through them and goes over to Queen Catty.

'Your Grace!' He swings off his hat and bends low so the gold chain round his neck nearly touches the floor. If he bends any more, his chins will get stuck in his great belly too.

'Ah, my dear Buckingham. We have been waiting for you. Rise, my lord, rise.' Queen Catty puts out her sparkle-covered fingers.

The grand man lifts his head and pushes his hat back over his thin brown hair. He walks forwards, blowing out air from his red, puffy cheeks. Then he kisses Queen Catty's rings on his thick fish-lips and squeezes them into a smile.

'I trust you are well, Your Grace?' His voice is all slippery and low.

'Very well, thank you.' Queen Catty dips her head and smiles back. 'And how was the journey from Kent?'

The grand man rolls his eyes and rubs his hand over his back with a groan. 'Long and hot and not without its troubles. The roads are teeming with vagabonds and cut-throats. My men had to dispatch several of the vermin with their weapons to clear the way. But Your Grace does not want to hear of that, I am sure.' His eyes blink round-and-about and fix on me. They are dark-grey and hard and make my insides go shivery-cold.

'And who, pray, is this . . . this person?' He wrinkles his nose as if I've made a privy-smell.

Queen Catty looks back at me. 'The maid? She is a poor innocent. I had the guards rescue her from a pair of villains who had set her to dancing with a crippled bear for their amusement.'

'A fool, then?' He says 'fool' the same as the man on the thundery-black horse, like it is a bad, ugly thing.

I am going to tell him he is wrong and that I am Queen Catty's special one, but she answers him back herself.

'Others may call her that, my lord, but I prefer to call her my songbird for reasons you will shortly understand.' She sends me a smile. 'Greet my lord with a curtsey as you have been taught, child.'

But I do not want to curtsey for this man. I want to be with Pippo. I call out his name. He twitches his ears, then he leaps from the bowl and runs spider-quick under the grand man's legs.

'God's nails, what the Devil?' The grand man jumps back with his eyes all round and goggling. He knocks into a table sideways and stumble-trips down on the floor.

The ladies-who-wait gasp out loud. Pippo dances and chitters about.

The grand man coughs and splutters, then he drags himself back on his feet. He looks like one of the nonnies' hogs, with his hair and his gold-knotty coat all stuck with stalks of grass.

I give a loud giggle. Some of the ladies giggle too.

Queen Catty's face goes into another frown. She pulls a small stick from her waist. I duck in case she is going to whip me, but then she shakes it and a paper wing flips out. She holds the wing close to her mouth and flutters it to-and-fro. From her eyes it looks like she is doing some giggling too.

The grand man's face is red as an 'R is for Radish'. 'Why, you little—' He kicks at Pippo with his great black boot.

'Leave my friend alone!' I bundle Pippo tight against me.

The Queen snaps the paper wing shut and flashes her eyes. 'Calm yourself, child.' She dips her head at the grand man. 'Forgive her, my lord. She means no harm – the monkey is her pet. Come, let my ladies bring you some refreshment, and while we are waiting, you will hear what a sweet voice she has and all will be forgiven.'

She nods to her ladies-who-wait. Lady Marjoree and another do a curtsey and patter off into the outside.

Queen Catty points the grand man to a chair. He dusts off his coat, still huffing and puffing, and sits with his hands gripping tightly on his knees. The Queen turns and waves with her fingers. 'Sing for us, Cat.'

The man looks at me with a stony-hard glare. I can tell he does not want to hear, and it is just as well, because when I open my mouth, no sound comes out.

He does a loud snort. 'It would seem that your songbird's voice has flown.'

Queen Catty's forehead frowns higher. 'There is nothing to fear, child. My Lord, the Duke of Buckingham is a friend.'

I shake my head. I know already he is not *my* friend.

Her lips press tight. 'Very well. Go and sit in the window until your voice has found you again.'

Her face looks sad. It makes me sad too. I take Pippo and drag my feet to where the night-gale is sitting in its silver box. It winks at me with its bright black eye and trills out a song, but my heart feels heavy and full of stones, as if I have done something very bad. What if I can't be The Queen's Fool any more?

Queen Catty and the Lord Bucket sit on their

chairs and talk. I try to listen in case they are talking about me, but it is all about 'ships' and a 'grand-meeting in France' and 'pepper-rayshuns'. Then the Lord Bucket moans on about a 'waist-of-money' and says some unkind things about someone called King Franswah and Queen Catty says in a more quiet voice she wishes they did not have to go.

I puff my cheeks and turn my ears to the sounds coming from the outside. There are birds squawk-ing and dogs barking and people shouting from far and below. I peer out.

They are a long way off, but I can hear what they are saying clear-as-clear: 'Make haste with those baskets, girl!' and, 'Careful with those goblets, turnip-head!' and, 'Watch what you're doing with that ladder, you clumsy great oaf!'

And now there's a clip-clopping sound too. It gets nearer and nearer, and nearer still, then a man on a horse comes riding under the gate-arch. I can only see the top of his black hat and cloak, but then he growls out at one of the green-and-white guard-men.

'Where is the duke? I have an urgent message for him!'

My heart flips over inside. It is him – the man on the thundery-black horse. I jump up and lift Pippo high on my shoulders. Queen Catty and the Lord Bucket are sitting together with their heads bowed, still doing talking. I slip-slide past them and the ladies bent over their sewing too. Even past the guard-men who are busy standing still as stones and looking at the wall. I am in the passage when Queen Catty calls out my name, but I can't stop or it will be too late.

I don't know the way to the outside, but when the stairs come, I hold tight to Pippo and bump down them. Heavy feet come after, but we hide inside a cloth on the wall and they go on another way. People look as we rush by, but they are too busy with their jobs of folding up cloths and putting things in chests to stop us.

There are more stairs and a door, and then we are in the outside. I spin about, but the man on the thundery-black horse isn't there. Did he go away again? I start to run over to the gate-arch, but then I stop, because now a big crowd is coming through it. There are green-and-white guard-men with axe-poles shining sharp in the sun, and men in black cloaks and hats, all fussing and bustling like a flock of noisy starlings. And in the middle of all is the big red-and-gold man – the one who was blowing his flute inside the golden boat.

The man's arm is hanging over the shoulder of another puffed-up man in a red gown and Holy-Cross necklace. He is talking loud-as-loud as if he wants not just the puffed-up one, but all the others to hear.

'See what the French make of our great palace of

glass, eh, Wolsey? I'll wager a bag of gold sovereigns they'll not be able to match it, nor a great many other fine things we will show them besides!'

I don't know what things he is talking about, but still, he might know where the man on the thundery-black horse is.

I put Pippo down on the ground, then I lift up my petticoat skirts and hurry off towards him.

· CHAPTER 12 ·

Jacques

I still can't believe I have met the Queen of England, or that I am working in the King's household. Though Queen Katherine spoke of the new peace between our two countries, from the way people here talk, you would think we were still at war. They call King Henry the rightful King of all France, even though all he rules over now is Calais and the small patch of land around it. As for King François, they curse at the very mention of his name.

I'm desperate to leave here and make my way back to London – begin a proper search for the one I've come here to find. Cat and Pépin will be safe at the palace. And if the Queen is as good as her word, she'll help reunite Cat with her sister too. It will pain me not to say goodbye – but it is for the best. Except that so far, there's been no chance of escape. We're treated little better than prisoners. *Maître* Gibson's assistants watch us like hawks during the day and we're kept locked in at night. All I can do is keep busy with cutting and stitching and bide my time.

The clothes we are making are for the entertainments when the two kings meet near Calais in a few days' time. No expense is to be spared according to *Maître* Gibson. King Henry wants only the finest of everything shipped across the Channel, from tents and horses, to food and clothes – and that goes for costumes and scenery too.

The others who work here say it's a sign of the English king's greatness, but all it makes me think of are the proud peacock birds *Papa* told me about that strut around the grounds of King François's palace, showing off their colourful feathers to impress and frighten their rivals.

As soon as *Maître* Gibson learnt I could use a needle and thread, he set me to work making costumes for the pageant of Robin Hood. Robin, he says, was a famous English outlaw and is the King's favourite character. He has made it clear that if I put a stitch wrong I will have His Majesty to answer to.

Now I've finished them to his satisfaction, he has ordered me to pack them in baskets and load them on to one of the carts outside. I run my fingers over the green velvet tunic the actor playing Robin will wear. It's the same forest green as my favourite cloak at home, but the bow and quiver that go with it are no match for my own. My heart cramps at the memory. They are surely gone for good now, taken by the guards when they brought me here.

A hand grips my shoulder and spins me round. I blink and look up into *Maître* Gibson's frowning face.

'Didn't I tell you to get those costumes loaded on to the cart?'

'Yes, master.'

My cheeks grow hot as the rest of the servants turn to look.

'Well, stop idling and get on with it!'

'Yes, master.' I give him a hurried bow. Packing the costume into a basket, I turn to go.

'Wait!' He swings me round again. 'A maid could carry more than that.' Glaring at me, he loads on two more baskets and pushes me towards the door.

Muffled sniggers sound behind me. I do my best to blot them out and stagger outside. The courtyard is full of servants hurrying to-and-fro, and dogs and ragged children on the lookout for bones and scraps of food. This could be my chance to slip away unseen . . .

I'm halfway to the cart when there's a clatter of horse's hooves. I jerk my head round to see a great black stallion careering towards me. Its rider must have seen me, but rather than rein the animal in, he's whipping it even harder. Heart pounding, I fling my load to the ground and leap clear with barely a moment to spare. As the horse thunders by,

I catch a flash of the man's face beneath his hat – the thick black beard, the full red lips, and eyes, green and piercing – like a wolf's. But then, as he swings round in the saddle and barks out a curse, I realize I'm mistaken. He's only got one eye. The left one is covered with a black patch – the red scar snaking from beneath it clue enough to its fate. I shiver and look away. When I look back again, he's cantering through the stable-yard arch, his black cloak billowing out behind him.

Stuffing the caps and tunics that have escaped back inside the baskets, I stack them on top of each other again and haul them over to the carts. There are five in total, each piled high with pieces of painted scenery, rolls of drapery and chests packed with yet more costumes.

I unload the clothes into a half-empty chest on top of the nearest cart and dart behind it. As I'm getting my bearings, a tramp of feet sounds in the distance. A clamour of excited-sounding voices echoes around the courtyard.

'The King is coming. The King!'

I peer round the side of the cart. Everyone has stopped what they're doing and has turned to look at the gatehouse arch. As I follow their gaze, a unit of guards marches beneath it. Striding behind is a tall, handsome man who, from his richly patterned gold doublet, crimson silk coat and red-gold hair, I am guessing must be King Henry. Hurrying along beside him is an older, plumper man, his face the same bright scarlet as the long robes and slippers he's wearing.

As they step into the light, men drop into low bows and women dip into curtseys. I'm about to bow too when a small figure in a green-and-white striped gown and cap tumbles past, closely followed by a furry grey creature bounding along on all fours.

My breath catches in my throat. Cat Sparrow! I glance at the two men. They're so busy talking, they haven't noticed her yet. I gulp in a quick breath and dash after her, but then, as I draw alongside her, a guard leaps out, barring our way.

'Halt, in the name of the King!' He forces us back with his halberd.

The royal party jerks to a stop. The man in the long scarlet robes sweeps forwards, brushing the guard aside. 'What is the meaning of this?' He looks us up and down with a haughty frown.

I stumble into a bow and make to drag Cat down beside me.

'No! I want to see him.' Wriggling free, she pushes past the man and comes to a wobbly stop in front of the King.

'Hello. I saw you through the window. You were floating like Noah in his boat and playing on your flute. I've got one too. Do you want to hear?' Before he has a chance to reply she pulls her bird-flute from her bag, gives it the usual rattling shake and plays her blackbird song.

The King's eyes narrow to two blue points and an angry-looking red tide rises up his face. I flinch, but instead of exploding with rage, he throws back his head and gives the loudest guffaw I've ever heard.

The man in the scarlet robes darts him a quick look, then follows his lead, though all he can manage is a hollow-sounding chuckle. The King's followers do the same.

Cat gives her gap-toothed grin and takes another step forwards. 'I can do more songs – Wren and Robin. Throstle too. But Blackbird is my best of all.'

The King laughs again and nods his head approvingly. 'The maid has talent, does she not, Cardinal Wolsey? And I like her monkey friend too.' He clicks his teeth at Pépin who is now clinging to the side of Cat's skirts.

The man in scarlet forces his lips into a tight smile.

'Tell me.' The King stoops forwards so his face is level with Cat's. 'Can you play other instruments besides your flute?'

She cocks her head. 'Instra-ments?'

I straighten up and run to her side. 'Forgive me, Your Majesty.' I give another hurried bow. 'But I do not think she understands your meaning.'

The King raises a pale gold eyebrow, but before he can say anything, the one called Wolsey rounds on me and fixes me with a furious-looking stare. 'How dare you address His Grace uninvited. The King has had his fill of rascal boys like you sneaking into the palace to thieve and make trouble. You are worse than a plague of rats, the lot of you. Throw him out!' He turns and waves a thick, ringed finger at the guard.

I toss my chin up and glare at him. 'I am not a rascal boy, I am—'

'Silence! Take him away.'

The guard steps forwards and makes to haul me off, but Cat stumbles out in front of him, Pépin *chee-cheeing* at her heels. 'No! You cannot throw him away. Jack-Bon is our friend.'

The King frowns and raises a gloved hand. 'Stop. I will hear what the boy has to say.' He signals to the guard to loosen his grip and peers down at me. 'Now then, explain yourself – who are you and what is your relation to this maid?'

Pulling myself to my full height, I draw in a breath and tell him. First, the story I made up for anyone who might ask about how I came here from France to seek my fortune, then fell in with *Maître* Tarleton and his players. And then how Pépin and I found Cat wandering all alone in the forest and how we ended up here. But I make sure I'm quick about it, because from the set of his jaw and the drumming of his fingers on the jewelled belt at his hip, he's clearly a man of little patience.

As I finish, the King's gaze turns back to Cat, who has picked up Pépin and is whispering loudly in his ear.

'So, maid, you live with Her Grace the Queen?'

Cat blinks up at him and nods. 'But I have to be kept with Mistress Bristles. She says it is because I have a soft head and cannot do things properly, but she is wrong. I can sing songs and play on my birdy-flute. Queen Catty knows. And Jack-Bon too.' She turns and throws me a small smile – the first since before what happened with Hotspur and the dogs.

I flash her one back. 'It is true, Your Majesty. Cat is very talented, in spite of what people might think.'

King Henry gives a grunt. 'The Queen's ear for music is almost as good as my own. Well, I will consult with her, and if your story is true, the maid shall accompany us to the meeting with our cousin, the King of France and provide some entertainment. And you, boy – what did you say your name was?'

'Jacques Bonhomme, Your Majesty.' I bow again.

The King's gaze hardens. 'Jacques Bonhomme you say? There was a French outlaw who went by that name. He led an army of peasants against the French crown.' His lips flatten into a grim smile. 'I trust it is not your intention to follow your namesake and do the same here?'

My cheeks prickle as the cardinal and the rest of the King's followers break into gales of mocking laughter. But I will not let myself be bested or put down, even if he *is* the King. I hoist back my shoulders and stand my ground. 'I am no outlaw, Your Majesty, but if I was, I would be like your own Robin Hood, and rob the rich to give to the poor.'

The guard angles the blade of his halberd towards me.

The King's eyes narrow. He fingers the small red-and-gold rose jewel pinned to his coat, then gives a nod of approval. 'You have spirit, boy, I can see that. My Lord Cardinal' – he turns to Wolsey – 'send word to the Serjeant of the Revels that the lad is to come with us too. He speaks the French language and may have a use beyond sewing costumes and painting scenery.'

As he gives the command, my chest tightens. If I do as he wishes, how will I ever find the one I'm looking for and keep the vow I made to *Papa*? But do I dare refuse the King of all England . . . ? And besides – I glance down at Cat and Pépin – after all we've been through, can I really desert my friends?

'Yes, Your Grace.' The cardinal bows low and waits for the King to sweep past. As soon as he has gone, he straightens and shoots me a sharp-eyed look. 'Make yourself useful and take this –' he bats a hand at Cat – 'this maid back to the Queen's household. If she is who she claims to be, her keeper will be missing her.' He puffs out his chest and turns to face the crowd. 'As for the rest of you, this is no time for standing about. Return to your duties at once! Their majesties leave for the port of Dover on the morrow and there is still much work to do.' He gives a loud sniff, adjusts the gold crucifix hanging from his neck and hurries off after the King, his robes swishing from side to side.

As I watch him go, the band round my chest grows even tighter. I heave a sigh. 'Come on, Cat. The Queen will be missing you.' I go to take her hand, but she pulls away from me and cradles Pépin against her.

'I don't want to go back to Mistress Bristles. She keeps me locked in and she's got a whippy-stick and—' She takes big a gulp of air. 'And she cut my hair off. See.' She fumbles with the strap on her cap and pulls it free. My stomach knots as I stare at the orange tufts sticking up from her pale white scalp – all that is left now of her beautiful copper-gold hair.

'Why . . . why would anyone do such a thing?'

But Cat hasn't noticed my shock. She sets Pépin down on the ground, holds out her skirts and sways from one foot to the other, the fear on her face replaced by a look of beaming pride.

'Because I am the Queen's Fool.'

'The Queen's Fool?'

'Yes.' She squats down, lifts up Pépin's front paws and jiggles them about.

A man wheeling a cart piled high with cheeses gives a loud snort as he trundles past us. 'She's that all right and more besides.'

I glare at him, then stoop and cover Cat's head with the cap before anyone else can see. 'But it is not right for people to call you that.'

She drops Pépin's paws and jumps up frowning. 'Yes it is. Queen Catty is my friend!'

'You might think that, but—'

Cat grips my arm, her face lit by a sudden smile. 'Will *you* look after me, Jack-Bon?'

'What?'

'Instead of Mistress Bristles?'

I lick my lips. 'I do not think the Queen would want a . . . a boy for such a thing.'

She pulls down on my jerkin. 'But we can ask?'

I throw a quick glance back at the gatehouse. London might be only a few short miles along the river, but with each passing moment it feels further away than ever.

'Jack-Bon?'

I swallow and do my best to sound encouraging. 'Yes. Yes, we can.'

Cat gives a happy-sounding sigh. Then, scooping up Pépin, she slips her fingers into mine and tugs me back across the courtyard and towards the door that leads to the Queen's apartments.

· CHAPTER 13 ·

Jacques

We are almost there, when Cat jolts to a stop and swings round.

'I didn't ask the King.'

'About what?'

'If he saw the man who took Meg.'

I frown. 'How could he have?'

'He's here.'

'That cannot be possible. Come.' I reach for her hand, but she pulls away.

'It's true! I saw him on top of his horse when I was with Queen Catty's night-gale. Pippo did too.' She looks down at the monkey and gives him a hug. He gives a loud *chee-chee* back as if he agrees.

An image of the one-eyed horseman on the black stallion gallops into my head. What if it's him? There's only one way to be sure. 'Very well. We will go and look in the stables.' I prise Pépin free and lift him on to my shoulder.

'Will he be there?'

'I doubt it, but it is where he would put his horse.'

She lets me take her hand again and we set off towards the stables, making sure to duck as we pass the sewing-room windows.

I hold Cat back at the entrance and listen for voices, but the only sounds coming from inside are an occasional snort or nicker. As we cross into the gloom, the sweet smell of dung mixed with horse sweat pricks my nose, bringing fresh memories of home and the time I spent rubbing Jongleur down after our rides. I blink them away and peer about me.

A line of earthen-floored stalls runs off to our right. There's a grey horse in the one nearest us, and a bay in the one beyond. The rest appear empty, but then an impatient whinny sounds from the stall at the far end.

'This way.' I slide towards it, tugging Cat after.

As we reach the entrance, my heart misses a beat. It's the stallion that nearly knocked me down. He's a giant compared to his stable-mates – at least sixteen hands high.

'Is this the one the man was riding?'

Cat nods, then freezes, her eyes round and start-led-looking.

'What is it?'

'Men are coming!'

'What?' I hold my breath and strain my ears, but I can't hear anything. I shake my head. 'You must have imagin—' But wait – she's right. Footsteps –

two sets, and heading this way.

'*Vite!*' I push Cat and Pépin into the neighbouring stall and bundle them down behind a large pile of dung. 'Hold him tight and keep quiet – both of you.'

'Mouse-quiet?'

I nod and press a finger to my lips. Cat does the same.

The footsteps draw closer, then grind to a stop. I slide back along the wooden wall and peer out. Two men are standing at the stable door, their figures silhouetted against the light. I can't see their faces, but the taller one is dressed in a cloak and riding boots while his companion, a weightier man, wears a hat and thigh-length coat.

'What ho! Is anyone in there?' the taller one calls in cold, barking tones. I snatch in a breath. It's the horseman from earlier – I'm sure of it.

A rustle sounds in the straw behind me. Cat is on her feet and staring over the top of the dung-heap, her eyes even wider than before. I signal for her to stay quiet and get down, then look back at the men. They've moved inside now, but they're still too wrapped in shadow to be able to see them properly.

The horseman speaks again, though quieter this time. 'It is safe, my lord. There is no one to hear us except a few dumb beasts.'

'Give me your news then, Mortmain.' The second man's voice is low, but it has the air of one who is used to ordering others around. 'And quickly, man. I am shortly to dine with my beloved cousin, the King, and he does not take kindly to latecomers – least of all me.' He spits out the word 'beloved' as though he means the exact opposite.

The horseman gives a quick bow. 'Yes, my lord. Our cargo is ready for shipping to France. I plan to set out for Dover tomorrow and will stow it on board myself.'

'Excellent. And remember, it *must* be kept under lock and key during the voyage. We cannot afford to lose it now.'

'Fear not, my lord. It will be safe with me.'

'It had better be. And what of the evidence?'

'My lord?'

The other man clicks his tongue. 'Must I spell it out for you, sir? The document proving our case. You have located a forger as we discussed?'

The horseman – Mortmain – clears his throat. 'Yes, my lord.'

'And after the work is done?'

'He is set to meet with an unfortunate accident on the way back to his lodgings.'

'A fatal one, I trust? Nothing must be allowed to risk our scheme's discovery before it has ripened.'

'I will not fail you, my lord. I swear it.' Mortmain gives another bow.

'You mean, like you did in France?'

'But my lord, I—'

'Do not plague me with your excuses, man. Your mission was simple. Sow doubt in the minds of the French about this glorious meeting between our two kings and do everything possible to undermine the so-called peace between us. But instead, you succeeded only in arousing suspicions about yourself.'

'I dealt with the problem, my lord.'

'So you say. I hope for your sake you covered your tracks behind you afterwards?'

'But of course, my lord.' Mortmain speaks as if through gritted teeth.

'Good, because nothing must be allowed to come between me and my true destiny – least of all you. Now I must away to the palace, or I shall risk the King's displeasure – and that would never do!' The other man gives an angry-sounding grunt, then turns on his heel and strides off without a backward glance.

I pull back against the wall of the stall, my mind spinning with all I've just heard. It's clear that Mortmain works for this other man – a nobleman from the sounds of it – and that they have some kind of mischief planned in France. But what? And what is the 'true destiny' his master spoke of? I take a deep breath to steady myself and peer out again.

Mortmain is still there, head bowed as though deep in thought. Then, all at once he clears his throat and snaps back into life. But instead of turning and heading outside, he comes marching straight towards our hiding place.

I dart back to join Cat and Pépin, but as I duck down beside them, Pépin gives a loud chirrup and breaks free. Before I can stop him he scampers up over the dung-pile and disappears from view.

A sudden shadow looms across the entrance to the stall.

'Who's there?'

Heart hammering, I clamp my hand over Cat's mouth and push her to the ground. A pair of feet crunches across the straw. If he comes any closer . . . I cross my chest and offer up a silent prayer. But as I brace myself for our discovery, there's a panicked whinny from the neighbouring stall and a sharp crack of hooves against wood.

'What the—?' Mortmain starts and strides off to investigate. There's more whinnying followed by a loud 'Whoa!' and a light pitter-pattering of feet.

'It's all right, boy! It's just a rat.' Mortmain's voice sounds relieved. 'Come, we must away to London to fetch our cargo and from there to Dover port.' He backs the horse from the stall and clip-clops it out through the stable door.

Cat wriggles against me, but I keep her pinned down until the sound of trotting hooves fades into the distance. She jumps up the moment I release her, her cap and gown covered in clumps of straw-filled manure.

'It is him! The man who took Meg.'

'Are you sure?'

'Yes, yes! We must go after and make him give her back.'

'Wait.' I grip her by the sleeve. 'It is too dangerous.'

'Dangerous?' She frowns.

'I know it is hard to understand, but those two men – the one you say took your sister – and the other one—'

'The Lord Bucket!'

I tighten my grip. 'You know him?'

'Yes. He is Queen Catty's friend, but he doesn't want to be mine. He spoke angry words at me when he came to see her.' Her mouth turns down in a grimace.

I run a hand through my hair. 'Well, whoever he is, they are planning something bad.'

'Is it to do with Meg?' Cat's eyes shine back at me, full of sudden fear.

'What? No, I think it is something to do with the journey King Henry and Queen Katherine are making to France, but—'

A shower of dust rains down on our heads. Coughing, I put a sleeve to my nose and peer into the shadows above us. Pépin is sitting perched on a rafter, picking fleas from his fur with his small black fingers.

'*Petit coquin!* You nearly gave us away.'

'But he saved us too.' Cat reaches up and strokes

the tip of his tail, then gives a loud sneeze.

I puff out a breath. 'I suppose he did, but what are we going to do now?' I ask her the question, though in truth I know it's up to me to decide.

'Tell Queen Catty. *She* will know.'

I shake my head. 'I do not think she will listen to us.'

'She will! I told you – she is my friend. And you are good in your heart, Jack-Bon, even if you did make Hosper die.'

A fresh surge of guilt rushes through me. 'I was only trying to keep you safe.'

Cat sighs, then gives me a quick hug which I think means I'm forgiven. I smile and hug her back. 'All right, let us go and find your Queen Catty and see what she will say.'

I clamber up the dung-pile and lift Pépin down on my shoulder. 'Come.' I steer Cat out of the stall and back into the daylight outside. We're halfway across the main courtyard when she stops dead in her tracks.

'What is it now?'

She gives a small shudder, then raises her hand and points a trembling finger. 'Mistress Bristles!'

A tall, angular woman in a black gown and white bonnet is striding towards us, her face pinched into a tight frown. She pulls to a stop as she reaches us, then juts her hands on her hips and glares at us with glittering black eyes. Cat gives a small cry and jumps behind me, her arms circling tight about my waist.

'It's no use trying to hide from me!' The woman's tongue is as sharp-sounding as her looks.

Pépin shrieks a warning. The woman shoots him a quick fear-filled look, then darts forwards, wrenches Cat's arms free and drags her to her side.

'I've been looking everywhere for you, Cat Sparrow!' She bends over her like a great black crow and wags a bony finger in her face. 'How dare you behave like that in the Queen's presence? And when she was entertaining the Lord High Constable of all England too.'

Cat blinks and shakes her head. 'He isn't the High Stable, he's the Lord Bucket.'

The woman's eyes flash like knives. 'Hold your foolish tongue, girl! And be sure never to let My Lord, the Duke of Buckingham, hear you call him that to his face. He is a proud and powerful man and does not take kindly to being mocked, least of all by a witless maid like you.'

Anger boils up inside me. 'She is not witless, *Madame* Bristles, she is different, that is all.'

The woman's cheeks flush from white to bright red. She raises a hand to her whisker-covered chin, then drops it down quickly and narrows her eyes. 'You may think it amusing to cheek me, boy, but you won't be laughing when I call the guards and have you thrown in the dungeon. Now be off with you!' She shoos at me with her skirts.

'But we have important information to tell the Queen. It is about a pl—'

'Did you not hear what I said?' Mistress Bristles – not her right name, I realize that now – scans quickly about her as if searching for a guard. I bite my lip and back away.

Her eyes flick back to Cat. 'Look at the sight of you, girl. Covered in muck and straw. T'will take me all night to clean it off. Come along.' She grips Cat's hand and makes to march her away, but Cat digs her heels in.

'I want to stay here with my friends.'

Mistress Bristles' frown deepens. 'You have no choice. I've told you before. You are the Queen's Fool and must do her bidding.'

That word again! I want to protest, but I daren't risk it. I dart forwards and squeeze Cat's arm. 'It will be all right. I will come and find you soon. Here.' I lift the monkey from my shoulders. 'Take Pippo.'

As I hand him over to her, I whisper hurriedly in her ear, 'Do not say anything to Queen Catty about Lord Bucket yet. It is better if I am there to help explain. Mouse-quiet, remember?' I put a finger to my lips.

Cat gives a loud sniff and nods.

'Good. Now, do your best to please the Queen and Mistress Bri— Er . . . this lady, and I will come to you as soon as I can, I promise.'

'But what about the man on the thundery-black horse?'

'We will find him again, and Meg too, I swear it!'

'That's enough!' Mistress Bristles pulls us apart. 'And if I hear one more peep from you, Cat Sparrow . . .' Her fingers slide to the thin wooden stick hanging from the belt at her waist.

Cat's eyes widen with fear. Shivering, she hugs Pépin to her and lets herself be led off.

My stomach cramps as I watch them go. I should have stood up to that woman. Stopped her from taking Cat away. And how am I ever going to find Cat's sister? But I have to try – I gave her my word.

I glance back at the stables. My best chance is to discover what Mortmain and his master, the Duke of Buckingham, are plotting and bring the proof of it to the Queen. Though how is another matter . . .

A sudden thought flashes into my head. If I succeed, perhaps I can ask for the Queen's help to find the one I'm seeking too? I feel inside my jerkin for the leather pouch. Gripping it tight, I close my eyes and whisper the words of my other promise – the one I made to *Papa* that fateful day and vowed I would keep, come what may.

Footsteps crunch across the cobbles towards me.

'You, boy! Get back to work!'

I snap my eyes open and give a silent groan. It is *Maître* Gibson – his face darker than a winter storm.

· CHAPTER 14 ·

Cat

Mistress Bristles hissed and squawked while she was getting me clean to go and see Queen Catty. She called me 'ungrateful wrench' and said I didn't know I was born. I do know because I had a ma and pa and I am here, but I didn't say in case she squawked some more.

She also said the Queen would have the furies because I ran away, but it isn't true. Queen Catty says The King told her all about seeing me and that he is coming to hear me sing and play when he has finished dinner. She has given me a green-and-white rope to tie on Pippo and now a paley-white girl with red coloured hair has come to be with us too.

The girl is called The-Lady-Mary and is The King and Queen Catty's daughter. She is four years old and smaller than me. She does not speak unless Queen Catty speaks first, but she likes making music and singing too. She plays on an instra-ment called the Verge-alls. When her fingers stroke it, music pipes out like all the birds' voices singing together. I wish you could hear it, Meg. You would love it! And Jack-Bon too.

And now The King has come and he wants us to play – The-Lady-Mary on the Verge-alls and me on my birdy-flute. But before we do that he is talking to Queen Catty about sailing on the water to France and the peace-and-friendship he is going to make with The French King.

'Our daughter will make an excellent wife for the Dauphin. Do you not agree?'

Queen Catty does not say anything, but her face goes more pale than The-Lady-Mary's.

The King's eyes shrink glittery small. 'Is something wrong, Madam?'

Queen Catty's fingers grip on her Holy-Cross necklace tight-as-tight. 'Oh, husband, do we have to go through with this meeting? My Lord, the Duke of Buckingham, says the French are not to be trusted, and—'

'Silence!' The King's voice comes out tight through his teeth. 'It is I, not my cousin Buckingham, who is king of this realm, even though he and his friends might wish it otherwise.'

The King does not like the Lord Bucket, I can tell, but Jack-Bon has said to keep mouse-quiet about all that and wait for him to come back, so I will.

'As for you, wife, you would do best not to interfere in matters that do not concern you and provide me with a son and heir instead.'

'Yes, Your Grace.' Queen Catty bites on her lip and does a low bow and curtsey. 'I am sorry, I did not mean anything by it.'

'Good.' The King pushes out his hand. Queen Catty kisses it and does another curtsey. 'Now make sure your women have everything packed. We leave for Dover at dawn.' He gives a growl, then puts on his hat and bangs away to the door.

I stumble-run after. 'But what about me and The-Lady-Mary playing for you?'

His face goes redder than the Lord Bucket's did. 'I am not in the mood.' He swishes his coat in front and stamps off into the outside.

I don't like him all cross and angry and I am sorry for Queen Catty and The-Lady-Mary too. I want to say it, but then Mistress Bristles comes and takes me back off to the tower room.

I look out through the window with Pippo in case the man on the thundery-black horse comes again. But he doesn't and nor does Jack-Bon. And Mistress Bristles says we must leave tomorrow and go off on a long journey to Dovercastle and over the sea to France.

I am the same as Queen Catty. I do not want to go, Meg. I want to find you and Jack-Bon so we can all go back together and live in the peace-and-quiet, and Nonny Sweet-Bee can teach me the rest of my letters and we can sing with the birds and spin round in the sun.

*

We rattled in the wagon for days and days and now we are here in Dovercastle, waiting to go on the sea. I do not like it as much as the other place. It is tall and grey and even more stony-cold. I shiver my arms around Pippo's basket and look out through my window-slit. Screechy white birds are swooping and swerving over the top of the water outside. I try hard-as-hard, but I cannot see the end of it. How long must we be on it for? I do not know, but now here comes Mistress Bristles to fetch me.

'Hurry up, Cat Sparrow. We do not want the ship leaving without us.' She pushes me out of the door and down the dark slippy steps.

Pippo jumps and screeches in his basket.

'Quiet, imp!' Mistress Bristles cracks her stick, but Pippo screeches louder.

As we go through the echo-y rooms and into the windy outside, people stare at us like always, with their eyes round as pebbles and their mouths all gapey-wide. They should be more careful in case the flies buzz in and can't get out.

We go through the gates and along the track past walls and towers and down to the growling sea. Mistress Bristles hurries me through all the other people who are busy hurrying too. When we get to the edge of things, my eyes go wide-as-wide because there are lots of boats – big ones and small ones – all bobbing and bouncing on the water.

Mistress Bristles points at the closest big one to us. She says it is the ship we will sail to France on and that we must go on another boat to reach it. The boat-ship has sides as high as the walls of Dover-castle, but it is made of wood not stone. Four tree trunks grow out of the top – two big ones and two small ones. They don't have branches and leaves, but there are thick ropes tied with fluttery cloths – white ones with red crosses, and others with green-and-white stripes like on my cap and skirts. Men are hanging from the boat-ship sides. They are pulling on ropes tied with sacks and baskets from small boats below. Other ropes have horses or people tied on. They take even longer to get up because of all the kicking and shouting.

I hug Pippo's basket close. 'Is it Noah's boat?'

Mistress Bristles' eyebrows go knotty and high. 'What are you talking about, foolish girl? It is the King's ship, the *Katherine Pleasaunce*. Noah did not enjoy such luxury.' She mumble-mutters the last bit in her breath, but still I hear it.

'What's a lucks-ree?'

Her eyebrows go even more knotty. 'Never you mind! Now, hurry, or we will get left behind.' She digs her fingers in and pulls me down the rest of the track.

The noises blow louder in my ears: the yells of the men climbing in the ropes and the others scut-tling around on the boat-ship tops; the horses neighing and the cries of ladies being loaded over the sides; and all mixed in with the scream of the birds and the splash and rumble of the sea. I search over all the ships and boats for The King. I cannot see him, or Queen Catty and her ladies-who-wait. But then I do see somebody else.

It is the man on the thundery-black horse. Except he is not on his horse but being rowed along by another man in a small boat. He is wearing a black cloak and there is a sparkle on his hat, the same as the gold knots on the Lord Bucket's coat. A girl is in the boat too. She is sitting fast asleep with her head in a cloak propped on his shoulder. I can only see part of her face, but still, I know who it is. My heart jumps high – higher even than the sides of the boat-ships and the walls of Dovercastle.

'MEG! MEGGY-PEG!'

I snatch away from Mistress Bristles and stumble-run down to the wall, with Pippo in his basket bouncing beside me. I shout again. You don't look, but the man with the thundery-black horse turns round and I see his black patch and beard. But he doesn't see me back, and then people get in between. I fumble for my birdy-flute and blow. *Peep, peep, PEEP-PEEP* – but your boat goes past the Catty-Pleasant and over to another big boat-ship rocking and creaking behind and you are . . .

. . . gone.

'No!' I put down Pippo's basket and push my

face in my skirts and go to-and-fro, fro-and-to. My head and heart are panging me so hard I don't hear the feet click-clacking behind, and then it is too late.

'There you are! I ought to keep you on a leash like that wretched monkey of yours.' Mistress Bristles drags me on my feet.

'But I saw her . . . I saw Meggy-Peg.' I point my finger to where the boat was.

Mistress Bristles' eyes shrink into two black pips. 'What are you talking about?'

'My sister. The man on the thundery-black horse has got her, but she was asleep and she couldn't hear, even when I blew on my birdy-flute, and now she is gone, like before.' I hug my arms round me and do another to-and-fro.

'Stop that!' Mistress Bristles shakes me up and down. 'I've had a bellyful of your nonsense, wench. If my dear, sweet Susan had had the chance to live half the life you are living now . . .' She drops down her hands and her eyes go soft and swimmy.

'Who is Sweetsusan?'

Her eyes snap back. 'Never you mind!' She snatch-grabs Pippo's basket and bangs it at me. 'Now put that ridiculous whistle away and *hurry*, or you'll feel the sharp end of my stick.'

Both ends of Mistress Bristles' stick are sharp, but I don't say because I don't want to feel them. She marches me down to the water and splashes me through it to a small, creaking boat. I am shivery-cold and wet, but she only lets go when I'm bundled down inside.

A man sitting on a plank with two long sticks rolls his eyes and gives a pig-grunt. 'So you're the Fool girl?'

'The *Queen's* Fool,' I say back to him.

'Proud to have you on my boat.' He bows down his head and grins with his broken-down teeth. But it is not a kind grin. I try to get back out, but Mistress Bristles climbs in and pulls me next to her on the plank.

More people jump in and then there's no more room. The man dips his sticks in the water and pulls. The boat whooshes forwards. My stomach does too. I hold Pippo's basket close and look round-and-about for the man on the thundery-black horse's boat, but there's no sign. We get close to the side of the Catty-Pleasant and a great thunder-boom sounds. Grey smoke puffs out over our heads. I duck and stick my fingers in my ears.

The man with the boat-sticks laughs out loud. 'Jumpy, ain't she?' he shouts at Mistress Bristles. Then he looks me hard in the eyes and says slower-than-slow, ''Tis only the cannon to say the King is on board his ship.'

I do not know what a cannon is, but I don't want to hear one again.

The man points at the Catty-Pleasant's wooden sides. 'Ready for the climb?' I look up, but there is nothing for holding on to. He scrunches an eye and gives another gratey laugh.

Mistress Bristles glares at him. 'Stop your jesting, man. T'will only make things worse.'

The man gives another pig-grunt and shouts something to the top of the Catty-Pleasant. Men's heads appear over the side. They tumble down a rope. Then the man ties it round my middle and the other men pull me into the air.

I yell and kick about. Pippo screeches too. But we keep on going higher and higher. I look down, but my skirt is flip-flapping about and I can't see the boat, or Mistress Bristles. The sea is far and away and getting more far all the time. The wind whirls and twirls me around and sends my head all in a spin; my insides too. But Pippo is making small, scared sounds. I have to look after him.

'Hush, Pippo.' I squeeze his basket tight and try to be like a bird, gliding through the air, but then two hands snatch at me and drag me down.

'Welcome aboard, little mistress.' A salty man in a red cap undoes the rope round my middle. He shines me a smile and lifts me on my feet. I blink and look about. More men in red caps are heaving baskets and barrels up over the sides and climbing ropes high in the sky.

Queen Catty and The King are here too. They are standing together at the top of some steps and look-ing back over to where Dovercastle is. They might have seen the boat with you and the man on the thundery-black horse in, Meg. I will go and ask.

I pick up Pippo in the basket, but I don't get far because then Mistress Bristles flies over the side. Her bonnet is down on her face and her hair is in rats' tails all whipping and tearing about her head. I let slip a giggle. The salty man gives a loud chuckle too.

Mistress Bristles pulls up her bonnet and gives us both a piercey-hard look. 'Untie me at once!'

The salty man undoes her rope and tries to help her on her feet, but she pushes him off and does it on her own instead.

'Unhand me, man. I don't need help from the likes of you! Now, which way to the lower decks?'

He points at some steps going into a big, black hole in the floor behind.

I want to go over and see Queen Catty, but then Mistress Bristles grabs my hand and drags me down them, into the deep dark below.

· CHAPTER 15 ·

Jacques

I'm sitting in the hull, wedged between two great rolls of cloth with only the rats and the sound of the ship's creaking timbers for company. We've been at sea for what feels like an age, pitching and tossing and rolling from side to side. I've already brought up the bread and cheese I had for breakfast, and now the candle has blown out in my lantern too.

As I brace myself for the next wave, memories of the night I left home come flooding back. The hours of sitting there in my chamber in the gathering shadows, waiting for the servants to retire to bed. Then of slipping out of the castle under cover of darkness and making the welcome discovery that Pépin – who I'd persuaded myself it was best to leave behind – had stolen after me. And of meeting *Papa*'s faithful groom, Pierre, in the stables, changing into the old clothes he'd brought and riding hard through the night to Calais and the ship that would take me to England.

Was it all worth it? I thought so then, but how can it be when I've ended up almost back where I started and further than ever from getting the justice for *Papa* I vowed to him I would seek. And what about *Maman*? I told myself I was doing this for her too, but to leave her all alone like that . . . ?

My eyes prick with sudden tears. I swallow hard and scrub my face with the back of my hand. *Papa* called me *Hirondelle* because he said I had a swallow's brave heart, but if he was here now, he would think me nothing but a coward.

I heave a sigh. One thing's for sure – sitting here in the dark feeling sorry for myself is going to help no one. Better to clear my head with some sea air. I haul myself to my feet and pick an unsteady path towards the stairs.

The deck above is lit by the glow from a line of swaying lanterns. I'm about to climb the next set of stairs to the top deck, when a man bounds down them, his cloak streaming out behind him. As he barges past me and turns down the gangway, the lantern-light catches the side of his face. My heart gives a sudden lurch.

Mortmain! I expected him to be with the Duke of Buckingham on the King and Queen's ship, not this one. I wait until he's gone further along the gangway, then take a deep breath and slink after him. He's in a hurry, but the pitch and roll of the ship is slowing him down and it's not hard to keep him in sight. It's not long before the gangway narrows into a dark, panelled passage, lined on both sides by small open store-rooms filled with wine-barrels and rounds of thick-rinded cheese.

Perhaps he's fetching something to eat? But he keeps going until he reaches a door at the very end. I pull back into the nearest store-room and wait. A few moments later there's the sound of a key rattling in a lock and a door being opened and shut.

I wait a little longer in case he reappears, then, heart bumping, I slide out, tiptoe up to it and press my ear to the wood. At first all's quiet, but then there's an angry-sounding growl and the noise of something heavy being dragged across the floor. It's followed by a dull thud and then silence again. What's he got hidden away in there? There's only one way to find out.

I slip back into the store-room and bide my time until at last, Mortmain re-emerges. Locking the door behind him, he lopes off down the passage again.

Prising a nail free from a damaged wine-barrel lid, I hurry back up to the door. I've never done this before – broken in to somewhere. But then there are plenty of things I never did in my old life which are second nature to me now.

Sliding the nail into the keyhole, I poke it about until the lock clicks. Then, with a quick glance behind me, I push on the door and step inside.

The room beyond is small, with a low ceiling, and is lit only by a small square of daylight which shines through a window-hole cut in the opposite wall. As my eyes get used to the shadows, I see rows of shelves, each one packed tight with baskets which, when I look inside, prove to be full of the things needed for a grand banquet – gold candlesticks, red silk tablecloths, jewel-studded jugs and goblets and boxes of slim-bladed knives and silver spoons. The only other items in the room are two pieces of furniture – a rickety-looking, three-legged stool and a long wooden chest with an iron lock-plate, of the sort for keeping coins and precious jewels in. Maybe secrets too?

I try the lid, but it's locked and this time the nail's not long enough to pick the lock. A blade might work though. I jump to my feet and snatch a knife from one of the cutlery baskets. As I jiggle it up and down in the lock, I spot the flattened edge of what appears to be a roll of parchment poking out from beneath the chest-lid.

Tugging it free, I uncurl it and hold it up to the light. The surface is covered in lines of small, closely written text. At the foot of the page beneath a blob of red wax, bearing the imprint of what is probably a holy cross, are two signatures. One, faint and spidery-looking, spells out the name 'Alys Godwin'. The other, full of curls and scrolls, looks like 'Hildegard'.

A sudden thought flashes into my head. What if this is the 'evidence' the Duke of Buckingham and Mortmain were talking about in the stables? If it is, then it's cost at least one man his life already. The question is, why? I peer at the first line. The text is in Latin and hard to read, but if I hold it to the light, I can just about make it out:

This is the final testament of Lady Alys Godwin, written in the last hours of her life on this the fourth day of April in the Year of Our Lord 1509. I do hereby declare that . . .

I sit back on my heels and frown. It doesn't make sense. What have the words of a dead woman got to do with Mortmain and Buckingham's plans in France? I'm about to read on when a pair of heavy footsteps creaks along the passageway outside.

Rolling the parchment up tight, I thrust it inside my jerkin and scan about me, looking for a place to hide. But there's nowhere . . .

The footsteps grind to a halt and a key rattles in the lock. There's a muttered curse, then the door swings slowly open. Heart pounding, I slip behind it and hold my breath.

The dark figure of a man edges into the room, the only thing visible about him a knot of gold-coloured metal pinned to his hat and the glint of a blade in his outstretched hand.

'Show yourself now, or you'll feel the kiss of my friend here.' A flash of silver slices through the air.

I shiver at the familiar sound of Mortmain's barking tones and tighten my grip on the knife.

'Very well, coward, then I will come to you.'

A wave of cold panic surges through me. If I stand my ground and try to defend myself, I'm bound to lose. My only chance is to create a distraction and run. I snatch up a basket of candlesticks on the shelf beside me and send the contents clattering to the floor.

Mortmain leaps to one side with a shocked cry. Seizing my chance, I dash past him and out through the door. But I haven't gone far when the ship lurches to the right and sends me tumbling to the ground. As I scramble to my feet, a hand grabs my collar and swings me round.

'A boy? What were you doing in there?' Mortmain's single eye gleams back at me, green and gold in the lantern-light.

Swallowing down on my fear, I slide the knife behind my back and force myself to meet his gaze. 'N-n-nothing, sir. I . . . I was looking for some food to take to my master, *Maître* Gibson. He is Serjeant of the Revels and—'

The scar beneath Mortmain's left eye twitches. 'A French rat, eh? I might have guessed! Enough of your lies.' He whips up his blade and presses the tip to my throat. 'Now, tell me the truth, or else . . .'

A dribble of sweat trickles down the side of my face. I need to find another excuse and quickly.

'My mother is sick. I was looking for things I could sell back home in France. I . . . I took this.' I draw the stolen knife from behind my back.

He stares down at it and frowns. 'That's all?'

'Yes, sir.'

He gives a low growl and relaxes his grip, but as he reaches to take the knife off me, his eye narrows. 'What's that you've got there?' He jabs a finger at my chest.

My stomach claws. The parchment is poking from the top of my jerkin.

'Nothing. I—'

'Let me see.' He makes a swipe for it. I twist away and lash out with the knife.

'God's teeth!' He drops his dagger and staggers backwards, right hand clutched to his chest.

It's only a flesh wound, but it gives me the head start I need. Heart thumping, I dash back along the passage and scramble up the stairs to the deck above. If I can only find *Maître* Gibson . . . I haul myself into the open and look towards the ship's stern, blinking against the light, but there's no sign of him there. As I spin about, a gust of wind knocks me sideways, straight into the path of a barrel-chested sailor.

'Stop him! He's a French spy.' Mortmain leaps out on deck and waves his dagger at me. The sailor makes a grab, but I jump to one side and pelt past him, weaving between stacks of barrels and coils of greasy black rope.

Footsteps thunder after me. I gulp in a breath and keep on running, but then suddenly the deck runs out. A timber wall looms up before me, a rough ladder nailed to its side. I glance behind. Mortmain and the sailor are gaining on me. If I don't scale the ladder now, it will all be over.

I fling myself on to the lowest rung and start to climb. The higher I go, the stronger the wind blows, tearing at my clothes and hair. If I fall now . . . I push the thought away and, pulling tight against the bars, keep on climbing, one hand over the other until at last I reach the top. I heave myself on to the upper deck and skim about me, legs braced against the lurching and bucking of the ship. I'm at the bow now and running out of places to go.

I throw another look behind me. A hat with a gold badge appears at the top of the ladder, quickly followed by Mortmain's dark-bearded face. He barks something at me, but the wind snatches his words away and bowls them out to sea. I dash across the deck towards the foremast, then grind to a stop. Three sailors have appeared from nowhere. They stomp towards me, faces scowling, arms spread wide.

I swing round. Mortmain and the other sailor are closing in fast. I fling myself to the rail. There's another ship coming alongside us. It's so close I can see the lords and ladies taking the air on deck.

I twist back again. My pursuers are circling in front of me like a pack of hungry hounds, blocking off all escape. Mortmain lifts his blade and takes a step forwards, his eye full of cold, hard cunning – the look of a wolf moving in for the kill.

I shiver and glance down through the salt-spray at the rolling water below. Pierre taught me to swim in our fishpond at home, but sea swimming is a different matter. Panic grips me, freezing me to the spot.

'Give yourself up, Frenchie!' yells one of the sailors.

And I nearly do. But then a voice sounds loud and clear in my ear.

You can do it, Hirondelle!

I swallow hard and look back at the other ship. Will I make the distance? I don't know, but I have to try. Shoving the roll of parchment deeper inside my jerkin, I scramble on top of the rail, suck in the biggest breath I can, and jump.

· CHAPTER 16 ·

Cat

It is loud out here, with the wind flip-flapping and the waves smashing and crashing and the sailor-men bawling and shouting fit to make my ears burst. But I'm glad I'm away from being down in the creaky dark with Mistress Bristles and all her groans and moans and sickly smells.

Pippo likes it better too. He is out from the basket and leaping and climbing like the sailor-men, but not too high because I am holding on to him by his special green-and-white rope.

A sailor-man told me we will be at France soon, but all I can see is the sky and the sea and more boat-ships. I look out at them in case you are in one, Meg, but they are too far to see, even the one in front.

It is a long way down to the sea. The water has changed from sparkly blue and white to green, but I don't like looking because it makes my head go all spinny and strange.

Then I hear the cry. It blows into my ears all faint and small, like a tiny bird.

Peep! Peep! Peeeeeep!

It is coming from down in the water. I scrunch my eyes, but I can't see where. Then it stops. I wait for it to come back and it does, but now it is louder and calling out a word – a strange one I do not know.

'*Au secours!*'

And then one I do.

'HELP!'

I peer and peer and then I see it – a dark wet head bobbing in the waves.

'Help! Help!'

Jack-Bon! It is Jack-Bon in the sea. Pippo knows it too. He is skitter-scattering along the side and shrieking down at the water. I bend over and cry Jack-Bon's name. His head goes back and his face looks up, pale-as-pale.

'Cat! Get help!' His arms are splashing, but his voice is all tired and gurgling.

I pull Pippo down and stumble-run to the nearest sailor-man – the same one that lifted me up the side. His head is down and he's busy winding up a rope. I drag on his sleeve. 'My friend is down in the sea.' I point over the edge.

The sailor-man frowns his face. 'Come, maid. Can't you see I'm busy?' He puts his head back down and goes on with his winding.

I drag on his arm again. 'But he needs help. Look!' Pippo bounces and chitters to tell him too.

The sailor-man's eyes go owly-wide. 'A monkey. So that's what was in that basket of yours. Where d'you get him from then?'

'He's my friend's who's in the sea. You have to pull him out – now!' I drag down even harder.

The sailor-man puffs a breath. 'All right. Show me then.' He drops the rope and bangs along after.

I look down, but Jack-Bon is gone. I scrunch my eyes and do more looking. 'He was there. I saw him.'

The sailor-man shakes his head. 'I knew it. Now stop your japing and get back down below. I don't know what that mistress of yours can be thinking, letting the two of you up here on your own.'

'Mistress Bristles is not my mistress, and I am not jay-pin. My friend is all alone in the sea and if no one helps him—'

Jack-Bon's head bobs out again coughing-and-spluttering. 'HELP! PLEASE!'

The sailor-man's face goes ashy-white. 'Saints preserve us! Hold on, lad.' He runs back and gets his rope. He ties an 'O is for Oak' in the end and swishes it hard over the edge. It tumbles like a brown snake and splashes down on top of the sea. Jack-Bon slaps his arms out, but he can't get it. The sailor-man snatches the rope back and swishes it down again.

The 'O' splashes next to Jack-Bon, but then a big wave comes and makes his head go back under.

I shout his name louder than loud. He bobs out again and reaches. He reaches some more. Another wave is coming, but then his fingers get hold of the rope.

'Put it over you!' the sailor-man calls.

Jack-Bon slides his arms and head in the 'O' and wriggles his body inside.

'Good lad. Now hold on tight!' The sailor-man turns and shouts behind. 'Hey! I need help here!'

Two other sailor-men run over and pull with him on the rope and Jack-Bon's body and legs come free of the sea. The sailor-men swing him up the side, then the first sailor-man drags him over the edge and he lands on the floor all dripping and wet like a fish from the nonnies' pond.

'Stand back!' the first sailor-man cries.

But I know he doesn't mean me or Pippo, because we're Jack-Bon's friends. I get down on my skirts beside Jack-Bon. His face is grey and his eyes are closed tight shut.

'Is he sleeping?'

The first sailor-man puts a hand over Jack-Bon's nose and mouth and frowns. He looks down at me and puffs his cheeks. 'I'm afraid he's gone.'

'Gone where?'

'To meet his Maker.' He closes his eyes and makes a slow Holy-Cross shape over his chest like the nonnies do when an orphling dies and goes to heaven.

My heart pangs. 'But he can't. It isn't time. Come back, Jack-Bon. Come back!' I hold him tight and shake and shake till I can't shake any more.

'It's no use, maid.' The first sailor-man tries to pull me off, but I won't let him. Then – all suddenly – Jack-Bon's mouth makes a groaning sound and a dribble of sea comes out. His chest goes in and out and even more sea comes. Then he coughs and spits and blinks his eyes wide open.

All of the sailor-men gasp out loud. Some lords-and-ladies in grand clothes hurry over and huddle round and everyone stares and stares.

The first sailor-man pushes back his cap and shines me a gappy-tooth smile. 'Seems you've brought your friend back to life, maid.' He bends and lifts Jack-Bon in his arms. 'We'd best get him down below so the surgeon can take a look at him.'

I trip along after, with Pippo following behind. People mutter and stare, but it doesn't matter about them. It only matters about Jack-Bon. When we get to the stairs to the down-below, the first sailor-man throws Jack-Bon over his back. Something drops down from his neck and plops on the ground. It's a bag on a string, all wet from the sea. I pick it up and put it in my own bag just in time, because then another sailor-man comes and takes Pippo and me down too.

He puts us at the bottom of the stairs and lets us

follow off after Jack-Bon and the first sailor-man. We go along in the creaky dark, then the sailor-man stops at a door. He does a loud *rap-rap* and goes inside. I hear him tell the person on the other side about Jack-Bon being in the sea and almost 'downing-in-the-deep' and being saved by 'the strange maid's keen ears'. When he comes out again, I try to go past, but he shuts over the door and says no, the Sir-John must look at Jack-Bon on his own, and he is going to take me back to Mistress Bristles now. But I don't want to go back to her. I want to wait here with Pippo and see my friend. I puff down on my skirts and fold my arms tight across me.

The sailor-man shakes his head. 'You're a stubborn one and no mistaking. All right, have it your way.' He pats my cap and goes off back where we came from.

I listen outside the shut door. I can hear a man's voice speaking low-as-low and lots of clinking and rustling. Then suddenly, the man gives a loud shout, 'The Devil take me!'

The nonnies say the Devil is bad. He can take the Sir-John if he wants, but I will not let him take Jack-Bon. I jump up and bang with my hand on the door. 'Let me in!'

The door cracks open and a whiskery red face pokes through. 'What? Who are you?'

'Is Jack-Bon all right?'

'Jack-Bon?'

'My friend. He is in there.' I point with my finger through the door.

The man's face furrows. 'Do you take me for a fool?'

'I don't want to take you, I want to take Jack-Bon!' I try to push through the gap, but the man bundles me out and locks the door with his key.

'Where are you going?'

'To fetch some dry clothes for *Jack*.' He curls his mouth and gives a pig-snort. 'Now wait outside, the pair of you.' He frowns a look at Pippo, then wipes his hands down his sides and hurries away into the dark.

I knock on the door and call Jack-Bon's name, but there isn't any sound. Perhaps he is sleeping. I wait and wait and then the Sir-John comes back again, his arms all bundled with clothes.

He sees me and Pippo and rolls his eyes, then he lock-opens the door and goes inside. I try to go in too, but the door shuts tight. The Sir-John does some talking and Jack-Bon answers back all peepy-small, but it is too quiet for even me to hear.

I bang on the door again. 'Let us in!'

It opens and the Sir-John's head pokes back out. 'Very well. You can come in now, but that creature' – he kicks a toe at Pippo – 'must stay outside.'

'But—'

'But nothing!' The Sir-John snatches Pippo's rope and ties it to a hook by the door. 'Now, I must go and attend to a matron with a bad case of sea-sickness on the lower deck. But when I return, rest assured I will be handing your friend over to the ship's master to do with as he sees fit.'

I want to ask him what 'rest-sure' and 'seas-fit' mean, but he bustles off into the doom and gloom. I wait for him to be gone, then I try and undo Pippo's rope. But it is no use because my fingers won't let me.

'I'm sorry, Pippo, but you have to stay behind.' I stroke his fur, then peep my head inside the door.

It looks like the cupboard in the nonnies' Infirmy. There are lots of pots and bowls and bunches of dried twigs and leaves. The smell is the same herby-sweet one, but mixed in with candle-smoke. A lantern is creaking and swinging above. Under the lantern is a bed with a person shivering and shaking in a blanket.

I come inside. The person coughs and looks at me with shiny, round, eyes.

'*C'est toi*, Cat?'

My heart squeezes. It is Jack-Bon's voice, but faint and small.

I tumble over and hug him tight. He gives a short, scrapey laugh and hugs me back. 'You saved me, Cat. I would have drowned if you had not heard me and fetched help.' He pulls a face and hacks out another cough.

'Why were you splashing about in the sea?'

Jack-Bon's face goes scared looking. He flicks his tongue over his lips. 'That man, Mortmain. The one who works for the Duke of Buckingham . . . He was on the other big ship. I took something from him and he chased me to try and get it back.'

My stomach goes all twisty-tight. 'What about Meg?'

Jack-Bon's eyebrows scrunch together. 'Meg?'

'My sister, Meg. She was in his boat at Dover-castle.'

'Are you sure?'

'Yes!' I push at him. The blanket falls down. I blink and step back. 'What are you in that for? The Sir-John has brought the wrong things. I will go and tell him.'

Jack-Bon puts his hand on my arm. 'No. They . . .' His face goes red and he gives another cough. 'They are the right ones.'

'But why?'

Jack-Bon blows out his cheeks and looks down. 'Because I am not who you think.'

My heart does a bounce. 'Not Jack-Bon?'

He lifts his head and does a big swallow. 'Not Jack-Bon, no, but Isabelle – Isabelle Boncoeur.' His face goes even redder.

My head feels all hot and spinny. I stumble-trip back. A pile of pots clatters down on the floor and smashes into pieces. It makes me jump. Jack-Bon too.

'I am sorry, Cat. I should not have kept it a secret from you.' He reaches out and squeezes my arm.

I look at him. My insides are tied with knots and tangles. 'But why did you wear boys' things?'

Jack-Bon's face frowns and his eyes go all faraway. 'So that no one could find me and make me go home before—' He stops what he is saying and shivers. Then he shakes his head and looks back at me. 'Besides, it is safer to travel as a boy. Though now the surgeon has found out the truth and turned me into a girl again.' He pulls at the brown kirtle-skirts he is wearing then drags the blanket over them and hunches down his head again.

I peer and peer at him, but apart from the kirtle, he looks just the same.

'Is-a-belle?' I sound the word. 'Queen Catty's ma is called that.'

He bites on his lip and nods. 'I remember.'

I reach out with my fingers and stroke his cheek. 'Your face is still Jack-Bon's. Your hair too.'

Jack-Bon creeps his own fingers over his sea-wet head. 'It used to be long like yours did, but I cut it off the night I left home.' He puffs another breath and stares in his lap. He looks sad – like I was when Mistress Bristles cut off all mine.

'It will grow long again.'

'I know. It is not that, it is just that . . . *Eh bien*, I wish things were different.' A tear squeezes from his eye and runs down over his cheek.

I nod my head. I do too. I wish we had found you, Meg, and I wish we could leave this boat-ship and be on the land again. The Catty-Pleasant gives a loud groan back at me, then everything rattle-clatters to one side – all the rest of the pots and bowls and the lantern too. I am falling the same way, but Jack-Bon grips my skirts and stops me. A white thing rolls out from his blanket and drops on the floor. Jack-Bon snatches it back. He undoes it and gives a loud cry.

'What is it?'

'The thing I took from Mortmain, but it is ruined!' He stares down, his face pale-as-pale.

I look too. It is a paper-roll like the ones the nonnies keep in their library. There are some words right at the bottom, next to a big red flower shape with a Holy-Cross in it, but the rest are scatters of letters – 'H is for Holly', 'C is for Cowslip', 'S is for Sage' – or else blobs and blurs. I want to ask Jack-Bon what it is for, but then his eyes go all wide and starey and his hands grab around his neck.

'*Mon sac*. Where is it?'

I remember about the thing that fell down on the floor when the sailor-man was carrying him. I reach inside my bag and pull it out. 'Is it this?'

He snatches it away and pulls a dirty cloth out. He hugs me and spreads it on his skirts and whispers a word which sounds like 'Mercy'.

I peer at the gold shape sewn on it. It looks like a . . .

'B is for Birch.'

Jack-Bon frowns his face. 'What?'

'B is for Birch. Bucket too.'

He holds it to the lantern and tips his head to the side. 'It does look like a B, I suppose. But there is a piece missing.'

'Did you take it from the man as well?'

'No, I—' He gives a loud swallow. 'I found it.'

I want to ask where, but then footsteps sound from the outside. Jack-Bon hears them too. He folds the paper-roll and stuffs it in the bag with the dirty cloth.

'*Vite!* We must go.' He grabs the bonnet lying on the bed and bundles me through the door.

Pippo is still sitting tied to the hook. He gives a loud chitter when we come.

'*Mon pauvre petit.*' Jack-Bon bends and undoes him.

'Wait! Where do you think you're going?' It is the Sir-John thumping back towards us.

'Run!' Jack-Bon grips my hand and drags me away. We run and run. The Sir-John runs too, but he is old and puffy and we leave him far behind. We turn round a corner and come to the stairs. Cries swoop down from the outside of 'Land ahoy!' and 'Get the ropes ready!'

Jack-Bon puts his head in his bonnet and we climb the stairs – him first, then me and Pippo after. When we get into the whooshing air, everyone is milling and spilling and trying not to slip and fall. I hold on tightly to Jack-Bon's hand, but a sailor-man pushes through us and makes me trip. When I get up again, Pippo is there, but Jack-Bon is gone. I call his name and spin about, but then a hand grabs my shoulder and stops me still.

I look round and my heart goes down like a sinking stone, because it is not Jack-Bon. It is Mistress Bristles, with her face all red and full of the furies.

As we come up on deck, I tighten my grip on Cat's hand, but a sailor barges into us and knocks us apart. I try to find her, but there are too many people jostling and pushing and I'm dragged away in a swirl of cloaks and skirts. When I see her again, she's in the clutches of that awful woman and being marched towards the other end of the ship. I call her name, but it's no use. She's too far away, and I'm penned in by a wall of lords and ladies all vying to get a view of the coast.

I elbow my way in between them until I reach the ship's rail. A cold shiver runs through me as I peer down at the rolling green swell below. If it hadn't been for Cat's sharp hearing and quick thinking, I'd be out there now somewhere, drifting lifeless on the waves. A fresh twist of guilt curls up inside me. She's my friend. I should have trusted her with the truth about who I really am.

I heave a sigh and stare out at the approaching coastline. The grey walls of Calais loom in the distance. The town and the land around were captured by the English in the wars which our two countries fought for a hundred years and more. But France and my home are just a short horse-ride beyond. It would be so easy to slip away and go back there when we land . . . I grit my teeth and push the thought back down. I made a vow to *Papa* and I'm determined to keep it however long it takes. And in the meantime, I must do what I can to help Cat find her sister.

I think back to what she said about seeing Meg at Dover. Supposing she was right? But then why would Mortmain have brought Meg here? And what other words did the parchment contain that made him so desperate to get it back?

I shake my head. There's still so much I don't know, but I'm too exhausted to try and make sense of it all now.

As I take in another breath, I become aware of my bodice digging into me. I've been so used to wearing my shirt and soft jerkin, I've forgotten what it feels like to be trussed up in a maid's clothes. Still, at least in this patched apron and skirts there's less chance of Mortmain recognizing me. A man like him won't give a poor serving-wench a second glance.

I grip the rail and fix my gaze on the harbour ahead. A flotilla of small boats and barges is ferrying people, horses and equipment from the ships at anchor to the shore. As our own anchor splashes down, people pull back from the rail and ready themselves for the landing.

A man dressed in the King's livery comes marching towards me. Before he can say anything, I curtsey and hurry off to join a line of servants bringing up crates of squawking chickens from the hold. Once all the birds have been safely transported to the shore, a sailor ropes us up and lowers us one by one into a waiting boat below. As the boatman rows us away, I overhear a woman in front of me gossiping with the man next to her.

'A French spy, or so they say. Rescued from the sea dressed as a boy, and now she's gone and disappeared. They should have left her to feed the fishes.' Her neighbour grunts in agreement.

Cheeks burning, I turn my head quickly and look out over the water at the procession of people and animals snaking its way up from the harbour towards the town walls. It's headed up by line upon line of guards dressed in the red-and-gold livery of the King. Next comes the King himself. He is mounted on a magnificent grey horse while the Queen rides a bay at his side. Trotting behind them is a great crowd of lords, ladies and bishops, accompanied by a whole army of lesser nobles and gentlemen and then more guards bringing up the rear. Dozens of horse-drawn carts stacked high with crates and baskets follow in their wake, together with a mass of servants hurrying along behind. Cat and Pépin must be in there somewhere, though trying to seek them out is like looking for two pins in a mountain of straw.

When we arrive at the harbourside, I clamber out of the boat and fall in behind a group of servants tailing a cart piled with tapestries and carpets. We toil up the cobbled slope towards the town gates, hurrahs and shouts of 'Long live the King!' echoing down to us from the streets inside. Hundreds of townsfolk stand in doorways or hang out of window casements waving green-and-white ribbons or flags marked with the English cross of St George. Though it is not my king they cheer, I can't help feeling a small glow of pride.

As we leave the town behind and strike out along a road between open fields, the afternoon sun pitches down, making my smock and hose stick to my skin. I'm desperate for a drink and something to eat, but I do my best to distract myself by listening to the servants' chatter instead.

"Course the Frenchie King ain't happy about meetin' our one on English territory,' a rough-shaven man with a limp says. 'If he'd had his way, we'd have been over the border in France, but you can't trust a Frenchie as far as you can throw him. I should know. I got this off 'em when I fought along-side the King at the Battle of the Spurs back in '13.' He pats the top of his right leg and sucks in a whistling breath.

There are grunts of agreement and sympathy, then a snaggle-toothed woman next to me chimes in. 'Rumour has it their King's a runt – half the size of King Hal and skinny as a weasel too. I 'spect the minute he sees him, he'll want to pull up his tent-poles and run off home!'

The others explode into loud guffaws and giggles. A tide of anger rises up inside me, but I stay silent. I don't want them turning their sharp tongues on me.

As we draw near to the site of the English camp, the excitement builds and people elbow and jostle to get a better view. Fearful of being trampled, I worm my way free of the crowd and drop down to the meadow which runs alongside the road. As the dust settles around me, my heart skips a beat. For there spread out in the valley below is a truly wondrous sight.

A great castle with brown stone turrets and red roofs stands on a low hill to the left. But more marvellous by far is the grand palace that has been built in front of it, its brick and stone walls topped by battlements and a sloping slate roof, its rows of arched windows – too many to be counted – glittering in the sun. Nearby is a magnificent golden pavilion, its pointed roofs decorated with colourful flags and painted beasts on poles, while pitched around it are hundreds of smaller tents, some covered in green-and-white striped cloth, others in red and gold. Beyond the tents, a grand stone arch leads to a large grass-covered courtyard with a railed-off track running down the middle. This must be the tiltyard *Maître* Gibson spoke of, where the knights will do their jousting.

There are people everywhere too. Men and women of all stations. Grand-looking ones riding on horseback, or sauntering about talking; servants pushing carts or carrying baskets and sacks, and guards everywhere, standing to attention, or parading up and down. And a whole host of animals as well. Horses, of course, but also pens of cattle and sheep and flocks of chickens, ducks and geese. It is as though the whole of Greenwich has been uprooted and planted here.

'A miraculous thing, isn't it? And much grander than the French camp across the fields, or so they say.'

I start. A man dressed in the black gown of a priest has appeared beside me, a prayer book in his hand. He waits for me to reply, but I'm lost for words and all I can do is nod.

He gestures to the grand palace in front of us. 'The King and Queen's quarters, with plenty of room left over for His Grace the cardinal too. Some call it the Palace of Illusions.'

'Why is that?'

'You will see when you get near to it. Let us hope

illusions are not the only thing this place will be remembered for.' He shakes his head, then clasping the prayer book close to his chest, he turns and rejoins the procession.

I frown, unsure of his meaning. But as I get closer to the palace, a warm breeze rises and its walls and gatehouse seem to ripple in and out. At first I think I'm seeing things, but the gasps from others around me say different.

I dart forwards and peer at the brickwork. The blocks at the base look solid enough, but when I stand on tiptoe and touch the wall above, it buckles beneath my fingertips. I snatch my hand back in surprise. And then I realize the truth of it. It's not brick, but canvas painted to look like it, though the great arched windows set into it appear real enough.

I follow the wall towards the gatehouse. The main entrance is topped by two huge red-and-white Tudor roses and a magnificent painted coat of arms – a great gold crown supported by a golden lion on one side and a red dragon on the other. But it's the grim-faced statues lining the walls of the gatehouse towers which draw my eye the most, each one clutching a boulder high above its head as if ready to hurl it down on those who dare to pass beneath.

As I step back to get a better view, I stumble against the bottom step of a huge brick and stone fountain behind me. Bunches of men and women are standing on the top step using the silver goblets chained to the fountain's brickwork to catch the sparkling red liquid spilling from the mouths of rows of snarling, cat-like beasts set around the sides.

I shake my head in disbelief. Palaces of painted brick, giant tents made from cloth of gold, and fountains running with wine? The priest was right. This place *isn't* real. But at least, if these are the King and Queen's lodgings, it means Cat and Pépin must be close by.

As I'm puzzling how to get past the palace guards, a pounding of hooves and a chink of bridles rings out behind me. I spin round to see a group of horsemen in coats of scarlet and black riding towards the gatehouse arch. A bunch of red-cheeked male servants dressed in the same colours are running along at their side.

This could be my best chance. Scooping up a half-filled jug of wine from the fountain steps, I gather my skirts and hurry after them. I keep my head down as I pass by the guards, but thankfully they're too busy admiring the men's horses to pay me any attention.

When I'm safely through the arch, I stop and look about me. I'm standing in a courtyard lined by cloth walls, each decorated with pictures of armed warriors and studded with yet more real windows.

Servants bustle to-and-fro across the stone pave-ment carrying piles of linen cloths and baskets of gold plate and cutlery. A door opens in the wall opposite and a boy in a brown tunic lumbers out, a yoke with two buckets balanced across his shoulders. Smells of roasting meat and baking bread waft out behind him, pricking my nose and making my stomach growl again. I close my eyes and breathe them in, imagining the taste.

'You, girl, if that's wine you're carrying, bring it here that I may quench my thirst!'

My chest tightens. That voice! I'd know it anywhere. It's the grand lord from the stables in Greenwich. I flick my eyes open. A proud-looking man on a chestnut mare looms above me, his black velvet coat studded with rubies which glint in the sun like hundreds of blood-red eyes.

So, this is him – the Duke of Buckingham, the most powerful noble in the whole of England.

He beckons to me impatiently with ring-encrusted fingers. I freeze, unsure of what to do. An elbow jabs me in the ribs. It's one of his serving-men. 'Quickly, maid! Do as his lordship commands.'

I hesitate, then scurry forwards offering up the jug. The duke swipes it from my hands and fixes me with a hard grey stare. My heart does a somersault. Has he recognized me? But that's impossible – he's never seen me before. Cheeks flushing, I bob a curtsey and dip my head, doing my best to hold my nerve.

When I dare to look up again, he's busy swigging

the wine straight from the jug. As I heave a sigh of relief, my gaze snags on the gold brooch pinned at his throat. I frown. I've seen that looping pattern somewhere before, I'm sure of it . . .

'What are you looking at, wench?'

I shake my head and lower my gaze.

The duke snorts and thrusts the empty jug back at me. 'Return to your duties before I have you whipped for your insolence.' Wiping his fleshy lips with the back of his hand, he swings himself down from his horse and marches away across the courtyard, scattering servants left and right as he goes.

As his men dismount too, I dart into the shelter of the doorway and do a quick scan of their faces, but there's no sign of Mortmain. I'll have to seek him out soon to stand a chance of learning what mischief he and his master have planned, but I need to find Cat and Pépin first.

And then I remember. That pattern on the duke's brooch – it's the same design as the gold knot I saw pinned to Mortmain's hat. But there's something else too.

An icy chill ripples through me. Sucking in a breath, I fish the leather pouch from my kirtle and pull the piece of torn kerchief free. As I stare down at the pattern of gold threads stitched into it, Cat's sing-song voice sounds like a bell in my ears.

'B is for Bucket.'

I trace a trembling finger over the loops and

curls. It isn't a 'B', but it could be part of a knot. The memory of Buckingham and Mortmain's secret conversation in the King's stables slides into my head again. They spoke about whatever they are plotting here, but also of an earlier failed mission Mortmain had made to France. Of suspicions he'd aroused and a 'problem' he'd had to deal with. My stomach gives a sudden, sickening lurch.

What if Mortmain's the one I've been searching for all this time? The man who killed my *Papa* in cold blood.

The ground whirls up about me and a flush of sour liquid floods my throat. As I go to steady myself, the jug slips through my fingers and smashes to the ground.

'Watch what you're doing, wench!' A pair of rough hands seizes hold of me and spins me round. A sweaty-faced woman in a grease-stained apron is glaring back at me from the doorway behind.

Balling the kerchief in my left fist, I take a deep breath and do my best to collect myself. 'I am sorry, I was just—'

But the woman isn't interested in my excuses. 'This is no time for idle hands. To the kitchens with you! We've a banquet to prepare for their majesties and they mustn't be kept waiting.' Before I can stop her, she snatches hold of me and drags me through the open door into the gloom beyond.

· CHAPTER 18 ·

Cat

This house is strange-as-strange. It has lots of sparkling windows which makes it feel like the outside. But the wall-stones are painted-on and they moan and groan like Mistress Bristles in the night.

We have been here for three nights and two days already. Sometimes Lady Marjoree fetches me so I can sing a song or play on my birdy-flute to Queen Catty. But mostly, I have to sit here with Pippo all alone in our room. Then Mistress Bristles comes squawking and fussing and gives me broth to eat or puts me away to bed. It makes me puzzle if to be the Queen's Fool is not such a good thing after all.

I dream about you all the time, Meg – when I am sleeping and when I'm awake as well. I blow to you on my birdy-flute too – even though Mistress Bristles tries to stop me – in case you hear it and come. But still you haven't.

And Jack-Bon hasn't too. I look through the window into the outside, but all I can see are men in tunics and ladies in aprons flip-flapping about and green-and-white guard-men standing straight and still with their shiny sticks.

Mistress Bristles says a special thing is going to happen very soon. It is a grand meeting with The Two Kings. She said the same as The King, that it is 'to seal peace between the English and the French' and that The-Lady-Mary will have to marry the French Dolphin when she is grown.

She says everyone is very excited, but worried too in case The French King, Franswah, is going to trick us and get his soldiers to fight ours. I asked what he would do that for and she said it was because the French had been 'our more-tall enemies' for a hundred years and more. I don't know if being more-tall means they will beat us, but from the way her mouth went all pinchy-tight, it might.

She has gone off now to get something, so I pull Pippo on my lap and sing him some songs. I have got to the end of the last one and then the door-lock rattles and Mistress Bristles comes in with a pile of clothes.

'See how Her Grace spoils you!' She shakes the clothes and holds them in my face.

They are even more shimmery than my green-and-white ones. There is a kirtle, all gold like the sun with an 'R is for Rose' on the front which Mistress Bristles says is The King's special sign. She drops it over my head and does it tight-as-tight. Then she fastens me in a red gown with sparkles and puts my head in a new red-and-gold cap too.

When she has finished tying and tucking, she looks at me with squinty-black eyes and click-clacks with her tongue. 'You'll do, I suppose.'

'Do for what?'

'Her Majesty has commanded that you be present with her and her ladies at the meeting between His Grace and the French King.'

'Am I going to meet them too?'

Mistress Bristles sniffs and huffs. 'Fie, maid! King Henry and King François have serious affairs of state to attend to. They will not want to be bothered with the likes of a silly, addle-headed maid like you.' She brushes her pokey-sharp fingers down over her skirts and makes her hood go more straight.

It doesn't make her look better, but I will not tell her in case she gets her whippy-stick out. I take hold of Pippo's rope and stroke his fur instead.

Mistress Bristles frowns her face, but she doesn't say I can't have him. 'Come on, or you'll make us late again.' She snatches my hand and bustles us through the door and off down the stairs.

The grass outside the painted glass palace is full with people. Red-and-gold guard-men in shiny round hats with archree bows like Jack-Bon's march up and down in the sun, and grand lords clip-clop about on horses in puffy coats looking big and fierce. Queen Catty is inside a gold box by the tower with the splashing red water and being held up by four green-and-white guard-men. She is wearing a black-and-gold gown and looking through the window with her hair hanging down in a shiny brown rope. Lady Marjoree and the other ladies-who-wait stand all together in gowns of red-and-black and with gold sparkles on too. I want to run to them and say hello, but Mistress Bristles drags us round behind.

A loud bang pains my ears. I jump and cry out. Pippo shriek-screeches as well. People look over. They point and laugh like always. Others frown their faces and look another way.

Mistress Bristles shakes hold of my arm. 'Quiet, maid! You're making a spectacle of yourself.'

I'm not making a speckle, or anything else, but my ears are full of clanging and banging. I pull Pippo tight and look round-and-about. 'Is it thunder?'

Mistress Bristles gives a puff with her soury-onion breath. 'No, cloth-head. 'Tis the cannon announcing His Grace's departure.'

Another one sounds from far away. She says that one is for King Franswah. Then a man's voice rack-ets out from the arch behind. 'Make way for His Majesty!'

The grand lords on horses and all the rest of the watchers mutter and push apart. A loud hoot-toot sounds and The King trots out. His coat is all silver-and-gold and covered with red sparkles and his hat has a long black birdy feather in it. His horse wears a coat too. It is a great gold one with bells as big as chooks' eggs that jangle and clang when it walks. We wait and wait while the guard-men and the grand lords on horses order themselves in front and behind, then a man shouts out and off we go.

We do a lot of walking and leave the palace far behind. The sun glares high in the sky. My kirtle is squashing me tight-as-tight and my mouth is parchy-dry. The ladies-who-wait have gone red in the face too. I ask about sitting down, but Mistress Bristles pinches her lips and makes us keep going.

I squirm my fingers under my gown and try to untie the ties, but it is no use. Then Lady Marjoree cries out she can see the French King and everyone flaps and flurries about like the chooks at feeding time. I want to see too. I drag my hand free from Mistress Bristles and squeeze through in front with Pippo.

Two men are sitting on horses. One is The King and the other is his friend, the one in the long red gown and Holy-Cross necklace who people call Candle Woolly. They are looking over the field to another man on a horse. He is wearing a gold cloak and his hat has a black feather in like The King's.

There are lots of grand lords on horses with him and more guard-men with shiny sticks and archree bows behind.

They sit and wait.

The King and Candle Woolly sit and wait too.

I puff a sigh. Is this all everyone has come to see – two kings on horses sitting and waiting? If it is, I am going to sit and wait the same as them. I make a space between the skirts of two ladies, but then a loud hoot-tooting shrills into my ears. I peer along the line. A group of men in tunics with 'R is for red Roses' are blowing with their cheeks into long gold pipes and banging with sticks on drums. Then a grand lord rides forwards holding a sharp silver sword-stick in front. The King and Candle Woolly follow. Another grand lord with a silver sword-stick starts off in front of King Franswah.

People curl their mouths and mutter things like, 'There are twice as many of them as us' and, 'If that French serpent tries anything . . .' and, 'God-preserve-His-Majesty!' All around us the grand lords on horses are looking fierce and the guard-men are keeping tight hold of their shiny sticks and archree bows.

But they are wrong to be scared, because when The Two Kings gallop up, they lift off their hats and clap their arms round each other and beam out smiles wide-as-wide. Then they jump off their horses and hug again. And Candle Woolly gets down too and they all go off behind two men carry-ing big Holy-Crosses and into an open house made from shimmery gold sheets. The Two Kings sit on tall chairs and chatter for a bit. Then some red-and-gold men hurry in with jugs and cups, and bowls piled full with food.

When the men pour a drink from the jugs, I lick my tongue over my lips. I am more thirsty now than ever, and my gown and kirtle are tight . . . so tight. The gold house sparkles and wobbles and then everything goes spinny and strange. I reach for the lady-next-to-me's skirts, but she gives a loud squawk and pushes me off. I stumble back, then my head bangs down on the ground and everything goes black-as-black.

• CHAPTER 19 •

Cat

Soft tickling wakes me. Two orange eyes stare out from the shadowy dark and tiny fingers pat at my cheek. My heart goes into a flutter.

'Pippo!' I hug him close and look round-and-about.

It is dark and hard to see, but the place we are in is very hot and small. Soft cushions are plumped under my head and shoulders. They smell of Queen Catty – all spicy-sweet and warm. But she is not here. No one is, only me and Pippo. I hold in my breath and listen. Voices hubbub from behind a black cloth. I get on my knees and drag it back.

Light is shining in through the open window and making it even more hard to see. I blink my eyes and look again. A strange tree is growing outside with gold branches and red-and-white flowers. There are 'C is for Cherries' too, but bigger and shinier than the nonnies' ones in the orchard, and wooden boards painted with birds and animals all clattering about in the wind.

Then the hubbubbing voices shrink down to nothing and there's a new sound of thundery hooves pounding, then a crash and a clank and a man crying out. The voices roar up again loud-as-loud – some groaning, some cheering.

I pick up Pippo and get ready to go out through the door and see, but then I stop because feet are thumping closer and closer, and a man's voice is speaking too. My heart bump-thuds. It is the Lord Bucket. I drag the cloth back over and show Pippo the mouse-quiet sign.

The feet stop. 'This is a safe enough distance from flapping ears and prying eyes. Now tell me, is everything ready for tomorrow?'

Another man answers. 'Yes, my lord.'

His growling voice makes me go shivery all-over. It is him – the man on the thundery-black horse.

'I have found a man in Calais to do the job – a scoundrel who suffered a whipping on the Queen's orders and bears her and the King a grudge.'

'Good,' says Bucket. 'And what of the document?'

The man on the thundery black horse gives a quick cough. 'I'm afraid . . . I'm afraid it is lost, my lord.'

'Lost? How?'

'A French boy stole it on the way across.'

'What!?' Bucket's voice goes all cough-spluttery. 'And where is this boy now?'

'Dead, my lord. He fell overboard and took the document with him.'

I gasp in a breath. He is talking about my friend, Jack-Bon. I want to shout out he is wrong and that Jack-Bon is alive. But Jack-Bon told me the men are dangerous, so I do what I told Pippo and keep mouse-quiet instead.

'Did he blab about it to anyone?'

'No, my lord. He didn't get the chance.'

The Lord Bucket gives a pig-snort. 'That is something, I suppose. Well, we will have to carry things through without it. But you must get a replacement made the moment we are back in England. While some will not question my word on the matter, others, like that proud popinjay, Wolsey, will take more persuading.'

'Yes, my lord.'

'And what of our own little bird? She is in good health, I trust, and none the worse for her confinement during the journey?'

'Yes, though when the sleeping draught wears off, she becomes . . . How shall I put it? More uncooperative.'

'There are ways and means to make her change her tune. I will leave it to you to devise something suitable. But be sure not to fail me again, Mortmain, or I'll send you down to the Devil myself.'

'I will not, my lord. I swear it!'

'Good. Now, I must return to the tournament

before His Grace and the Queen miss me.'

A pair of feet go stomping off.

I breathe in another breath then slowly, slowly poke back the cloth and peep out. The Lord Bucket is marching to where the cheering and groaning are coming from. The man on the thundery-black horse pushes back his hat with the gold sparkle and looks after, his face all red and fury-filled. Then *he* marches off too, but going the other way.

I frown my face. I don't know most of what they said, but I've found the man on the thundery-black horse, and I mustn't let him go.

'Come on, Pippo.' I take hold of his green-and-white rope and tug him into the outside.

When I look round behind I can see the small, hot place we were in is Queen Catty's gold box. The green-and-white men have all gone and Queen Catty and her ladies-who-wait are nowhere too, but I can't look for them now because the man on the thundery-black horse is getting away. I stumble-run after him with Pippo bouncing behind.

The ground is bumpy and it is hard to go fast, but I do my best. We pass a big round oven with fires coming out through its holes and lots of men with puffed red cheeks shovelling bread on sticks. After that there are lines and lines of green-and-white cloth-houses with pinned-up door-flaps and straw beds inside. The man on the thundery-black horse hurries past them too. Then he gets to one on the edge of things with its door-flap fastened across. He undoes the ties and looks back behind with his glittery green-gold eye.

I don't want him to see us, so I pick up Pippo and spin us about like the grand lords-and-ladies when they dance to their tunes. After a bit, I stop and look back. The door-flap on the cloth-house is down and the man on the thundery-black horse has gone. I wait in case it opens again, then I scuttle up close and listen.

A small voice pipes on the inside – faint and faraway. The man on the thundery-black horse makes a growling noise.

'Stop your whining and drink!'

There's coughing and spluttering and then everything goes quiet. I slide round the side of the cloth-house and wait, but he doesn't come out.

Pippo bounces about, picking up beetles and cracking them in his teeth. My stomach grumbles. The last food I had was my breakfast bread. He sees me looking and holds one out. I shake my head and push it back. Beetles are for munkees, not girls.

I do more waiting and belly-grumbling, then the door-flap snaps open. I drag Pippo close and keep down low to the ground. The man on the thundery-black horse comes into the outside. He is holding a jug. He looks about with his narrow green eye, then ties the door-flap over and marches off.

I wait until he's a small black speck then I trip

round to the front and call hello. I strain my ears, but no one answers. I drop hold of Pippo's rope and fumble at the ties, but I can't make them come undone. Pippo chitter-chats from round the side. He is rocking on a wooden stick which is fixing the cloth-house into the ground. He rocks it some more and makes it fall out, then he wriggles under the cloth so all that's left is his tail.

I plop down and squeeze myself after. My nose tickles. It is hot inside and smells of the straw on the parchy-hard ground. A brown cloth hangs in the middle with a straw mattress in front and a bowl with some leftover pottage. I scoop some up. It is cold, but it tastes good. I scoop up more, but then a snuffle sound comes from behind the cloth. I put the pottage down and peep my head round to the other side.

There is another mattress with someone lying in it. They are all wrapped in a blanket and pointing the other way. I sneak-creep over. I'm nearly there, but then they give out a moan and roll over, and my heart does a swoop.

Because this time I am as sure-as-sure . . .

It is my own dear Meggy-Peg. My chest fills to bursting with whistles and tunes. I want to sing and spin about like we do at the nonnies', but you have to do it with me too, Meg.

I pull on your arms, but you flop back and lie there still as stone.

'Meg. It is me – Catty. Open your eyes!'

I shake your shoulders. You give out a groan, but your eyes stay shut. My heart pangs. Why won't you wake?

A thought flies in. I pull my birdy-flute out from my bag and blow the notes of Blackbird's song. Your eyes flitter-flutter and you give another moan. I keep on blowing, but it's not working. What shall I do? What shall I do?

The water comes in my eyes. I stop blowing and go to-and-fro, fro-and-to instead. Then Pippo jumps on my lap with bits of pottage all on his face. He reaches up and chitters in my ear.

I stop going to-and-fro. He is right. Jack-Bon will know. I have to find him.

I put my birdy-flute back safe in my bag and bend over you. 'I have to go now, Meg, but I am going to come back soon – criss-cross my heart!' I do the sign and press my lips on your paley-white cheek. Your face frowns, but your eyes stay shut fast.

My heart pangs again. I puff a breath, then I slip down on my front and crawl back into the outside with Pippo close behind.

· CHAPTER 20 ·

Isabelle

I've been slaving so long in this hot smoky kitchen I've almost forgotten what the daylight looks like. The cook, Mistress Sowerby, is a hard task-mistress and has kept us working all hours so the King and Queen and their guests will not go hungry – though with all the animals and birds here and the stores full of the finest food and wine, I doubt there's any danger of that.

All I can think about while I toil at churning lakes of milk into butter, making mountains of pastry and kneading never-ending piles of dough, is of finding Mortmain and proving my suspicions that he killed my father are right. The question is, how? There's been even less chance of getting away from here than there was of escaping *Maître* Gibson's workshop back in Greenwich.

I've almost given up hope when a royal messenger arrives. Fresh supplies of tarts and sweetmeats are required by their majesties at the tiltyard, and Mistress Sowerby wants me and two of the other kitchen-maids to take them over.

As we load up the handcart, the other girls mock me for my 'Frenchie' accent and the ragged line of cropped hair poking out from beneath my bonnet. I want to answer back, but I bite my tongue instead. Thankfully they soon grow bored and start babbling on about which king has the longest legs, which the squarest shoulders and which the finest clothes – though how they can tell when they've never seen either of them I don't know. If I did choose to speak, I'd tell them this: that it's not what a person looks or sounds like that matters, but what's on the inside.

My heart cramps as I think of how others treat Cat – calling her names and tormenting her, or keeping her shut away to perform at their command. And all because she's different to them, and sees the world in a different way. I glance at the gossiping kitchen-maids and heave a sigh. Perhaps if we were all just a little more like her, this world might be a kinder place . . . Poor Cat. She must be wondering why I've deserted her. But I've got to track down Mortmain and discover the truth. Then, if I'm right, I'll make him pay twice over – for stealing Cat's sister away, and for taking dear, sweet *Papa* from me and *Maman* too.

And suddenly, here come the memories again, rushing in like a pack of baying hounds, dragging me back to the time and place I've been trying so hard these past few weeks to escape.

I close my eyes and do my best to fight them off. But it's no use. This time they're too strong . . .

It is a fine early spring day. We are galloping towards the forest, *Papa* out in front on Montjoy, me on Jongleur close behind, my bow hooked over my right shoulder, my quiver strapped tight to my back. As we course along the side of the frost-filled valley, the wind snatching at our clothes and hair, I imagine myself as a swallow, skimming through the air, the whole world set out below me, and for those precious few moments, anything is possible.

'Whoa!' *Papa*'s cry jerks me back down to earth. He has reined in Montjoy at the top of a rise and is peering down to the edge of the forest below.

I crest the slope and draw Jongleur alongside. 'What is it?'

He frowns. 'I thought I saw something in the trees down there.'

Lifting up from my saddle. I follow his gaze, but all I can see is a crowd of rooks circling above their nests in the topmost branches.

He skims the tree-line for a moment longer then grunts and shakes his head. 'I must have been mistaken. Let's go on, *Hirondelle*. If we don't catch that fine buck I promised your mother for the dinner-table, she will never forgive us.' He flashes me a smile. Then, with a quick dig of his heels against Montjoy's flanks, he gallops away off down the slope and towards the trees.

I'm about to ride after him when a shadow slips across the sun. I glance up. When we set off from the castle earlier, the sky was a beautiful blue, but now dark clouds have bubbled up as if from nowhere and are lowering angrily overhead. I'm filled with a sudden sense of cold dread.

'Wait for me!' I kick my heels against Jongleur's belly and spur him on, but by the time I reach the forest edge, *Papa* has already disappeared inside. Heart pounding, I sit tall in my saddle and peer into the trees, through the tangle of brambles and moss-covered branches.

'*Papa*? Are you there?'

The only reply is a rustle of dead leaves and the harsh cries of the rooks still circling high above. Reluctantly, I lift the reins and urge Jongleur forwards, into the shadow-filled depths beyond.

No! I shudder and snap my eyes open. I can't go back there – not now. I blink and look about me. The two serving-girls have finished loading the handcart and are busy trundling it towards the gatehouse arch. I draw in a quick breath and hurry off after them. I might as well follow them to the tiltyard. It is where all the grand lords and ladies will be, including Buckingham. And where the duke is, surely Mortmain won't be far.

As we near the tiltyard entrance, I catch sight of a strange-looking tree, its branches and trunk wrapped in cloth of gold. It must be the Tree of Honour the servants were chattering about in the kitchen this morning. It's false, like so much else here, with twigs decked out in artificial cherries and silk flowers – hawthorn for England and raspberry blossoms for France – while on its lower branches hang the painted shields of those pledged to fight in the jousts, the two kings included.

Small groups of English noblemen and women stand beneath it, making admiring comments and pretending not to stare at the small groups of French noblemen and women doing the same. One of the other girls calls back for me to catch up and help with the pushing, but I pretend not to hear.

And then a cry goes up that King François is about to compete in the joust. The crowds around us surge forwards, but I make sure to hold back until the two girls are out of sight. I'm about to set off again when I spot two small figures up ahead, wriggling in between the would-be spectators.

Cat and Pépin. What are they doing here? My stomach knots. I want to go on and find Mortmain, but the crowds are so thick and swirling, the pair of them might be crushed at any moment . . .

Heaving a sigh, I pick up my skirts and dash after them.

· CHAPTER 21 ·

Cat

I am still looking for Jack-Bon. I haven't seen him, but there are lots of other people all milling and spilling about. I push through their tangled bodies and arms. Pippo gets caught in a lady's skirts. She jumps and shrieks out piercey-high. It pains my ears, but I pull him back off and we carry on squeezing to the other side.

The sun shines out from the sky above. I cover my eyes over and look about. There's a green square, like Nonny Sweet-Bee's herb garden, only lots bigger. It has a fence along the middle with a gap underneath and more fences all around the sides. There are guard-men everywhere – red-and-gold ones on one side; black-and-white-and-orange on the other. They are all carrying silver sticks or archree bows and frowning their faces under their shiny round hats.

Everyone is staring at two men in metal suits. One is on top of a blue-and-gold horse and the other is on a red-and-green one. They are busy prancing and bowing in front of a long barn where The King and two ladies are sitting high on a bench in the middle of things. The ladies have gold sparkles on their heads. One I don't know, but the other is Queen Catty. *She* will make the Lord Bucket and the other one give Meg back. She is my friend.

The men in metal suits finish their prancing. They go on different sides of the fence, with one at one end and one at the other. Other men fuss about and give them gold cups to drink from and long sticks and wooden boards painted the same colour as their horses. Suddenly there's a loud hoot-tooting. The men throw their cups away and hold their long sticks and boards out in front. People yell and shout all around.

I press my hands over my ears. I don't like it here but I have to get to Queen Catty now. Pippo screeches and jumps on my shoulder. I pull him down to my chest and stumble-run into the square.

People don't see us, but then they do. They shout things like:

'Get away from there!'

and:

'Stop her!'

and:

'Come back, you fool!'

Hands snatch on to my arms and skirts, but I spin-and-twist free and keep on going.

The man on the red-and-green horse thunders

along the side of the fence with his long stick. And now the one on the blue-and-gold horse is coming along the other way too. We have to hurry.

I grip Pippo tight-as-tight and run out and past the red-and-green horse and through the space under the fence. But the other horse is thundering closer and closer and the people are roaring louder and louder and it is all going to be . . .

. . . TOO LATE!

I scream and go down in a ball. The horse squeals up and pounds with his hooves. There are cracks and crash-bangs and wails and shrieks. My ears and head are paining me fit-to-burst. I scrunch my eyes shut and say a prayer-to-God.

When I open them, the blue-and-gold horse is dashing and kicking and the man in the metal suit has thrown away his long stick and board and is tipping to-and-fro on top. The guard-men try to catch him while all the others jump about waving their arms and shouting things like: 'Monjoo!' and 'Sackblur!' and 'Is the King injured?'

I don't know what to do, so I shut my eyes again. I start to sing 'la-la-la' to make it all go away, but then a hand shakes me and a voice sounds loud in my ear.

'Cat!'

I look round. It is Jack-Bon in his new girl clothes. I try to tell him about Queen Catty, but he drags me on my feet and scuttles me away, past the shouting men and the shrieking ladies and the guard-men all red in the face and running about with their shiny sticks. We keep on going, out through the arch, past the golden tree and over the field. My puff is nearly all gone, but then Jack-Bon says it is all right to stop. He puts his hands round his middle and does puffing too.

The people going past stare and point like always. Then Jack-Bon stops doing his puffing and stares as well.

'What were you doing, throwing yourself in front of King François's horse like that? You could have been killed!'

'I was trying to get to Queen Catty—' I huff and puff some more. 'To . . . to tell her about Meg.'

Jack-Bon frowns his face. 'Meg?'

'Yes. She is shut in a cloth-house fast asleep. I tried to make her wake, but it was no use.'

Jack-Bon's eyes grow owly-wide. 'What? But how did you find her?'

'I was all alone inside Queen Catty's gold box with Pippo and then the Lord Bucket and the man on the thundery-black horse came and talked outside. When they finished I followed the man to the cloth-house. Then he went away again, so I squeezed inside and there was Meg, all wrapped tight up in a blanket.'

Jack-Bon snatches my hand. 'What did Bucking-ham and Mortmain talk about?'

I shake my head. 'It's hard to tell it all.'

'I know but you have to try, Cat. Please.'

I scrunch my face and try to hear all the things they said. 'Well, the Lord Bucket asked was it all ready for tomorrow.'

'Tomorrow?' Jack-Bon's fingers dig in.

'Ow!'

'Sorry!' He makes his hand go loose. 'And then what?'

'The man on the thundery-black horse . . .' I sound the name. 'Mort-mane?'

'Mortmain, yes . . .'

'He said he had found a man-in-calay for the job and that you were dead and gone. But he is wrong, Jack-Bon because you are here and walking about.'

'Yes, I know, Cat. What else?'

'The Lord Bucket was full of the furies about you taking the dog-you-meant and said he had to get another. And then Mort-mane said Meg was sleeping in a draught and being un-copatif, or . . . or something.'

Jack-Bon shakes his head. His face has gone all frowny again.

'Did I do something bad?'

He blinks, then squeezes my hand. 'No, Cat. You did very well. It is just that I wish I had been there to hear with you.'

'I do too.' I pull down on his apron. 'Can we go and get Meg back now?'

Jack-Bon flickers his eyes round-and-about and gives another frown. 'Did you see where Mortmain went after he left the tent – I mean, the cloth-house?'

'No, but he had a jug for water.'

Jack-Bon's tongue licks over his lips.

'Are you thirsty?'

'What? No, it is not that. I am thinking. Do you remember the way?'

I look round-and-about too. There are lots of cloth-houses and horses and people, and I'm not sure. But then I see the smoke and flames coming from the big round oven. 'Over there.' I point with my finger.

Jack-Bon nods. 'Good, but we must hurry.' He lifts Pippo off me. 'Can you run again?'

I nod back. He takes my hand and we do more hurrying so my chest grows achy-sore and I am nearly all out of puff again. And then there is the cloth-house, right on the edge of things.

'There!' I point over.

Jack-Bon stops and looks back and forwards with his eyes all darty-sharp, then he waves for me and Pippo to follow.

The door-flap is tied shut like before. Jack-Bon puts his finger on his lips and makes the mouse-quiet sign. We creep nearer and listen. Something is making a peeping noise inside, but it is not a bird.

My heart pangs. I look at Jack-Bon. He has heard it too. We wait some more. The peeping stops and it goes all quiet.

Jack-Bon jumps down on his knees. He works his fingers at the door-flap knots then lifts the corner and slides through. I go after, but he turns round and pushes me away. 'No, Cat. You must keep watch in case Mortmain comes.'

I fold my arms. 'But I want to see Meg. Pippo will do it.'

Pippo chirrups to say yes. Jack-Bon looks at him and back to me. His face goes into another frown. 'All right.' He takes Pippo and ties him to a stick in the ground. 'Do not let us down, *mon ami.*' He pats Pippo's fur, then pulls me with him into the inside.

The cloth is still hanging in the middle. More peeping comes from the other side. Jack-Bon creeps over. He looks beneath, then he pushes the cloth away and my heart does a jump, because there you are again, Meg, but wide awake and sitting with your hands tied to a pole. I am so glad you are all right. I go over to hug you, but when I try, all you do is make more peeping sounds and twist and turn your head.

'What is wrong, Meggy?'

'Wait.' Jack-Bon pulls me away. He bends and takes a long, red rag from inside your mouth.

You gasp and cough and spit bits out. Then you look at me and your eyes go swimmy-bright. 'Oh, my little Catty. Is it really you?'

187

I want to say, 'Yes, Meggy-Peg, it *is* me.' But my heart is panging and panging, so I push my arms back round your middle and hug you tight-as-tight instead.

· CHAPTER 22 ·

Isabelle

My chest tightens at the sight of Cat hugging her sister. I close my eyes and remember how it felt the last time *Papa* and I embraced. The smell of warm leather as I pressed my cheek against his doublet. The steady beat of his heart in my ear, and the light brush of his lips as he kissed the top of my head. I miss him so much. *Maman* too. A hot tear trickles down my cheek. I brush it away before the others see. This is not the time . . .

Meg pulls back her shoulders and stares up at me, her eyes full of bewilderment. 'Who . . . who are you?'

As I look down at her, I'm struck by how different she and her sister are. Her hair is dark while Cat's is coppery-red. Her eyes are the colour of hazelnuts; Cat's are bright blue. And while Cat's nose and cheeks are scattered with freckles, Meg doesn't have a single one.

Cat jumps in. 'He is Jack-Bon, my true friend.' She gives me a gap-toothed smile.

'And you are mine, Cat.' I flash her a quick smile in return.

Meg's eyes dart to my skirts and apron. 'Jack?' She looks even more confused now than before.

My cheeks flush with sudden heat. 'I was in disguise when Cat and I first met. My name . . . my *real* name is Isabelle Boncoeur.'

'But why—'

I give a quick cough. 'It is a long story and not for telling now.' I throw a hurried glance over my shoulder, fearful that Mortmain might soon reappear, though there's no peep yet from our watchman outside.

Meg frowns. 'But I don't understand. What is Cat doing here? Why isn't she with the holy sisters?'

Cat lifts up on to her knees. 'I ran away to find you, Meggy, and Jack-Bon tried to help. And we went to the King and Queen's palace and Queen Catty said I could come and live with her. And I was made into the Queen's Fool and I liked it at first, but I don't like Mistress Bristles because she broke your spindle in pieces and she has a whippy-stick and cut off all my hair. And now –' she takes a gulp of air – 'now I want to be just Cat Sparrow again and—'

'Hush, Cat!' I reach out and grip her arm. 'You can tell Meg later. We have to get her away from here, before Mortmain comes back.'

Meg shivers at the mention of his name.

I give her shoulder a quick squeeze. 'Do you know where he went?'

She shakes her head. 'He talked about having some business to do. But he said he wouldn't be long.'

'Then we must hurry.' I scramble round behind her. The rope binding her has been knotted three times over. It is going to take time to undo it – time we may not have. But I've got to try. I flex my fingers and start working the first knot loose.

'Why did Mortmain take you from the holy sisters?'

Before Meg gets a chance to reply, Cat leans forwards and flings her arms around her sister's neck. 'I tried to go after you, Meg, but Holy Mother Sharp-Tongue wouldn't let me.' She starts to sob.

'I'm sorry, Catty. I didn't want to leave you either, but—' Meg's voice shrinks into a choked whisper. 'But I had no choice.' She draws in a breath, then answers my question. 'The new Prioress, Holy Mother Agnes said I was wanted to work as a servant in the house of a rich and power-ful lord in London.'

I shake my head. 'But that is nonsense. Why would he take a girl from a nunnery when he could have had his pick of girls in London?'

Meg heaves a sigh. 'I know, but I had no reason to think the Holy Mother would lie. And she was determined his servant – Mortmain – would not leave empty-handed.' Her voice quavers.

I drop the rope and slide round to face her. 'So why did he really take you?'

She gives a gulping swallow. 'I . . . I don't know. After we left the nunnery, Mortmain gave me something foul to drink that made me fall asleep. When I woke up, I was in a small dark room, tied to a chair.'

'And then?'

'A grand man dressed in the finest silks and furs came to see me and . . . Well, he told me something.' She shudders and sucks in another breath.

'What?'

'He claimed that I am of –' she dips her head and speaks the rest in another whisper – 'of royal blood.'

My heart jolts. I stare at her open-mouthed. 'Is it true?'

She jerks her head back up, cheeks flushing. 'Of course not! I told him so too. That I was just Meg Sparrow, a poor orphan-child, taken in by the nuns after my parents died of the sweating sickness when I was very young. But he laughed and said it didn't matter what the holy sisters had told me. He said that gold could be found in the most barren ground, and that when the news got out it would—' She swallows again. 'It would change everything.'

I frown and sit back on my heels. 'Did you ever learn his name?'

'No, but he was old and red in the face, and his

eyes were cold and grey, like a fish's.' She wrinkles her nose and gives another shudder.

Buckingham. There's no doubting it. I am about to tell her, but Cat gets there first.

'It is Bucket!' She scrambles up and dances about us. 'The Lord Bucket!'

Meg gapes back at us. 'The Lord Bucket. But who—'

'The Duke of Buckingham. It is Cat's name for him. He is Mortmain's master and cousin to the King.'

Meg's eyes grow wider still. Before I can tell her more, Cat jumps in again. 'We heard them planning bad things, didn't we, Jack-Bon?'

'What sort of bad things?' Meg's face is full of fresh fear.

I shake my head again. 'We do not know exactly, but the duke talked of his destiny being fulfilled.'

'What destiny?'

'He did not say, but it is something to do with upsetting things here in France, I am sure of it.'

Meg stiffens. 'We're in *France*?'

'Yes. You did not know?'

'No. I can't remember anything, except being made to drink more foul-tasting potion by Mortmain and waking up somewhere hot and dark and not being able to breathe. Then I went back to sleep again and when I woke up I was here in this . . .' She blinks and looks about her. 'This house of cloth.'

My heart does a quick somersault. 'So it was *you* Mortmain had shut up inside the chest?'

She frowns. 'Chest? What chest?'

'The one in the locked cabin. I followed him there when I discovered he was on the same ship as me. I had no idea you were in there, or I would have—'

Cat stamps her foot. 'I told you I saw Meggy-Peg with him in the boat at Dovercastle!'

Meg's eyes widen again. 'You saw me, Catty?'

'Yes. You were sleeping and I told Jack-Bon after he came out from the sea and—'

'You were right, Cat. I am sorry. I should have believed you.' I reach out and touch her sleeve as I speak. I'm about to start back on working at the knot when a sudden thought strikes me. Reaching inside the pouch round my neck, I pull the piece of parchment free and hold it out in front of Meg. 'Do you recognize this?'

She scans the water-stained page and shakes her head. 'No. What is it?'

'The last testament of someone called Lady Alys Godwin. Cat and I overheard Buckingham ask Mortmain to get a false document made when we were at the King's palace in Greenwich. I think this might be it. I pulled it from under the lid of Mortmain's chest, though I did not have the chance to read it before it got wet.'

Cat pokes her head over my elbow and peers at the parchment. 'It fell in the sea with you, didn't it,

Jack-Bon?'

Meg's mouth drops open. 'In the sea, but how—?'

'It does not matter about that now.' I heave a sigh. But as I go to put the parchment away, Meg jerks her head up.

'Wait! My reading is not good, but that word at the bottom.' She nods at the second signature.

'Hildegard?'

'Yes. It was the name of the old Prioress at the nunnery. The one before Sister Agnes took over.'

'Are you sure?'

Cat chimes in. 'Holy Mother Hildy, yes! She was good and kind. Not like Holy Mother Sharp-Tongue.'

I stare down at the name, but before I get the chance to think what it might mean, a loud *chee-chee* sounds from outside. My throat tightens.

'Pippo. I will get him.' Cat turns to go.

'No! Stay here with your sister.' Jumping to my feet, I hurry over to the door-flap and peer out. Pépin is up on his hind legs making nervous chittering sounds. My stomach knots as I follow his gaze. The figure of a man in a black cloak and hat is marching towards us. He's too far off to be able to see his face yet, but there's no mistaking his long, loping walk and the raven-black hair and beard.

I tug Pépin's rope free and pull him inside. Meg gives a small cry of wonder, but there's no time for explanations now.

'Mortmain is coming!' Dropping back down on my knees again, I scrabble desperately at the rope binding her, but it's no use – I can't undo it. I curse at my own feebleness and for letting myself be distracted by talk of Buckingham and Mortmain.

Meg straightens and takes a deep breath. 'Go, before he captures you too.'

Cat pulls at her sleeve. 'But you are coming with us, Meg?'

'I can't, Cat. Isabelle has tried, but the knot – it won't come loose.'

'No!' Cat flings her arms round Meg's waist and buries her face in her lap.

'Please, Cat. You have to go. NOW!' Meg throws me a desperate look.

'Listen to your sister.' I prise Cat's fingers free and drag her struggling towards the door-flap. As we reach it, she turns back and cries Meg's name in great gulping sobs.

'Shhh, or he will hear!' Clamping my hand across her mouth, I lift up the flap and peer out again. An old woman with a tray of pies has stopped Mortmain and is pestering him to buy one. While he's busy trying to fend her off, I take my chance and bundle Cat and Pépin round to the back of the tent.

Cat wipes her nose on her sleeve and blinks up at me, her cheeks wet with tears. 'What are we going to do about Meggy?'

My throat tightens. I don't know, but I can't tell

her that. 'We . . . we must find somewhere to hide until Mortmain has gone.'

'Like in the game?'

I frown. 'What? Yes, that is right.' I dart a quick look around. To our left is the broad, open field which separates the English and French camps. To our right a maze of brightly coloured tents stretches as far as the eye can see. Snatching Cat's hand up again, I tug her towards them. There are groups of people sitting in the smaller ones, gossiping or lounging about on straw mattresses, most of them clearly the worse for drink. As we pass by, my stomach heaves at the sour stink wafting out. It smells like they've been using the tents as privies too. Then, as we round the corner, we come upon something more promising – a large red-and-gold pavilion, its door-flap lifting slightly in the breeze.

Signalling to Cat to keep back, I pull open the flap and peer inside. As my eyes get used to the dim red light, my heart lifts at the sight of the painted wooden trees and flowers and the great golden sun leaning against the canvas walls. There are chests of costumes and props too. *Maître* Gibson's stores – all of them transported here from the palace at Greenwich. It's the perfect place to hide – for now at least.

I call back to Cat. She scoops Pépin up and follows me into the dusty warm gloom.

She looks about her, sniffing loudly. 'Why are we in here?'

'I told you. We must not let Mortmain see us. And after what happened at the tiltyard earlier, there will be people looking for you too.'

Her eyes fill with tears again. 'But what about Meggy? She is back there and all on her own.'

A fresh stab of guilt spikes my chest. I drop down in front of her and grasp her firmly by the arms. 'We will save her, Cat. I promise.'

I speak the words to comfort her, though in truth, I still don't have the slightest idea how.

· CHAPTER 23 ·

Isabelle

Cat's stomach makes a grumbling noise.

'Are you hungry?'

She nods. I cast about, though I'm doubtful of finding anything to eat in here. But we're in luck. Someone has left a half-eaten loaf and a piece of hard cheese on top of one of the costume chests. And there's a jug of some sweet-smelling liquid and a cup too.

I break the bread and cheese and pour a drink from the jug. Soon we are sitting side by side on the chest, munching and slurping, making light work of the unexpected feast.

When she's finished, Cat gives a loud burp. Pépin *chee-chee*s and bolts up the side of a painted tree. Cat burps again and lets out a giggle and soon we're both clutching our bellies and shrieking with laughter. But as we fall silent, my thoughts turn back to Mortmain. I'm no closer to proving my own suspicions about him. But whatever he and Buckingham are planning to do tomorrow, it is something dreadful, I am sure. And it isn't just Meg who's in danger.

A tide of fear rises up inside me. I take a deep breath and force it back down. It is time to live up to the name *Papa* gave me. To be his brave *Hirondelle* . . .

I wipe my mouth on the back of my sleeve – a habit of Jack-Bon's that seems to have stuck – and jump to my feet. Cat stares up at me, her blue eyes wide and shining.

'We are going?'

'Not you.'

'But I want to come.' She scrambles up beside me.

'No, you might be recognized. You must stay here and look after Pépin instead.'

She frowns. 'But—'

'Please, Cat. It is important.'

She gives a small sigh and hangs her head.

'Promise me?'

She sighs again and makes a wobbly cross sign over her heart. 'I promise.'

'Thank you.'

'I will play on my birdy-flute. Meggy might hear it too.' She reaches in her bag and pulls out the flute.

'Yes, but softly, Cat. And if you hear anyone coming, you must go behind the sun and hide.' I point to where the gold-painted sun stands propped against the back wall of the tent. 'And remember, mouse-quiet, yes?' I put my finger to my lips.

She nods and does the same.

'Good. I will come back as soon as I can.' I pull Pépin down from his perch. 'Look after her, *mon petit ami.*' I kiss the top of his head and hand him to Cat. Then, with a quick check to make sure no one's about, I take a deep breath and step outside.

The late afternoon sun is warm on my face, but the breeze has strengthened and is buffeting the canvas walls of the tents so they ripple and swell like a galleon's sails. I weave in between them, doing my best to go back the same way we came. But the narrow grass alleyways all look the same. I've almost given up hope when I turn a corner and find myself out in the open, a few short paces from Mortmain's tent. I'm about to creep closer when the door-flap opens and a tall dark figure emerges.

It's him, though he's wearing a different hat and has a muffler pulled up over his nose and chin. I pull back to the safety of the last tent and watch as he fastens the flap then turns and strides off in the direction of the tiltyard. I waver for a moment, torn between following him or going back inside to try and rescue Meg again. I promised Cat I'd save her, but if I don't go after Mortmain now, I won't stand a chance of finding out what he and his master are up to until it's too late.

Forcing the feelings of guilt back down, I tail him at a safe distance, ready to duck out of sight if he turns. As I pass among the crowds, snatches of conversation confirm my worst fears. Guards on both sides are hunting for the 'scoundrel' who nearly unhorsed King François. Some say it was a jest gone wrong, but there are other, darker mutterings that it was an attempt on the King's life and the culprit, when caught, will be tried and put to death. I shiver and murmur a quick prayer that Cat keeps her promise and stays out of sight until I get back.

As I near the entrance to the tiltyard, a clash of metal followed by cheers and loud clapping carries towards me on the breeze. I glance through the arch and see two knights in armour circling each other with raised swords. It seems they are back to fighting their mock battles for now. But there are even more French and English guards on duty than before, all of them fully armed and busy watching the crowds. Each other too.

I ready myself to follow Mortmain inside, but he marches straight past the tiltyard and makes for a low, dingy-looking building on the far side instead. From the look of the crumbling plasterwork and the sunken, moss-covered thatch, it's been here a lot longer than the rest of this strange, make-believe city of cloth. Men are sitting on rows of wooden benches outside the door, drinking from pewter tankards and gambling with dice, though I know from what *Maître* Tarleton said when Gobbo and Bardolf used to play, it is a game forbidden to the ordinary folk.

As Mortmain approaches the tavern – for it's clear that's what the building is – he pulls the muffler down then stoops beneath the door frame and disappears inside. Plucking up all the courage I can muster, I dart after him into the darkness beyond.

A sour-sweet smell of ale mixed with soot and sweat pricks my nostrils and makes my stomach churn. I swallow hard and peer about me. More groups of men are sat around upturned barrels talking and drinking, their faces lit by the glow from sputtering tallow candles and dusty shafts of daylight shining through the holes in the roof. Two serving-maids are busy refilling the men's tankards, while an older woman who must be the ale-wife, fills more jugs from a large keg resting on a table at the back.

I cast about for Mortmain. At first I don't see him, but then I do. He's sitting next to a fireplace in the far corner, half-hidden by a wooden screen. There's another man with him too, tucked deep in the shadows against the wall. The Duke of Buckingham? No – a grand man like him would never lower himself to enter a place like this.

I glance over at the ale-wife. She's got her back turned. Now's my chance. Heart thumping, I pull down my bonnet to cover more of my face and sidle as close as I dare. Mortmain is speaking in a low voice, but if I stand with my back to him and pretend to be collecting empty tankards, I can just about hear.

'So, you know what to do?'

His companion gives a grunt of agreement.

'Good! Here's your disguise – and the weapon too.' There's the rasp of something metal being slid across a table top.

The other man makes a low whistling sound. 'A pretty piece, and with a nice sharp point on it.'

My eyes widen. That voice. It's horribly familiar . . . I curl my fingers and hold my breath.

Mortmain gives a low growl. 'It ought to be. See the *fleur-de-lis* on the handle? It's the mark of the French King. These blades are given only to the most trusted members of his bodyguard.'

'How come you got hold of it then?'

My stomach shrinks up inside me. It can't be . . .

'That is none of your concern. And don't go getting too attached to it either.'

'Why's that?'

'Because it's the evidence that the French are to blame. When you've done the deed, you must leave it behind at the scene.'

The other man makes a clicking noise with his tongue. 'Seems a shame. A man could earn a tidy penny for a piece like that.'

And then I know for sure. Gobbo! What's he doing here?

There's a sudden sharp scrape of chair legs. 'Listen to me, idiot!' Mortmain snarls the words through gritted teeth.

I drop my head and busy myself with rearranging the tankards.

'There's no need for insults. Just because I'm down on my luck and—'

'Do you want the job or not?' Mortmain's tone is iron-hard.

''Course I do. My pa and his friends died fighting for Good King Richard against that rat of a pretender, Henry Tudor, at Bosworth Field. But 'twas all in vain, and now his high and mighty son sits on the throne with that Spanish mare alongside him. They deserve bringing low, just like they've done to me and mine.'

'Keep your voice down, man. If we're discovered . . .'

Gobbo sniffs loudly. 'All right, but there's one thing that's bothering me.'

'What's that?'

'How will I get out of here, after? The King's guards'll be everywhere and if I'm caught' – Gobbo sucks in a breath – 'well, 'twill be a traitor's death for me, whereas you will get away scot-free.'

'I told you before, I've arranged for a distraction. It will give you plenty of time to strike the blow and make your escape too.'

There's a pause, then Gobbo speaks again. 'I want half the money up front.'

Mortmain gives another angry-sounding growl. 'We agreed on a quarter, and the rest when the deed was done.'

'Well, I'm sorry, sir, but it seems only fair what with me taking all the risk an' all.'

Typical Gobbo! Money's the only thing he cares about. That and tormenting innocent children and animals.

'Gah! Very well!'

There's a chinking sound followed by a wheedling snicker from Gobbo. 'Thank you, sir. *Most* generous. By the way, you never did tell me your name.'

'It's none of your concern. But remember this – if, for some reason you should have a change of heart and decide not to go through with things tomorrow, I will hunt you down, string you up and draw and quarter you myself.'

'I-I won't let you down, sir. I swear it on my pa's mouldering bones.'

'See to it you don't. Or else . . .'

'Yes, sir. I-I mean no, sir.'

There's a fresh chink of coins and the sound of a chair being drawn back. I slip quickly behind the wooden screen and peer out. Moments later, the scrawny figure of my old enemy, William Gobbo appears. He darts a nervous look about him then slings the sack he's carrying over his left shoulder and scuttles off towards the open door.

I stand there, buried in the shadows, head reeling from what I've just heard – the dagger Mortmain gave him; Gobbo's talk of revenge and his fear of dying a traitor's death. There's only one thing it can possibly mean. Buckingham and Mortmain are plotting nothing less than the assassination of the King and Queen of England! And they mean for the French to be blamed. I've got to do something, while there's still time . . .

Before I have the chance to think what, a hand seizes hold of my apron and yanks me round.

'You there!'

A green-gold eye glitters back at me from the darkness. The eye of a hunter who will stop at nothing to bring down his prey.

CHAPTER 24

Isabelle

Mortmain leans forwards, his eye raking my face. My stomach lurches. What if he's recognized me as the boy from the ship – seen through my maid's disguise? I duck my head down and take a quick step back. But instead of dragging me closer, he thrusts a battered tankard at me.

'Ale, and be quick about it.'

I dip into a curtsey, doing my best to hide my fear. As I turn from him, a voice inside me tells me to run. Leave him. Alert the guards about Gobbo instead. But what if this is my one chance of discovering whether it *was* him who killed *Papa*?

There's only one way to find out. Gritting my teeth, I reach for a nearby jug. But then, as I go to pour the ale, I miss the tankard and tip it in Mortmain's lap instead.

'What the—?' He jumps up, wiping angrily at his hose and breeches.

I have him off guard. Time to act. In one swift movement, I reach in my kirtle for my pouch and pull the piece of cloth free. 'Here, sir. Your kerchief. You . . . you dropped it – earlier.' I thrust it at him.

He plucks it from me then throws it to the ground. 'What are you talking about? It's nothing but a dirty rag.'

My heart fills with a mix of disappointment and relief. I was wrong. It isn't his. I snatch it up and take a step backwards. But a curl of doubt snakes up inside me. It's dark in here. I have to be sure.

I grab a nearby candle and hold the cloth in front of the flame. 'Are you . . . are you sure, sir?'

Mortmain bares his teeth. 'Stop wasting my time, girl.' He makes to push me aside. But as the gold threads catch the light, a strange look flickers across his face. 'Where did you get this from?' He reaches for the kerchief again, but I twitch it quickly away.

'I . . . I found it on the floor. I thought it was yours. I'm sorry, I must have been mistaken.' I crumple it into a ball and take another step back.

'Give it here!' Mortmain makes another swipe for it. I jump to one side, dropping the candlestick, which clatters to the ground.

There's the sound of hurried footsteps. The ale-wife pushes past me and thrusts herself between us. 'Is there a problem, sir?'

For a heart-stopping moment, Mortmain's glittering eye scours my face again, like a hunter's knife seeking the weak spot to slice into and lay bare what lies beneath. Then he gives a low, snarling growl, pulls his cloak about him and strides out through the door without saying another word.

But he doesn't need to. After what's just happened, I know now my suspicions about him are right.

I ball my fingers into fists. If I was as brave as *Papa* said, I'd find a weapon and run after him. Reveal my true identity and challenge him to confess his crime, then get the guards to arrest him so he could be tried by his King or mine – it doesn't matter which. But I'm not. I couldn't save *Papa* that day, and I'm too weak and cowardly to confront the man who killed him now.

As I slump against the table, head bowed, a hand grabs me by the shoulder. 'You've got a cheek, girl.'

I blink and look up. The ale-wife is standing over me, her mouth pressed into a thin, hard line.

'Who do you think you are, coming in here and upsetting my customers. Be off with you!' She swings me round and shoves me out through the door.

As I stagger into the grey daylight, the wind whips at my clothes and a fat drop of rain splashes against my cheek. I shiver and clutch my arms about me. A storm is coming. But it's nothing compared to the one that's raging inside me.

I stumble to the back of the building and collapse against the wall, head spinning, eyes half-closed. Then the world whirls up in a darkening blur and before I can stop it, I'm being dragged back into the forest to witness it all over again. The hooded man lurking in the shadows, the arrow hurtling through the air, the horse rearing up and *Papa* – my brave, handsome *Papa* – lying face down, his lifeblood seeping into the dirt from the single deadly wound in his back.

The familiar feeling of cold guilt claws at my chest. It's my fault, *Papa*. I should have stopped him before he could loose his arrow. Run at him and knocked him to the ground. And now – now I've missed the only chance I had to keep my vow and get the justice for you that you deserve. Hot tears prick at my eyes and trickle down my cheeks. A low rumbling sounds above me. I blink and look up. The sky is full of dark, boiling clouds. A sudden fork of lightning rips through the air and strikes the top of a nearby tent. A woman screams and a flock of geese waddle past, honking in terror.

Heart pounding, I pick up my skirts and hurry off back towards the main camp. As I approach the first set of tents, a funnel of wind spirals up from the ground and roars into them like a giant serpent, snapping their masts and ripping up the stakes that fix them to the ground.

Screams of panic pierce the air. Door-flaps lift and men and women come running out. Some grapple with the ropes, doing what they can to try and tie the canvas back down. Others fly towards the shelter of the castle walls. But the wind-storm is getting stronger all the while, and now it's picking up objects – buckets, stools, straw mattresses – and hurling them through the air too. A pair of men's breeches sails past me, quickly followed by a torn sheet of canvas and a tangle of flailing ropes.

A riderless horse comes pounding towards me, eyeballs rolling, nostrils flared. I dash clear and run straight into the path of a fleeing guard instead. He careers into me, sending me sprawling to the ground. I lie there for a moment, all the breath knocked out of me, then my eyes close and I know no more.

I'm wakened by a barrage of cold raindrops soaking into my hair and clothes. I sit up, wiping my face with my apron. The storm has passed, but it's left a trail of destruction behind it – tangles of wrecked canvas and frayed ropes, sheep and other livestock wandering loose, and bunches of dazed-looking people huddled together or else stumbling about in the fading daylight collecting their scattered possessions.

My stomach twists up inside me. Cat and Pépin. They could be in there somewhere – injured – or worse . . . I have to find them. Battered and dazed, I drag myself up on my feet and set off through the wreckage, praying that they will be all right.

· CHAPTER 25 ·

Cat

Jack-Bon has gone now and I am on my own with Pippo. I blow on my birdy-flute in case you might hear it, Meggy. But my heart is sore with panging and the notes come out all wrong. Instead of Blackbird and Robin and Wren, it is more like Crow and Maggie-pie and Chook-in-a-flummock.

Pippo leaps about and screeches for me to stop, so I put my flute away and look round-and-about instead. Apart from the sun for hiding in, there is a white smiling moon and some trees and flowers too, but not the same as the ones in my letter-learning.

The wind is blowing the walls in and out, like the grand house where The King and Queen Catty are staying. I want to go back there and ask Queen Catty to save you. But Jack-Bon said to wait for him, and I made a criss-cross on my heart, so I had better keep it.

I open the lid on a big wooden box. It is packed full with clothes. All the colours of the woods and the trees – browns and yellows and greens. I pull them out. Some are kirtles and bonnets and some are coats and breeches, but they are all soft-as-soft. I stroke them with my fingers to help stop the panging, then I lift the lid on the next box along.

There are strange paper faces inside, with holes for the eyes and mouth. They are painted in bright colours and some have got green-and-silver sparkles on. But my best of all is the one with feathers, all red and blue and shiny gold. There's a feather-cloak too. It is better than the old dove-coat Gobble and Badulf made me put on; better than the new clothes from Queen Catty as well. I want to try it, but my fingers won't do the ties.

I look inside another box. It is full of archree bows, and arrows with birdy-feathers and sharp points, like the one that stuck into Hosper and made him die. My heart starts panging again, but I know Jack-Bon spoke the truth. He didn't mean to hurt Hosper. It was all Gobble's fault. I didn't like that one. He called me names and was unkind to Jack-Bon and Pippo, and I am glad he is gone.

I puff a breath and open another box. But then my ears prick at a horse-and-cart noise in the outside. It rattles closer then stops. Two shadow-men thud down and one speaks, all scratchy and creaky like the cart.

'This be the one.' A shadow-hand goes to the door-flap.

My stomach scrunches. We have to hide like

Jack-Bon said. I bundle up Pippo and stumble-run over to the big sun. I push behind and press my cheek in Pippo's soft munkee fur.

The men clump into the inside, then one of them whistles his lips. 'You mean we got to shift this lot by ourselves?'

'Yes, 'n' all before sundown too. Master Gibson's waitin' for it over where they've been buildin' the chapel and banketin' hall. If it's not ready in time for tomorrow's royal entytaynments, he'll have our heads on a spike, make no mistake.'

'But what's it all for?'

'I told yer. The gran' finallee of everythin', afore we push off home agin. Prayer-sayin' first in the chapel, then a great feast of fine foods, all topped off by singin' and dancin' and King Harry's faverit play.'

'What's that then?'

'You know, the one about ol' Robin Hood and his band of Merry Men.'

The footsteps thump closer. I keep hold of Pippo and poke my head round the side of the sun, and low to the ground. There are two men standing there. One is old and bent with a white tufty head and the other is tall with short yellow hair and eyes all quick and darty.

The darty-eyed one walks to a box. He swipes a brown cloak and puts it to his chin. 'Who's going to be there then?'

'Why the two kings and queens of course! Plus the card'nal and all the grand lords and ladies from both sides.'

The darty-eyed one throws the cloak away and snorts out a laugh. 'If King Harry and the Frenchie King are still speaking. I heard King Harry challenged him to a wrestling match and got thrown to the ground for his trouble, and the two queens had to step in quick and blow kisses about before the pair of them started fighting for real.' He does more snorting.

The old one frowns his face. 'If you ask me, the Frenchie King were tryin' to get his own back after that divil dressed in King Harry's colours jumped him and his horse at the joust.' He rolls his eyes and makes a shivery-hissing noise.

The other one's eyes go thin and piercey. 'Devil? I ain't so sure about that. I saw the whole thing happen. She looked like a real flesh-and-blood maid to me. A strange one, I'll grant you, but still . . .'

'Well, divil or maid, there's a purse of gold sovereigns for whoever finds 'em – and that spidery creature they had on 'em too.'

My chest goes tight and knotty. I want to jump out and shout it was me, Cat Sparrow and not a divil or any other name they want to say. But I promised Jack-Bon to keep mouse-quiet, so I stay down behind the sun.

The darty-eyed one does another whistle. 'There's plenty a man could do with a bag of gold, like tell old Gibson what he can do with his rotten costumes and pretend trees.'

'Come on, stop yer dreamin' and give me a hand with this.' The old one lifts the end of a clothes-box. The darty-eyed one does more grumbling, then he gets the other end and they puff it into the outside.

I sit and wait still-as-still while they go in and out, taking trees and flowers and more boxes. The wind in the outside growls louder, and the walls do more blowing. My ears are paining and I'm scared in case the two men come for the sun, because then they will find us, even if we are more quiet than all the mice together.

I wish you were here, Meg, and Jack-Bon too. But you're not. It is only me and Pippo. I grip him tightly-fast, but he doesn't like the wind sounds too, and he twists and turns and gets away. The men are outside, so I call Pippo's name, but the walls are creaking and groaning and it is too much for him to hear. He jumps in the open clothes-box and pushes himself down inside.

Then the men come back in, all gasping and groaning.

'Storm's getting up,' the darty-eyed one says. 'I reckon we should take what we've got and come back for the rest when—'

The old one jumps and grabs at his arm. 'Did you see that?'

'What?'

'Over there in that chest! Beneath the cloak. Somethin' movin'.' He points a finger at Pippo's box.

'You're imagining it, my friend. Too much talk of devils and the like.'

'There's somethin' there, I'm tellin' yer.'

'We'll see about that.' The darty-eyed one creeps to the clothes-box. My heart pitter-patters. I want to go and stop him, but I promised Jack-Bon.

He gets there and looks in and his eyebrows go up into his hair. He claws out his fingers and does a cat pounce. 'Got you!'

Pippo gives an ear-piercey shriek. The old man shouts and stumble-trips and rushes out through the door-flap. But the darty-eyed one stays standing. He lifts the cloak in the box. Pippo's head sticks out. He shrieks again and shows his teeth. The man's mouth goes gapey-wide, then he bundles Pippo in the cloak tight-as-tight.

I have to make him drop him, whatever Jack-Bon said. I push with my hands on the sun and scream loud-as-loud. 'AHHHHHHHHH!'

The man's darty-eyes go wild and white. 'Wh-who's that?'

I push again. The sun rocks to-and-fro, fro-and-to and falls to the ground with a crash. But the man is too busy running off into the outside with Pippo to see.

'Pippo. No!' I run out after, but the racketing wind sucks all my breath and throws me on the ground. I try again, but it's no use because the wind won't let me follow. And now my last friend has gone and there is nothing I can do.

I crawl back on the inside and climb in the box where Pippo was. My head and chest are achy-sore and my eyes won't stop crying. I cover the clothes over and poke my fingers in my ears. Then everything shrinks down into quiet and I fall fast to sleep.

CHAPTER 26

Cat

BANG!
I flick open my eyes. Someone is inside the cloth-house, clattering and crashing about. My heart bump-thuds. What if it is the men who took Pippo? I stay mouse-quiet in the clothes-box and listen.

'Cat? Are you there?'

Jack-Bon! I push off the clothes. Two eyes gleam down from out of the pitchy-dark.

'Thank goodness! I thought the wind might have blown you away.' Jack-Bon puts his arms out and lifts me from the box. 'What are you doing in there?'

'Hiding from the men.'

'What men?'

I hang down my head. 'The ones that took Pippo.'

'What?' Jack-Bon's voice goes raspy-high. He grabs hold of my shoulders. 'Tell me what happened!'

'They came to take the trees and the boxes. The

old one said it was because of a grand-finally happening tomorrow, but then they talked about me and Pippo. They said we were divils and if they could find us, they would get a bag of gold soft-rings.'

Jack-Bon's fingers squeeze harder and his eyes go owly-wide.

'Ow! You're hurting.'

He drops down his hands. 'I am sorry. Go on.'

'It wasn't true what they said about us, but I stayed mouse-quiet behind the sun. And then Pippo got away and the one with the darty-eyes caught him and now—' My eyes go all blurry-wet again. 'And now he is gone.'

'Hush!' Jack-Bon strokes my cheek and puts his arms round me. He is wet and warm and full of fresh rain smells. He holds on for a bit, then pushes me back and frowns his face.

'Did the men say anything else?'

I sniff and wipe my nose on my sleeve. 'They said there was going to be prayers-to-God in the chapel and feasts and entytaynment in the blanketing hall, and then everyone would go back home.'

Jack-Bon's eyes grow wide as two suns put together. 'That is it, Cat! That is when they are planning to kill the King.'

'Kill The King? You mean, make him dead?'

'Yes. And the Queen too.'

'Queen Catty? No!' My heart scrunches.

'I think so, yes. I heard Mortmain talking to Gobbo—'

'Gobble?' My heart scrunches more tightly. 'He is here?'

Jack-Bon nods. 'He is Mortmain's assassin.'

'Ass-assin?'

'It means Mortmain is paying him to kill the King and Queen. And then, the Duke of Buckingham will blame it on King François.'

'But that isn't right!'

'I know, but it is what they are going to do.'

'Why?'

'To cause trouble between the French and the English. But there is more to it than that, or else why make Meg their prisoner and bring her here?' Jack-Bon furrows his face into another frown. 'And what did Buckingham mean when he said she was of royal blood? It does not make any sense . . .'

'Meg! Is she still there in the cloth-house?'

Jack-Bon slumps his shoulders and hangs down his head. 'Yes.'

'Did she hear my birdy-flute?'

'I . . . I do not know. But if she did, I am sure it will make her feel better, knowing you are near.' He pushes his mouth into a crinkled smile, but his eyes stay down and frowning.

'We have to go and tell Queen Catty.'

Jack-Bon gives a puff and shakes his head. 'Even if the guards let us see her, I do not think she will listen, Cat. Not when she finds out it was you who jumped in front of King François's horse.'

'What can we do then?'

He stares over the top of my head and far away, then his eyes flutter back and he puffs another breath. '*Eh bien*, there is only one choice. We must stop them ourselves.'

'Ourselves? You mean, you with me?'

'Yes, but it is going to be difficult.' Jack-Bon pulls off his bonnet, all wet from the rain, and wraps himself tight in a cloak from the box. 'People are searching for you, Cat, and if those men are right, they will get lots of money for catching you. And there is a danger that Mortmain will recognize me too.'

'But he thinks you are dead and down in the deep

Jack-Bon's tongue licks over his lips. 'Yes, but now he has seen me again, dressed like this.' He tugs on his kirtle-skirts.

'How?'

'I spoke to him after Gobbo left. I suspected – I mean I thought he had done a bad thing to my *Papa*. I . . . I needed to be sure.' His voice is all chokey-small.

'What bad thing?'

Jack-Bon's eyes go shiny bright. A tear trickles down and plops on his kirtle-skirts. He puffs another breath. 'I cannot tell you, Cat. Not now.'

I slump my shoulders. I want the old Jack-Bon back.

'When are you going to put on your real clothes?'

He wipes his apron on his face and stares at all the clothes-boxes. 'That is it!' He looks at me with his eyes all owly-wide again.

'What is?'

'If we can fool them into thinking we are players, they will let us in for the entertainments. And after that . . . well, I do not know yet, but at least we might have a chance.'

My stomach goes all twisty-turny. I am fed up of hearing that word 'fool'. I stamp my foot down. 'I am not a fool and no one can make me be one – not you, or Queen Catty, or Mistress Bristles too!'

Jack-Bon frowns his face and takes my fingers inside his. 'I know you are not a fool, Cat. But it is not what I meant.'

'What did you?'

'That we can trick them by dressing up in these costumes.' He peers round-and-about. 'It is too dark now. We will have to wait until first light and pray those men do not come back.'

'They won't. They are too frighty-faced and scared.'

Jack-Bon squeezes my fingers tighter. 'I hope you are right. Now we must try and sleep.' He pulls more clothes out from the box and throws them over the ground, then he lies on them and pats the space beside him.

I lie down as well, but I am too busy being awake to sleep. I turn my face to Jack-Bon. 'I can sing a song if you like?'

He gives a shivery yawn. 'I would like that, Cat. But quiet as a mouse, remember?' He makes the sign.

I nod, then soft-as-soft I sing our sleeping song.

'Hush! Hush! Little Jack-Bon
Sleep your sleep until the morrow
Still and quiet, in my arms
I will keep you safe from harm.'

When I've finished, I whisper Jack-Bon's name. But he is still and quiet, like in the song, with just his chest going in and out. I sing the song with Pippo's name, and then with your name, Meg. And then I say my prayers-to-God and ask Him to keep us *all* safe from harm.

A cock-a-doodle in the outside crows me awake. I get on my knees and look for Pippo. And then I remember about the men. My heart pangs. Poor Pippo. What have those two done with him? I stare at Jack-Bon. His eyes are tight shut and his mouth is puffing and blowing.

'Jack-Bon.' I shake his arms.

His eyes flick open. '*Quoi? Je suis où?* Oh, Cat – it is you!' He rubs at his face and sits up.

'The morning has come. We have to put on the clothes and fool them.'

He blinks. 'Yes, you are right, and we must hurry too. If they come back and find us here . . .' He gets on his feet and snatches a brown shirt and breeches from the clothes-box. 'Too big!' He throws them away and looks some more.

I run to the box with the painted faces. The red-and-blue birdy one is there, and the feathery cloak too. I tug them out and put the birdy-face over mine. 'Found one!'

Jack-Bon looks from behind a mound of cloaks and hats. His face frowns, then he turns it into a smile. 'A mask. Yes, to keep your face hidden will be good. I have found something too – look.' He swishes out a leaf-green coat and holds it to his neck. 'It is for the part of Robin Hood. I sewed it myself when I worked for *Maître* Gibson. The tunic is too long, but there is a belt.' He shows a leather belt. 'And a hat too.' He pulls a pointy brown hat down on top of his head. 'The only thing missing is a bow and arrows.' His face frowns again.

Something flickers inside my head. I run back to the box with the archree bows. 'Here. Look!' I open the lid to show him.

Jack-Bon hurries over. 'Let me see.' He clatter-rattles through them and gives a loud gasp.

'What's the matter? Did you get a spike?'

He shakes his head, then he puts his hand back in

and pulls out a bow. It is long and curved like the others, but the wood is pale-gold and there's a shiny silver bit on it too.

He holds it out. 'This is *my* bow. The one *Papa* gave me for my birthday. Look, it has our family's badge on it – a swallow.' He points to a bird shape marked in the silver and strokes over it with his fingertip. His eyes fill with water again, but he wipes it before it comes out. 'I wonder . . .' He hunches down and rattles through the rest of the box. *'Eh bien, oui!* My arrows too.'

'Did you put them there?'

He shakes his head. 'One of the guards took them, after . . . after I tried to stop the dogs.' His cheeks go red and glowy and he slides his eyes down to the ground.

My chest pangs. 'Hosper was brave.'

Jack-Bon puffs a breath. 'He was. And now we must be too.' He grips his hand on my shoulder. 'Are you ready?'

I nod my head.

'Bon. Come. We must get dressed.' He picks the arrows out and puts them with the bow, then he changes his maid clothes for the Robin-Hood ones.

My heart flit-flutters. 'You are Jack-Bon again!'

He looks down, then he shines me a smile. 'You are right, Cat. I am. Now – your turn.' He ties the feather-cloak over my skirts and pokes my hands and arms in the holes, then he fixes the birdy-face on. 'Can you see?'

I peep through the eye-holes. 'Yes.' I flip-flap my arms and swoop about.

'*Très belle!*'

'What?'

'Sorry. I mean you are very beautiful.'

My chest swells to bursting. Only Meg and Nonny Sweet-Bee have said I was that. I pull out my birdy-flute and make it sing. But not like Blackbird, or Robin or Wren. Like me. Cat Sparrow.

Jack-Bon claps his hands. I am going to do it again, but then I hear voices – voices I know.

I gulp a breath. 'It is them – the men. They are coming back.'

Jack-Bon's face goes pale-as-pale. '*Vite!* We must hide.' He grabs on to my hand, but then the door-flap opens and there is nowhere left to go.

· CHAPTER 27 ·

Cat

The men stare at us, then the old one steps over and thumps his hands on his sides.

'What are you two doin' in here?'

Jack-Bon gives a spluttery-cough.

'Well?' The man's face is all cross and knotted.

I flap my arms and jump in front. 'We are going to be in the Robin-Hood play. Where have you put Pippo?'

His face knots tighter and his eyes shrink beetle-small. 'Pip who?'

'No. Pipp-O.'

'Stop foolin' with me, you little—'

'I am not foolin', I am—'

'Pshhht!' Jack-Bon gives me a 'watch out!' look, then he coughs again and makes his voice go lower. 'She means nothing by it, sir. Master Gibson ordered us to come and fetch our costumes so we can practise our parts.'

The other man drops the door-flap down and comes closer. He flickers me over with his darty-black eyes. '*You're* a strange one.' He makes a snatch-grab at my birdy-face.

'No!' Jack-Bon leaps in between. 'You cannot. The mask – it is very fragile. If any of the feathers come off, Master Gibson will be furious.'

The old man holds on tight to the darty-eyed one's arm. 'He's right. The master's in a foul enough temper as it is, what with the mess the wind and rain made of things yesterday and all the repairs that have needed doin' since.' He shakes his head. 'That storm was an omin. There's bad things comin', you mark my words.'

The darty-eyed man rolls his eyes. 'You and your superstitions, old man. All right, but they can help with loading up the cart, though from the look of this one –' he sticks me with a pokey finger – 'she'll be less use than a mule in quicksand.'

I want to say I am not a mule and stick him back, but Jack-Bon grips my hand in his. 'Yes, sir. Very good, sir.' He drags me to the clothes-boxes and pushes me down.

I look back over at the darty-eyed one. 'He took Pippo.'

Jack-Bon pulls me back round. 'Quiet or he will hear. Help me put these away.' He piles the clothes on the ground.

After they are all inside the boxes, the darty-eyed one makes us put them in the horse-and-cart. Then he and the old one bang-and-crash the sun and moon in and get on top. We try and do the same, but the men make us walk behind.

The sun shines down on the cloth-houses all around. Some have been knocked down in the wind and rain. I'm scared in case your one is too, Meg, but Jack-Bon says not to worry and that it is still there. He saw it on the way back yesterday. My heart does a small skip when he tells me. My prayers-to-God must have worked.

People come out through the door-flaps, yawning and rubbing at their eyes. When they see us, they blink hard-as-hard. Some shake their heads and roll their eyes like always. Others snort and crow. But I don't care because I am all belle-and-bootfull in my feather-cloak and birdy-face – Jack-Bon said.

You would say it too, Meg. I promise we will come and rescue you – criss-cross my heart. And Pippo as well, but now we have to go and save Queen Catty and The King.

We trundle on behind the cartwheels. Jack-Bon holds on to my hand, but his face has gone all frowny and his eyes are far off and away. Bells clang and bang ahead and more people come – lords with feathery hats, and ladies with sparkles on their dresses. They hustle and bustle towards the bells. Some of them point at us and titter, but most are too busy chit-chattering to look.

The cart rumbles on and goes past more

cloth-houses and in through the arch where the men in their shiny metal suits were fighting, and King Franswah nearly fell down from his horse. Jack-Bon grips my hand tighter and makes a gasping noise.

'*C'est pas vrai!*'

'What?'

He points to an open cloth-house with a pointy roof. It is where the noise of the bells is coming out from.

'A chapel. They must have built it during the night. And look over there. That gold tent with the tables all set for a feast. It must be the banqueting hall.'

I do my best to stand on my toe-tips, but there are too many people milling and spilling about to see.

Jack-Bon tugs on my feather-cloak. 'We must get closer and watch for Gobbo.' He pulls us away from the cart so the two men can't see and takes us in between the grand lords-and-ladies. We get nearer to the cloth-chapel and then a loud hoot-tooting noise makes us jump. There are cries of 'Their Majesties!' and 'Make way for the Kings of England and France!' The guard-men stand straight and squash all the grand lords-and-ladies back.

I follow along the line to where everyone is looking. Candle Woolly is coming along on top of a white donkey in a red-and-gold gown and cape. The donkey is like the one Stewer Boneyface uses to help grind the corn at the nonnies' mill, but with a cushion for the Candle to sit on and two gold hoops for holding his red sparkled shoes. It is puffing and blowing, but Candle Woolly doesn't care. He is too busy holding a big cross and nodding and smiling all pleased-as-pleased from beneath his shiny gold hat.

The Two Kings come behind riding their horses side by side. Our one – The King – is wearing a red-and-gold coat and a black hat with a white feather – bigger than the biggest goose feather. There is a red-and-gold 'R is for Rose' round his neck and gold sparkles on his fingers too. The other one is King Franswah, but instead of his metal suit, he is wearing a silver-and-blue coat and a hat with a feather to go with his black hair and beard.

Behind The Kings come two more horses. One has Queen Catty perched on the side. She is all dressed in gold-and-black-and-red and looking belle-and-bootfull as a swan. The other has another grand lady in a silver gown with gold showing through. She looks younger than Queen Catty, but she is not so bootfull – more of a wood-pidgie or a duck.

They trot up and there are bows and curtseys all around. I flap my arms at Queen Catty, but she isn't looking and Jack-Bon pulls them back down.

'No, Cat.'

'Why?'

'She will not know you with your mask on.

Besides, we are here to find Gobbo, remember?'

Candle Woolly and The Kings and Queens clip-clop to a stop outside the chapel. Guard-men rush to help the queens climb off their horses and then all of them go into the inside. The grand lords-and-ladies follow behind. But there is no sign of the Lord Bucket and Mort-mane, or Gobble either.

Jack-Bon looks round-and-about. 'Where is he?' He pushes closer to the chapel, but then a guard-man blocks the way.

'Where d'you think you two are going?'

Jack-Bon stands tall-as-tall. 'To pray.'

The guard-man gives a roaring laugh. 'Not looking like that you're not! Only the great and the good are allowed inside, and *you* are neither.' He shoves Jack-Bon back with his hand.

Voices blow out from inside the chapel, but not like the nonnies all wailing-and-groaning. These ones are pipey-sweet, like a whole flock of night-gales. My heart swoops up inside, because it is bootfull – more bootfull than all the Blackbirds and Robins and Wrens put together. I close my eyes and spin myself round and round.

'What's wrong with your friend?'

I blink my eyes open and stop still. The guard-man is pointing his stick at me and his eyes have gone all tight and hard. Jack-Bon's face is pale-as-pale.

'Nothing. She . . . she likes the sound of the music, that is all.'

The guard-man jabs the stick again. 'Fools, the pair of you! Be off or I'll have you thrown in the castle dungeons.'

I stare back at him. He is the one who is the fool, pinching his mouth and poking his stick. Why doesn't he do dancing instead?

Jack-Bon grabs my feather-cloak. 'Yes, sir. Come on, Cat.' He pulls me away.

'But what about Gobble?'

He keeps on going without answering, but when we have left the guard-man behind, he turns round and looks back at the chapel with frowny-dark eyes. 'I do not think they will let Gobbo in there either. Which means he will have to make his attack during the banquet.' He points over to the golden cloth-house.

People are hurrying and scurrying about putting things on the tables outside. There are boards full of bread loaves and cheeses and bowls of red-and-gold fruit – 'C is for Cherries', 'P is for Peaches' and 'A is for Apples' as well. Water comes up in my mouth because we didn't have breakfast, or supper too.

On the nearest side to us, the trees and the flowers from the other cloth-house have been planted like a garden in the grass. The sun and the moon are there too.

Jack-Bon tugs me towards the closest tree and slides us down behind. 'We can keep watch from here.'

'What if he comes?'

'We must do everything we can to stop him from reaching the King and Queen. But do not do anything until I tell you. You understand?' Jack-Bon gives me a piercey-sharp look.

I shiver and give a nod.

'Good.' He flickers me a smile and looks out from behind the tree.

I puff on the ground and wait. The sun boils down from the sky above. My feather-cloak is making me all hot and bothered and my birdy-face is stuck to my nose and cheeks. I close my eyes over and droop my head.

'Wake up, Cat.' Jack-Bon is shaking me hard-as-hard.

I blink and sit up. 'Is it Gobble?'

'No, but they are arriving for the banquet. Look.' Jack-Bon points round the side of the tree. I push next to him and hold in my breath.

The tables outside the golden cloth-house are even more full of things now, with bowls of cooked chooks and silvery fish, and rows of gold knives and spoons.

The King is leading the pidgie-queen to the highest one that is all covered in a shimmery gold cloth and red 'R is for Roses'. She only reaches his middle and she walks with a round back and as if one shoe is paining her. But she has a kind face and smiley-bright eyes.

Queen Catty is being led by King Franswah. She is smiling and laughing too, but the sound is high and honking, like a goose warning off a fox. After them comes Candle Woolly, but not with his donkey, and then all the grand lords-and-ladies from the chapel.

The ladies-who-wait are there too. Lady Marjoree and Lady Boleyn and . . . Mistress Bristles!

My stomach goes all squirmy-tight. I want to tell Jack-Bon, but then a black shadow grows over us.

'Well, well,' a voice sneers and snarks. 'And what've we got here?'

CHAPTER 28

Isabelle

My heart sinks. It is one of the men from the tent – the sly-faced one Cat says took Pépin. His eyes dart from me to Cat and back again.

'What are you doing skulking about back here?'

I grip the stave of my bow and lift slowly to my feet. 'We . . . I mean, I—'

There's a rustle of feathers as Cat jumps up beside me. 'We're looking at the kings and queens, aren't we, Jack-Bon?'

I draw back my shoulders and look him full in the face. '*Oui*. I mean, yes. It is the first time we have seen them so close.'

The man's lips curl into a sneer. 'A Frenchie. I thought as much.' His eyes catch on my bow and quiver. 'And an armed one too.'

'Yes, but that is only for the play. I told you before, we are going to be in Robin Hood.'

'A pretty story!' He gives a loud snort.

'But it is true. Ask Master Gibson.'

'Now there's an idea!' The man throws a quick

glance over his shoulder. My chest tightens as I follow his gaze. My former master is standing a short distance away barking orders at a bunch of men dressed in the costumes of Robin Hood's outlaws.

The man's eyes narrow. 'What's wrong? Changed your mind?' He snatches hold of my tunic sleeve.

Cat jumps between us, arms flapping. 'You took Pippo. Give him back!'

The man stumbles back in surprise. As he reaches out to steady himself, his foot catches on the base of the tree and he crashes to the ground.

'Quick!' I make to grab Cat's hand, but she pushes past me.

'Gobble!'

'Where? Show me.'

Instead of answering, she gallops off towards the crowd of people now gathered in front of the banqueting tent. I chase after her. As I catch her up, she jerks to a stop and slides her bird-mask up over her forehead. 'Look! There.'

The man she's pointing at is dressed in a French gentleman's clothes – blue silk shirt and breeches and a blue velvet cloak with a border of gold *fleur-de-lis* sewn round the hem – but he looks the same height as Gobbo and he's got the same skinny legs too. As I stand on tiptoe to get a better view, the air around us darkens. People turn and throw puzzled looks about them. The man who might be Gobbo does the same.

My stomach squeezes. Cat's right. It *is* him – I'd know those bony cheeks and mean lizard-eyes anywhere. Before I can do anything, the air grows darker still. People are staring up at the sky now, eyes wide and startled-looking, mouths gaping. I follow their gaze and freeze.

There, hovering above us, is a giant winged monster, its legs and body covered in green-and-gold scales, its long, writhing neck topped by a narrow head and a pair of blazing orange eyes. But worst of all are the blood-red lips pulled back to show rows of jagged yellow teeth and a flickering black-and-gold forked tongue.

It hangs there for a moment longer then swoops down towards the crowd, jaws snapping, tail thrashing. Cat screams and flings her arms about me. All around us people dash for cover – nobles, servants, guards, the man who took Pépin too – all of them yelling and screaming, shoving their neighbours to the ground and tripping over their own feet in their hurry to get away.

All except Gobbo, who appears to be ignoring the monster now, and is busy ducking and weaving his way towards the open tent instead. Why isn't he fleeing too? I frown and look back up. The creature's jaws are wide open now, and spouts of orange flame are shooting between its fangs. But instead of blood-curdling shrieks and roars, the only sounds coming from it are a few sharp pops and bangs and a loud flap-snapping noise – like the tent-canvas in yesterday's storm.

The words Mortmain spoke to Gobbo in the tavern echo in my ears: *I have arranged for a distraction. It will give you plenty of time to strike the blow . . .*

And then I realize the truth. It isn't a monster but some sort of fire-spitting kite instead.

I prise myself free from Cat's grip. 'Stay here.'

'No!' She throws her arms round me again, but I push her away.

'I have to stop Gobbo, or it will be too late.' I swing my bow down off my shoulder and slide an arrow from my quiver.

Cat clutches at my tunic. 'But the snake-bird will eat me.'

'It is not real, Cat.'

'Not . . . not real?' Shivering, she stares back up at the monster dipping and diving above our heads.

I snatch up her hand. 'We are friends, *non*?'

She turns to look at me again and gives a hurried nod.

'Then you must trust me. Go and hide behind the tree. I will come for you, I promise.' She hesitates for a moment, then clutching her bird-cloak about her, she stumbles towards it, shoulders hunched, eyes fixed firmly on the ground.

I glance over at the banqueting tent. Gobbo has

got past the crowds and is sliding towards the entrance. But the handful of guards who've remained to protect the royal party are too busy gawping at the sky-monster to have noticed. It's only me who knows where the true danger lies – but I have to get closer to be sure of hitting my target. I tighten my grip on my bow and arrow and dart forwards, doing my best all the while to keep Gobbo in my sights. But then, as he closes in on his prey, a second figure in a black cloak and hat appears and sets off in pursuit.

Mortmain! A fresh ball of anger tears through me. I should shoot him in the back now, like he shot *Papa*. But can I really kill a man? And what about Gobbo? I flick my gaze back on him. He's nearly in striking distance of the King and Queen. If I don't act now, it will be too late.

Sweat pricks at my forehead. My eyes dart between Gobbo and Mortmain. What should I do, *Papa*? What should I do?

You know the answer, Hirondelle.

He's right – in my heart of hearts I do.

I nock my arrow, then pulling myself to my full height, I raise my bow and draw the bowstring taut. Narrowing my eyes, I take aim at Gobbo's right leg and with a quick prayer, let the arrow fly. I hold my breath as it speeds through the air, willing my aim to be true.

As it finds its mark, there's an ear-piercing shriek

and Gobbo staggers sideways, one hand clamped to the top of his leg, the other clutching the edge of a tablecloth. As he slides to the ground, goblets and trenchers clattering about him, a man's voice shouts, 'Their majesties. Look to their majesties!'

The remaining guards spring to the defence of the royal party, circling around them, swords and halberds drawn.

I scan around me looking for Mortmain. At first, I don't see him, but then I do, head down and hurrying towards the tiltyard arch. If I can wing him like Gobbo, he'll face the King's justice alongside him, and my vow to *Papa* will be fulfilled. I snatch another arrow from my quiver, but as I go to nock it, I'm barged from behind and sent thudding to the ground.

'Got you!' A guard glares down at me, his booted foot digging into my chest. I wriggle against him, but it's no use – I'm caught hard and fast. Another older-looking guard appears at his side, sword drawn, mouth pulled into a tight grimace.

'It's the assassin, Captain.'

My heart does a quick somersault. Assassin? What's he talking about?

'It was not me, it was him.' I try to lift up and point Gobbo out, but the first guard shoves me down again.

'*Je vous en prie.* You do not understand! I was trying to stop him. I—'

The captain signals to my captor. 'Throw him in the dungeons.' The guard grabs my collar and drags me choking to my feet. I struggle against him, but his grip grows tighter still.

My throat closes over.

I can't breathe . . . I can't breathe . . .

'Please, I can't brea—!' I stumble sideways, head spinning, then a wave of darkness washes over me and I crumple to the ground.

· CHAPTER 29 ·

Cat

Jack-Bon told me to stay still and hide, and I was going to, Meg – criss-cross my heart. But the snake-bird's tail came swishing and snapping and I got scared and jumped away.

And then I saw Mort-mane going towards the golden cloth-house. People were shouting and pointing to the snake-bird and running all over, but he didn't look once. Instead, he was holding a shiny sword-stick and creeping after Gobbo. But then Jack-Bon fired an arrow like when he was trying to stop the dogs from biting me and Hosper, and Gobbo fell down. And now the guard-men are coming and Mort-mane has put his sword-stick away and he is pounding back off with his eye flashing and his face all stormy-dark.

Jack-Bon tried to stop Mort-mane too, but a guard-man has caught him, so I will have to try instead. But I don't have an archree bow like Jack-Bon – I only have my own self and . . . Wait – I know!

I pull my birdy-face back on and reach in my feather-cloak for my flute. I give it a rattle, then I get my lips ready to blow and wait for Mort-mane to come.

Close . . .

Close . . .

Closer . . .

And . . .

NOW!

I fly out and sound Blackbird's warning loud-as-loud.

Shriiiii! Shriiiii! Shriiiiiii!

Mort-mane jump-stops and glares with his glittery green eye. 'Out of my way, fool!'

'I am not a fool. I am Cat Sparrow!' I puff my cheeks to blow again. He growls and pushes me off, then goes even faster.

I tumble-run after, blowing and blowing so my heart goes bursty-tight. But no one looks. They are all too busy running away from the snake-bird. I keep on going, but then there's a loud crash-crack behind. I stop and spin round. The snake-bird has dropped out of the sky and is lying all tattered and torn on the ground. Everyone else stops their running too. Some slink over and stare with mouth-open faces.

I want to go and see as well, but I have to stop Mort-mane. I whip back round. He is standing and staring like the rest. I drag hold of his cloak and shout louder-than-loud so everyone will hear.

'You are a bad man. You took Meg, and now you and the Lord Bucket are trying to hurt The King and Queen Catty.'

People look round at us with their eyes all owly-wide.

The snake-mark on Mort-mane's face goes red and angry. His green eye flashes and flares. 'Quiet, you little idiot!' He snarls the words through gritty-tight teeth, then he grabs my neck and pulls my bird-face off my head. 'Wait.' His eye shrinks down in a gold-green slit. 'I know you! You're that numb-skull from the nunnery.'

'I am not a nun-skull!'

'Gah! I haven't the time for your clowning!' He snatch-grabs my birdy-flute and smashes it to the ground, then thunders off with his black cloak swooshing out behind.

My stomach goes sick and squirmy. I drop down and find my little bird, but the head is broken from the body, and when I blow it, nothing comes out. I press it to my chest and close my eyes and go to-and-fro, fro-and-to.

I do it so hard that my head bumps down on the grass, and then voices go 'ooh' and 'ahh' and one does quacking and another clucks. But I don't care – I only care about my birdy-flute. I shrink in a ball and try to stop from hearing.

'Cat Sparrow!' A voice squawks maggie-pie

sharp in my ear.

I snap open my eyes and give a shiver.

Mistress Bristles is standing side-by-side with a red-and-gold guard-man, both of them frowning down hard-as-hard.

'You led us all a merry dance, girl, causing all that fuss and bother at the joust and then running away like that. Where have you been all this time?'

I open my mouth, but the only thing that comes out is a tiny-high peep. Mistress Bristles clicks her tongue and snatches my hand in her bony claw-fingers.

'No!' I twist and turn and try to get free, but she holds on tighter-than-tight.

'Whisht! You are coming with me, girl, like it or not.'

'Coming where?'

'To see Her Grace the Queen. You have some explaining to do.'

I don't want to do ess-playning. I want to go after and stop Mort-mane. But it is no use, because the guard-man has got hold of me tightly-fast and is dragging me off behind.

· CHAPTER 30 ·

Cat

Mistress Bristles marches off without saying another thing. When we get to the big cloth-house, we climb the stairs to a room full of sparkling windows and walls covered with tree-green cloths all stitched with The King's 'R is for Roses' and The Queen's 'P is for Pomegranate fruits'. The only other things inside are a big black chair with a golden cushion and a lady in a red dress who is standing by a window and looking into the outside.

As we go in, she turns round and my heart does a bump. But it is a good kind of bumping, because it is Lady Marjoree and even better, she is holding . . .

'Pippo!' I tug my hand free from Mistress Bristles and tumble-run so fast I nearly trip on my skirts. But I don't and then I am there and Pippo has jumped on my shoulder and he is chit-chattering so loud it makes my ears whistle and my head and heart sing. I press my face in his munkee-fur and say his name over and over. Pippo chirps and cheeps and Lady Marjoree joins in with giggles and coos.

Then Mistress Bristles tries to ruin it. 'Put that nasty creature down before—' But she doesn't get to say any more because suddenly a guard-man calls out in a loud boomy voice, 'Her Grace, the Queen!'

I spin round with Pippo and see Queen Catty swishing in at the door with all the rest of her ladies-who-wait. Her eyebrows lift when she sees me, but she keeps on going until she gets to the big black chair. When she turns back round, Mistress Bristles curtseys low and drags me down too. Queen Catty sits on top of the golden cushion. She fiddles with her fingers on her Holy-Cross necklace and gives a small cough.

'Bring the girl forward.'

Mistress Bristles goes down even lower, then she pushes me out in front.

Queen Catty waves her hand. 'Thank you, Mistress Bristol. You may leave us.'

'But Your Grace—'

'I said, leave us.'

Mistress Bristles pinches her lips and makes a small huffing noise. Then she falls down in another curtsey and steps back and back and out through the door until she is gone.

Queen Catty flutters her grey eyes on me. 'Well, Cat Sparrow, and what do you have to say for yourself?'

I do not want to say anything for myself. I want to tell her about Meg and Jack-Bon and Mort-mane and the Lord Bucket. But there is too much of it and I don't know where to start from. I bite on my lip and hold Pippo tighter.

Queen Catty frowns her face. 'Very well. Shall we begin with what happened at the joust yesterday? It was you, wasn't it, who ran out in front of King François's horse?'

I look at the ground and nod.

The ladies-who-wait hold their hands over their mouths and give loud gasps and cries.

Queen Catty coughs again. 'I thought so. His Grace and I did not see clearly ourselves, but there were rumours the person responsible had some sort of creature with them. Then, when that man came here yesterday with your monkey and tried to claim the reward . . .' Her face goes even more frowny. 'Why did you do such a foolish thing?

I curl my fingers round Pippo's furry-soft tail. 'I was coming to get you to help.'

Queen Catty's eyebrows go up again. 'Help? With what?'

I look around at the ladies-who-wait. They have stopped their twitterings and are staring at us with their eyes all owly-wide. I shake my head. It is only for Queen Catty to hear.

She sees me and waves them back. 'You may go.'

The ladies-who-wait mutter and fuss and give

lots of upset looks. The one called Lady Boleyn goes over and whispers low-as-low in Queen Catty's ear, but I hear anyway.

'Your Grace, are you sure we should leave you on your own with this . . . this troublemaker?'

Queen Catty looks back at me and nods. 'Yes, quite sure.'

The other ladies-who-wait shake their heads, then all of them hustle and bustle away. Lady Marjoree goes too, but she turns round and flutters me a smile from the door.

Queen Catty waits for everyone to go, then she stands and swishes towards me. 'So why did you need my help?'

'To get my sister, Meg, free from the Lord Bucket.'

Queen Catty's face frowns again. 'Lord Bucket?'

'The one with the fish-eyes who tripped on Pippo and didn't want me to sing.'

Her eyebrows fly high. 'The Duke of Buckingham?'

'Yes, him and his friend – the one called Mort-mane. They are bad men. They have got Meggy and they are trying to hurt you and The King, and—'

Queen Catty puts her hand in the air. 'What nonsense is this? My Lord Buckingham is the King's noble kinsman and a loyal friend.'

'But it is not non-sense, it is true! Me and Jack-

Bon heard them talking all whispery-quiet in the place where the horses are kept. They did it some more when I was all hot-and-bothered inside your gold box. Lord Bucket went off, but I followed after Mort-mane and found Meg shut in his cloth-house. Mort-mane is the one who took her from me and the nonnies, but the Lord Bucket ordered it. Meggy said so, and she never tells any lies.'

I gulp a breath and look back at Queen Catty. Her eyebrows are still high, but her eyes are round and listening, so I carry on with my telling.

'Mort-mane was the one who got Gobble to try and kill you and The King when the snake-bird was flying about. But he didn't manage it because Jack-Bon stopped him with his bow-and-arrow. And I ran after Mort-Mane again, but Mistress Bristles caught me and now Mort-mane is gone. So . . . so I couldn't rescue Meg and . . . and it is all too late.' Water comes in my eyes. Some runs down my cheek and plops on Pippo's head.

Queen Catty's face goes paler-than-pale and her fingers grip tight on her Holy-Cross necklace. When I have finished she presses her mouth shut and swishes over to the window. She looks through it for a long while, then she lifts her shoulders and swishes back.

'Where is this man, this . . . this Mort-mane, keeping your sister?'

'It is on the edge of things, near to the big round

oven where the men shovel in the bread.'

'Very well.' She nods and shakes out her skirts. 'Guard!'

The door opens and one of the red-and-gold guard-men steps in.

'Ready my litter at once.'

The guard-man gives a low bow, then he clatters about and hurries off into the outside.

Queen Catty takes hold of my hand. 'Come. You will show me, but if you are lying . . .' Her eyes go black as thunder-clouds.

I am not lying – I am telling the truth. But I don't say because soon she will see for herself.

We go along the passage and back down all the stairs. When we get into the outside, Queen Catty's gold box is there with more red-and-gold guard-men waiting to lift it. We climb in and Queen Catty bangs on the roof and we bump and bounce away. But she doesn't say anything. Instead, her eyes stare straight ahead and her fingers stay gripped on her Holy-Cross necklace.

I stroke Pippo in my lap and watch out of the window at all the people stopping and staring. We do lots more bumping and bouncing, then we get to the edge of things. I poke my head into the outside. At first I can't see where the right cloth-house is, but then I do. My stomach goes topsy-turvy.

'There!' I point with my finger.

Queen Catty bangs on the floor. The box thumps down and a guard-man's face shows at the window.

'Majesty?'

Queen Catty speaks through pinchy-tight lips. 'Go and check the tent.'

The guard-man bows his head and clatters away. Queen Catty drags over the window-cloth and looks ahead again with her face all paley-white.

The topsy-turvy feeling grows bigger. I hug my arms tight round Pippo and start going to-and-fro. But soon there's more rattling and pounding and the guard-man's face shows again.

'There is no one, Your Grace.'

My heart scrunches. 'Not Meg?'

The guard-man frowns with his eyebrows, even though I spoke the words clear-as-clear.

It is no use. I can't wait any more. I will go and find out myself. I jump through the door with Pippo chit-chitting behind.

The guard-man tries to snatch us, but we get past him and all the others too. Queen Catty calls my name, but I pretend I can't hear. I hurry over to the cloth-house and push through the door-flap into the inside. But the guard-man was right – there is no one. All that is left is an empty blanket and some piled-up ropes. My heart pangs so hard it feels like it will break. I stumble-run back into the outside and spin round-and-about.

'Meg. Meg. My Meggy-Peg!'

But there is too much neighing of horses and hubbubbing of people for you to hear. I reach in my bag for my birdy-flute, but it is no use because it is all smashed in pieces. There is only one thing left I can do. I lift my head and puff in a breath and sing our safe-together song.

> '*The rain doth rain*
> *The wind doth blow*
> *The ice doth freeze . . .*'

But my voice is pipey-small, like a chickling left all alone in the nest. I stop and sink down in my skirts and curl myself into a ball. It is too late. It is all too late . . .

'Cat?'

A voice sounds from far away. I shut my eyes and put my fingers in my ears. I am fed up of seeing, and hearing too.

The voice sounds again, but louder.

'Cat!'

A hand curls over my shoulder.

I take my fingers back out from my ears and blink open my eyes. A person is crouching down in front and shining me the biggest smile of all. And my heart swoops and soars, because it is the one I love best in the whole widey-world.

It is you, Meg. YOU!

We hug and hug, and hug some more.

Then you say about Mort-mane coming to take you again and how you tricked him to think you were asleep and got away.

I tug your arm. 'Come and tell Queen Catty, Meggy. Tell her about Mort-mane locking you in, and the Lord Bucket and the thing he said about your blood.'

'The Queen?' Your eyes dart over to the gold box and go all big and worried.

I squeeze your hand like you do to me when I'm feeling small and scared. 'It will be all right. She *is* The Queen, but she is good and kind.'

You swallow in a breath. Then you pull your bonnet right and flutter me back a smile.

We get to the gold box and Queen Catty peers out from the dark inside. She opens her mouth to say something, but I bob a quick curtsey and speak instead.

'This is my sister, Meg. She can tell you all about everything and then you will know I am speaking the truth.'

Queen Catty's eyebrows raise. She skims her grey eyes over Meg, who goes low into a curtsey too.

'Very well.' She clears her voice. 'But if you speak false to me, you will both be in grave trouble.' She waves her hand to one of the guard-men. He opens up the door and lets us in.

As the rest of the guard-men lift the box and carry us away, Queen Catty sniffs in a deep breath and nods. 'Well then, tell me everything.'

So, taking one turn after another, we do.

· CHAPTER 31 ·

Isabelle

I'm woken from my daze by a thud of approaching footsteps followed by the scrape of a key in a lock. A door in the opposite wall creaks open and a guard marches in carrying a flaming torch in his hand.

'Get up, traitor!' He seizes the front of my torn tunic and hauls me to my feet.

My stomach clenches. 'I am not a traitor. I . . . I was trying to save them. Please, you have to believe me.'

'A likely story.' He tightens his grip and shoves me out through the cell door into the dark, dank passage beyond.

I twist my head round. 'It is true! There were two of them. I wounded one with my arrow, but there was another . . . Mortmain. He works for the Duke of Buckingham. He—'

'Enough of your lies, unless you want a taste of this?' The guard presses his gloved fist to my cheek.

I flinch and shake my head. 'But . . . but where are you taking me?'

'You'll find out soon enough.' He bundles me along the passage, then up a narrow stone staircase and out through a doorway into dazzling bright daylight. At his signal, two more guards fall in on either side. They march me away in grim-faced silence, across the castle courtyard, out over the drawbridge and down the track that leads to the English camp.

As the King's cloth-and-glass palace swings into view, taunts of 'French devil' and 'Traitor!' echo out from the growing crowd. I swallow hard and do my best to ignore them, fixing my gaze on the way ahead.

As we tramp beneath the palace gatehouse, the sight of the dragon on the King's crest conjures fresh memories of Mortmain's fearsome, fire-breathing kite and the chaos it caused at the banquet. If it hadn't been for Cat's sharp eyes, Gobbo would have gone unnoticed and the King and Queen would be dead.

But where is she? And what about Meg? Now their plot has failed, the duke and Mortmain will surely want to be rid of her, which for ruthless men like them can mean only one thing . . .

An ice-cold shiver rushes through me. Whoever I'm being taken to, I've got to make them believe me – not just for my sake, but for Cat and Meg's as well.

*

Our journey ends in a grand hall, the likes of which I have never seen – not at home, or at the King's palace in Greenwich either. I draw in a breath and gaze about me. Shafts of gold sunlight flood through the great arched windows on to walls lined with cloth of gold hangings and chests laden with jewel-studded platters and goblets. The floor is covered in richly patterned carpets, while above our heads hang swags of green-and-white silk twined about with clouds of gold-painted roses.

It is only as my eyes get used to the dazzle that I become aware of the people gathered inside – a hundred or more lords and ladies dressed in the finest silks and velvets, who, as I'm marched between them, glare at me and exchange shocked-sounding whispers.

My face burns hot, but I pull back my shoulders and stare past them. I've done nothing wrong – I need to remember that.

As we advance, the courtiers fall back on either side to reveal a cluster of grander-looking lords with the familiar figure of Cardinal Wolsey at their centre. The lead guard jolts me to a stop in front of him and gives a quick bow.

'The prisoner, My Lord Cardinal.'

The cardinal looks me up and down with disdain, then waves the long gold staff he's carrying at the guard. Cutting the rope which binds my hands, the guard thrusts me into a low bow. There's a swish of coats as the cardinal and the other lords step to one side and the room falls deathly quiet. Then another voice rings out cold and clear. 'Well, traitor, what do you have to say for yourself?'

As I lift my head, the breath freezes in my throat because there, looking down at me from his seat on top of a raised platform, is the gold-coated figure of none other than Henry Tudor, King of all England.

The King's eyes bore into me, ice-cold and full of contempt. I shiver. What chance do I have of getting him to believe me? But then, as I hunch my shoulders and drop my eyes down to the floor, a familiar voice sounds soft in my ear.

Courage, Hirondelle!

I start and look about me. But *Papa's* not out there. He's here, in my heart, like he's always been.

And the best way to honour him and right the wrong done to him is to speak up and tell the truth – for it's not only my life that depends on it, but Cat and Meg's too.

Gripping my fingers into fists, I tilt back my head and force myself to meet the King's hard, blue gaze. For a moment his eyes widen and my hopes are raised that he's recognized me, even if the cardinal hasn't. But they're quickly dashed as his look hardens again and an angry red flush colours his cheeks.

'I am waiting.' He drums his jewelled fingers against the arm of the chair.

There's no time to try and remind him now – I

must say what I need to say, before it's too late.

'Please, Your Majesty, I am not the assassin. It is a man called William Gobbo. I shot him in the leg to stop him, but your guards, they—' I swallow hard. 'They arrested me and locked me up instead.'

The courtiers mutter among themselves and there are whispers of, 'Lying foreigner' and, 'French cur.'

I raise my hand and cover my heart. 'But it is the truth, I swear. He was hired to kill you by—'

'Majesty! Please forgive this interruption, but I must speak.' A figure dressed in a coat of gold and silver almost as fine as the King's elbows me aside. As he doffs his ruby-studded cap and scrapes into a low bow, my heart gives a sudden lurch at the sight of the large gold knot embroidered on the shoulder of his cloak.

King Henry raises a pale eyebrow. He exchanges a quick glance with Cardinal Wolsey, then clears his throat. 'Very well, My Lord Buckingham, but make it brief.'

'Thank you, Your Grace.' The duke sweeps into another exaggerated bow then turns and glares at me, his bulbous fish eyes shrinking to two glittering grey chips. 'It is quite plain this boy – this *French* boy – is doing his best to make fools of us all. This Gobbo character he names is an invention, designed to throw us off his scent and convince us of his own innocence.'

Heads nod and the room fills with more mutterings. The King's gaze grows even icier. My stomach clenches, but then I hear *Papa*'s voice again.

Keep your head, Isabelle, but speak from your heart.

I curl my fingers tighter and draw in a breath. 'Gobbo is not an invention. He is real. But it was not his idea.' I glance at Buckingham, a bead of sweat trickling down the side of my cheek. 'There are others more powerful than him who wish you harm, Your Majesty. If you would grant me permission to speak with you alone—'

Buckingham spins round and seizes hold of my tunic. 'Silence! How dare you address His Grace in such a fashion? It is clearly some kind of French plot, Majesty. I had fears such a thing might come to pass, as I know others in our company did too.' He glances around the room. Several of the older-looking nobles nod their heads and murmur their agreement.

'Enough!' King Henry raises his hand for silence. Rising from his chair, he steps off the platform and plants himself in front of me, hands on hips, legs splayed. 'Do you have proof of what you claim, boy?'

My mind flits to the parchment. But what use is it when it can't be read? I heave out a sigh. 'Only . . . only my word, Your Grace. But please – you have to listen to me. Your life may still be in danger if you do not.'

The Duke of Buckingham gives a loud snort. 'You really expect our great King would be so – please forgive me, Your Grace – so foolish as to believe the word of a lying French snake-in-the-grass such as you?'

The King hesitates for a moment, then his frown deepens and his mouth pinches into a tight red bow.

'As you, our loyal subjects, know' – he gestures to the courtiers gathered before him – 'we came here to this so-called Field of Cloth of Gold to meet with our cousin, the King of France and to celebrate the peace agreed between our two great countries. But now, alas, the act of this French assassin has put it in the most serious jeopardy. Take him away, My Lord Buckingham, and do with him as you see fit.'

'I am innocent, I swear it! Please—' I stumble forwards, hands clutched tight together.

But it's too late – the guards are already closing in. Buckingham throws me a look of scornful triumph. 'Hanging is too good for him. Bind his hands and feet and drown him in the castle moat like the base dog he is.'

'I beg of you, no!' I try to twist free, but the guards are too strong. As my arms are thrust behind me, I call to *Papa* silently for help.

But this time there's no reply. Instead my ears fill with a fresh barrage of voices crying 'Traitor', 'Coward' and 'Devil'. My stomach wrenches.

Buckingham has won. I was a fool ever to hope my word could count more than his. And now . . . My throat grips. Now I must pay with my life. Knees buckling, I close my eyes and suck in a juddering breath.

'Stop!'

I snap my eyes open again. A small figure in a striped hat and a grubby red-and-gold gown is running towards us, a spidery grey shape trailing a silk cord bouncing along at her side.

My eyes widen. Cat? But how . . . ?

She comes to a wobbling stop and plants herself in front me, arms stretched wide to shield me. 'Leave my friend alone!'

'What is the meaning of this?' The Duke of Buckingham's voice rings out, hard as an iron-clad fist. Before anyone can give an answer, there's the sound of marching feet and a small group of armed guards appears at the doorway. Then, two more figures hurry between them into the hall. The first, short and plump and dressed in a black-and-gold gown, is Queen Katherine. The second – a pale-faced girl in a dirty-looking smock – I realize with a jolt is Meg.

At the sight of the Queen, the courtiers pull back in low bows and curtseys. The Duke of Buckingham bows too, but Queen Katherine ignores him and sails on towards the King. As she draws in front of him, she dips her head and clasps her hands to her pearl-studded bodice. 'Your Grace, I would speak with you in private on a matter of great importance.'

King Henry frowns. 'It will have to wait, wife. The cardinal and I have urgent matters of our own to discuss.'

Queen Katherine's lips purse into a tight pink line. 'Begging your pardon, Your Grace, but I am afraid it cannot.'

The King growls and huffs out a breath. 'Very well. Leave us, all of you.' The courtiers sink into more bows and curtseys, then slide off out through the doors until only the Duke of Buckingham and Cardinal Wolsey remain.

Buckingham snaps his fingers at the guards. 'What are you waiting for? Take the prisoner away.'

'No!' Cat throws her arms tight about my waist. 'You cannot take Jack-Bon. He hasn't done anything.' The guards waver, unsure of what to do.

King Henry's frown deepens. 'Is this some kind of jest, Madam?'

The Queen shakes her head and draws closer still. Standing on tiptoe, she cups her hand and whispers something in the King's ear. His eyes widen. He glances at Buckingham, then turns to the guards.

'Let the prisoner go.' They bow and release their grip.

The King draws himself to his full height and

turns to face Buckingham again. 'Your presence is no longer required, my lord.'

The duke's face flushes bright red. His eyes swivel from the King and Queen to me and Cat, then back again. 'But, Majesty—'

'I said, go.'

'Your Grace!' Buckingham gives a quick bow, then snatches his coat about him and strides smartly from the room.

The King waits for the guards to pull the doors shut before he speaks again.

'Now, tell me, what has my kinsman, the Duke of Buckingham, got to do with any of this business? And what, wife –' he casts a suspicious-looking glance over the Queen's head – 'is this rag-tag of maids and monkeys you bring dancing in with you?'

'Patience, husband. All will become clear soon enough.' The Queen gestures for him to sit, then signals to Cat and Meg to come forward.

'Jack-Bon and Pippo too.' Scooping up Pépin's lead, Cat hooks her arm through mine and tugs us along with her.

There's a sudden flash of red as Cardinal Wolsey steps out in front of us, blocking our way with his staff, but the King waves him aside. He turns to the Queen and presses his mouth into a small, tight smile.

'So then, Madam, begin.'

· CHAPTER 32 ·

Isabelle

The King's eyes widen as he listens first to Queen Katherine and then, at her request, to Cat and Meg.

When they have finished, he sits back in his chair and frowns. 'So, you are asking me to believe the words of a poor orphan, a fool and this French –' he stares at me again – 'this French Robin Hood?'

My cheeks flush with sudden anger. 'I am half-English, Your Grace, and Cat Sparrow is no fool. She saved my life and has helped save yours and the Queen's too!' Pépin scrambles up on my shoulder and gives a loud *chee-chee*.

'Less of your impertinence!' The Queen shoots us both a warning look. 'Remember, it is the King of England you address.' She bows to the King. 'Your Grace, this man – William Gobbo – is the same one I had whipped and sent away for causing the disturbance with the bear outside our palace in Greenwich. I suspect this could be the reason he was so ready to act against us.'

The King gives a loud snort. 'That and a bag of gold from my cousin, Lord Buckingham's coffers. At least that is what this boy here claims.'

I want to tell him that he is mistaken. I am not a boy. I am Isabelle Boncoeur. But I hold my tongue. What matters now is getting the King to believe us.

His eyes narrow. 'But what of this other business concerning the maid's so-called royal blood? It is nonsense, of course.' He casts a quick glance at Meg then touches a hand to his own red locks. 'She does not even faintly resemble me. But if, for whatever motive, My Lord Buckingham wanted others to believe such a story, he would need to produce the evidence.'

A sudden thought curls up inside my head. The document! Buckingham told Mortmain he wanted it to – what did he say? – 'prove his case'. What if his purpose for having it forged was to prove Meg's supposed royal blood? It's true the parchment is badly damaged, but still, if I show it to the King – tell him it's meant to be the last testament of a lady called Alys Godwin – he might understand something more from it I cannot . . .

Setting Pépin down, I fish it from the pouch tied round my neck. 'Pardon, Your Majesty, but I have something that might help.' I bow and hold it out to him.

The King's frown deepens. He signals to one of the guards to pass it to him, then opens it out and scans it with a look of growing impatience. But as he reaches the bottom of the page, he pales suddenly, and taking a sharp breath, flutters his eyelids shut.

The Queen steps forwards and touches his sleeve with a look of concern. 'What is it, Your Grace? Are you unwell?'

He flicks his eyes open again. Instead of answering, he gives a small cough and motions for her to step back. Then, folding the parchment into a tight square, he fixes me with a suspicious-looking stare. 'Where did you get this from?'

'The store-room on board ship, Your Majesty – where Mortmain was keeping Meg prisoner. I . . . I think it might be a forgery.'

The King raises an eyebrow. 'A forgery, eh? Was it like this when you found it?'

'No. It . . . it got wet.'

His eyes shrink to two blue points. 'But did you read it before that happened – assuming a boy like you *can* read?'

My face burns with indignation. 'I know my letters, Your Grace.'

'Answer me then, and be quick about it.'

I lick my lips. 'I . . . I only had time to read the first line or two, but it said it is the last testament of a Lady Alys Godwin. As Your Grace can see, it has her signature on it, together with someone called Holy Mother Hildegard.'

'Holy Mother Hildy, yes!' Cat jumps up and down beside me. 'She was the one in charge before Holy Mother Sharp-Tongue.'

Queen Katherine clicks her tongue. 'Shhh, child. You will anger the King.'

I glance back at King Henry, but instead of showing any sign of irritation, he is staring into the space above our heads, a strange wistful look on his face.

Cardinal Wolsey bustles to his side, staff in hand. 'Is something wrong, Majesty?'

The King blinks. 'What? No!' Clearing his throat, he slides the parchment inside his sleeve and turns his gaze back on me. 'I have never heard of this . . . this Alys Godwin before.' He coughs again then pulls back his shoulders and beckons Wolsey closer. 'There is something I would have you do, My Lord Cardinal.'

The two men speak in low voices, then pull apart. The cardinal sweeps into a low bow and hurries out of the hall, the gold crucifix round his neck swinging from side to side.

Cat frowns. 'Where is Candle Woolly going?'

The King's face flushes a fresh shade of red. 'Candle Woolly?'

I exchange a worried glance with Meg. She pulls Cat quickly behind her, but instead of losing his temper, the King throws back his head and gives a loud guffaw.

'I like that. It suits him!' He slaps his thigh, then

his face grows stern again. 'I have asked the cardinal to have my guards search for this Gobbo. If what you and Robin Hood here say is true, a man with an arrow-wound in his leg cannot have gone far.'

I am about to ask about Mortmain, but the Queen gets there before me. 'And the duke's man, Your Grace? He is still at large too.'

'Yes, Mortmain too, though he has a head start and may be more difficult to apprehend. Which leaves our cousin, Buckingham.' The King's nails dig into the wood of his chair as he speaks the duke's name. 'He made it plain he did not like this peace with France, and I have not been deaf to the rumours that he covets my throne. But I never believed he would act against me – until now. Still . . .' He steeples his fingers and frowns. 'We must tread carefully. He is a slippery fish and has powerful allies among the other lords at court. I will instruct the cardinal and his men to dig for more evidence. Until then we must keep our suspicions to ourselves and our powder dry.'

A bubble of hope springs up inside me. 'So . . . so you believe us, Your Grace?'

'I did not say that. Let us wait and see what your friend Gobbo has to say.' His lips tighten again.

The bubble bursts, replaced by a ball of fizzing anger. I want to shout that Gobbo is not my friend and never has been, but before I get the chance, a distant fanfare sounds.

The King stiffens and glances towards the doors. 'Our guests! Guards, remove the prisoner and these others from our view.' He bats a hand at us then stands and offers his arm to the Queen. 'Come, Madam, we must ready ourselves to greet them.' She dips her head and allows him to help her to her seat.

The guards march us off to the far corner of the hall. As we reach it, the doors are flung open and Cardinal Wolsey sails back in followed by the Queen's ladies-in-waiting and a small party of the more important-looking nobles and their wives, though Buckingham is not among them.

Another fanfare sounds. Cat cups her mouth and makes a loud tooting noise. The guard next to her mutters a quick curse and drags her hand back down, but no one else notices. They are all too busy staring at the troop of French guards marching two-by-two into the hall. As the guards come to a stop, each pair draws apart to face one another, eyes straight ahead, halberds resting at their sides.

A man's voice cries, 'Their Majesties, King François and Queen Claude of France!' and a hush descends as two richly dressed figures appear at the doors. The figures pause then, heads held high, they advance slowly between the two lines of guards.

King François is dressed in even greater finery than he was earlier. His blue velvet coat is trimmed with white ermine, and the silk tunic beneath is embroidered with blue-and-gold *fleur-de-lis*, its neck and hem studded with rubies and pearls. Queen Claude limps beside him wearing a shimmering gown of blue and silver silk, her pale hand resting lightly on his outstretched arm.

A group of French noblemen and ladies file in behind and take their places alongside the English courtiers, who recognize them by sweeping into exaggerated bows and curtseys. Cardinal Wolsey glides forwards and bows to King François and Queen Claude, then escorts them to join King Henry and Queen Katherine on top of the platform. As they nod and bow to each other and take their seats, Cat tugs on my sleeve.

'Can we go and see them too?'

The guard next to her bends down and gives her a rough shake. 'Quiet, you.'

'I don't want to be quiet. I am Cat Sparrow and—'

'I said, quiet!' He grabs her round the middle and clamps his hand across her mouth. She twists and turns, but he holds her fast.

Pépin gives a loud screech and bares his teeth. I thrust him at Meg and struggle with the guard, doing my best to prise Cat free. 'Leave her alone, you great bully!'

'What is the meaning of this disturbance?'

I spin round, heart thumping. King Henry is on his feet, but it's not us he's shouting at. A guard is kneeling before him, his helmet clutched under his arm. Cardinal Wolsey puffs over, staff thudding against the carpet and speaks to the man, then approaches the platform and whispers in the King's ear. King Henry frowns. He takes his seat again and leans in close to speak with King François, then straightens and nods to the cardinal.

'Very well. Have him brought in.'

Two more guards appear at the door dragging a scrawny figure in a ripped blue silk shirt and breeches between them. My heart skips a beat. Cat gives a muffled gasp and I know she's recognized him too.

Meg throws me a quick glance. 'Is it him? Gobbo?'

I nod, but before I get the chance to take another look, the cardinal's voice echoes out across the room.

'Bring the boy forward – now!'

· CHAPTER 33 ·

Isabelle

The men guarding us stand to attention. The one nearest me seizes me roughly by the collar and marches me back across the carpeted floor. As I'm shoved down alongside my old enemy, he lifts up his head and stares at me, his eyes out on stalks.

'*You!* But . . . but how—'

Cardinal Wolsey thumps the ground with his staff. 'Silence! William Gobbo, you have been brought here to answer a claim by this boy that you were part of a plot to assassinate their royal majesties, King Henry of England and his beloved queen, Katherine.'

There's a rustle of silk and shocked cries of 'Fie!' and '*C'est pas vrai?*'

The cardinal holds up a hand and the room falls quiet. 'What say you to this charge?'

Gobbo clasps his scabby hands to his chest and bows as low as he can. When he speaks his voice is high and wheedling. 'Please, I beg of you, Your Grace – don't believe this Frenchie's lies. It's him who's the traitor, not me. I . . . I took his arrow in my leg to save your majesties' lives.' He jabs a trembling finger at the bloodstained rag wrapped around his skinny right thigh.

More gasps and mutters echo around us. King Henry frowns back at me. My heart lurches. Surely he doesn't believe Gobbo's lies? Not after all we've told him.

I struggle free of the guard and jump to my feet. 'It is not true, Your Majesty! *He* is the one who is lying.'

Gobbo's eyes shrink to two gleaming slits. 'Where's your proof, Frenchie?'

I swallow hard. Gobbo's right. What proof do I have? I glance at his clothes, but without his *fleur-de-lis* hemmed cloak, there's not even the evidence to say that he's wearing a disguise. And then it dawns on me.

'His knife. The one Mortmain gave him. He told Gobbo it was special.'

The King's frown deepens. 'Special? How?'

'It . . . it had a *fleur-de-lis* on it. He said it was a type given only to the most trusted members of King François's bodyguard.'

King François, who has been listening intently all the while, stiffens at the mention of his name. Before I can explain that the knife was part of Buckingham's plan for laying the blame on the French, he springs to his feet, brown eyes flashing.

'*Mon Dieu!* But what are you saying, boy? That I am somehow responsible for this attempt on my cousin, the King of England's life?'

Fresh cries of horror and outrage ring out all around. The French guards tighten their grip on their weapons. The English ones do the same.

I take a step forwards. '*Non*, please Majesty, that is not what I meant, I—'

King François hesitates, then signals to his guards to stand down. King Henry motions his men to do the same. The two kings speak together in private for a moment, then King François swings round to face me again. 'The knife, it has been found?'

The cardinal turns to Gobbo's guards. 'Well?'

One of them nods. He pulls a small cloth-wrapped bundle from his jerkin and stepping forwards, presents it with a low bow to the French King.

King François unfurls the cloth to reveal a slim-bladed dagger, its handle decorated with the three gold petals of the *fleur-de-lis*. He turns the blade over, examining it more closely then looks up frowning.

'It is true that it has the same appearance as the weapons I give to my bodyguards, but . . .' He taps his top lip with a pale finger and shakes his head.

King Henry gives an impatient-sounding cough. 'What is your meaning, cousin?'

King François draws in a breath. 'At first glance

it could be mistaken for what this man says it is. But my weapons master engraves each blade with the royal salamander, and as you can see –' he tilts the knife towards King Henry – 'this one has no such mark.' He waits for his nod of agreement then, with a loud sniff, hands the knife back to the guard. 'It is a forgery, and a poor one at that.'

Relief rushes through me.

Next to me, Gobbo gives a strangled cry. 'But . . . but I don't understand. The one who gave it me said it would be the thing that made sure the Frenchies were blamed for—' He snaps his mouth shut, eyes filling with sudden panic, but he's said too much already.

Shouts of 'Murderer' and '*Traître*' echo around the room. With a wild look about him, Gobbo twists free of the guards and tries to run. But his injured leg gives way beneath him and he falls crashing to the ground.

As the guards drag Gobbo back up on his knees, King Henry gestures to King François and the two men take their seats again.

'So, cousin, it would appear that I and my beloved Queen owe our lives to one of Your Majesty's loyal subjects.' King Henry dips his head in my direction. 'And as we now have the proof and this devil's confession, we must step up our efforts to find the others involved.' He coughs again and scans the room. 'Pray, where is my noble lord, the

Duke of Buckingham, when I most need him?'

Cardinal Wolsey steps forwards, a look of sharp cunning dancing across his face. 'I understand My Lord Buckingham has been called away on urgent business, Your Grace.'

The King's eyes narrow. 'How unfortunate! But it matters not. We will catch up with him on our return to England. As one of our closest and most loyal kinsmen, I am sure he will be only too ready to lend us his assistance in hunting down the remaining culprits.' He rises to his feet again and steps down to stand in front of me. 'As for you, Robin Hood . . . Or perhaps I should call you Jacques Bonhomme?' He gives me a knowing smile.

My eyes widen. So he *does* recognize me . . . 'Yes, Your Grace?'

'You and your merry band of maids and monkeys are free to go.'

'Yes, Your Grace. Thank you, Your Grace.' I make to dip into a curtsey, but catch myself and turn it into a clumsy bow instead.

Light footsteps sound behind us. I twist round to see Cat tripping towards me across the carpet with Meg and Pépin a few steps behind. As she reaches me, she flings her arms around my waist.

'Jack-Bon! Jack-Bon!'

'*La Sainte Vierge!*' King François jumps to his feet a look of horror on his face. 'But what is the meaning of this?'

King Henry turns to him and frowns. 'Is there something wrong, cousin?'

He jabs a ringed finger at Cat. 'It is her! *Le petit diable* who almost knocked me from my horse!'

King Henry rests a hand on his arm. 'Wait. There is an explanation, cousin. She is not a devil, only the Queen's Fool.'

A voice lifts up behind him. 'No, Your Grace.'

The whole room turns and watches as Queen Katherine steps down from the platform and comes to stand alongside us. 'This French boy is right. She is no fool. She is Cat Sparrow – a brave girl who sees the truth and is not afraid to speak it to anyone – even the greatest lords and ladies in the land.' Raising her hand, she touches it gently to Cat's cheek and smiles.

Cat turns and points to us. 'Jack-Bon and Meg are brave as well. And Pippo too.' She pulls the monkey from her sister's hands and cradles him lovingly against her chest.

As King François's eyes light upon Pépin, the flicker of a smile plays across his lips. He reaches out a finger and tickles the top of his furry grey head.

'I had such a creature once myself. But he was a mischief-maker and kept stealing things, so I gave him to a dear friend of mine instead – a man I trusted with my life, though alas, his own was cruelly taken from him but a few short weeks ago.' His eyes cloud over suddenly.

My throat tightens. 'Do you mean Jacques Boncoeur, Majesty?'

King François's eyebrows shoot up. 'What? Yes! But how do *you* know that?'

My eyes blur. I bite my lip and draw in a breath, but it's no use – the tears are already spilling down my cheeks.

'Because, Majesty, I . . . I am his daughter.'

'His daughter?' He looks me up and down. 'But then why are you dressed as a boy?'

'He's not a boy, he's a girl!' Cat bounces up and down beside me. 'The Sir-John on the ship said he was when he got pulled out from the water.'

'Hush, sister.' Meg slides her arm round Cat's shoulders and pulls her gently to her side.

King François's eyes widen. 'Does your mother know you are here?'

I gulp in another breath. 'No, Majesty. I left home in secret not long after my father . . . After he died. I made a promise to—'

Before I can finish my sentence, there's a fresh disturbance at the doors. Another guard steps in to the hall. He approaches Cardinal Wolsey and speaks with him. The cardinal shares a few hurried words with the two Kings, then nods to the guard who marches swiftly back the way he came. As the royal party returns to their seats, two more guards march into the hall dragging a man in a dusty black cloak and breeches between them. The man's head is covered with a sack – but I don't need to see his face to know who it is. I curl my fingers into two tight balls.

As the guards shove him alongside Gobbo and pull off the sack to reveal the dark, wolfish face beneath, my stomach churns with the familiar mix of loathing and cold fear. I steel myself. I can't falter now. I made a vow to *Papa* and I'm going to keep it, come what may.

I ready myself to accuse him, but Gobbo jumps in instead. 'That's him. The one who gave me the knife. I'd recognize him anywhere.'

King Henry gives a loud snort. 'It would be hard not to when the man has only one eye.'

The sound of laughter echoes around us, but it shrinks into silence again as Cardinal Wolsey steps forwards and pokes the end of his staff into Gobbo's scrawny chest.

'Speak again, traitor, and I'll have you executed on the spot!' He turns to face Mortmain. 'As for you, sir, you stand accused of hiring this man to murder our noble King and Queen. What do you have to say in your defence?'

Mortmain glares at Gobbo, then shifts his glittering green eye to the platform where the Kings and Queens sit looking down in stony silence.

'Your Majesties.' He gives a low bow. 'I have never seen this wretch in my life before, I swear it on the good cardinal's Holy Cross.'

Surprised murmurs ripple around the room. As the Kings and Queens exchange puzzled glances, Cat pushes out in front.

'He did! I saw him. He was chasing after Gobble with his sword-stick when the snake-bird fell from the sky. Then he ran back and I went after to stop him, and he broke my birdy-flute. Look!' She pulls the two pieces of her flute from her bag and holds them high above her head.

'Shut your blabbing mouth, you little—' Mortmain makes a lunge for Cat, but Meg pulls her to safety and the guards rein him back in.

I step alongside her and draw in a breath. 'What Cat says is true, and as Your Majesties know already, I witnessed him pass Gobbo the knife.'

'More lies!' Mortmain spits back at me, but his eye narrows and darts over my face and ripped costume, searching furiously for a clue as to who I might be.

A cold shiver runs through me, but then I hear the voice again.

This is your chance, Hirondelle. Be brave and find your mark.

I grit my teeth. *Papa's* right. I'm not going to be beaten – not this time. I raise myself to my full height and speak loud and clear so that all may hear.

'I am telling the truth, Your Majesties. But this man is not only guilty of plotting to kill the King and Queen. He was also a spy, sent to the French court by his master—' King Henry gives a loud cough. I shoot him a look to reassure him I will not speak Buckingham's name. 'To prevent this meeting from happening and to ruin the peace. But my father discovered what he was up to, so Mortmain killed him to stop him from telling our King.' I turn and bow to King François.

Gasps of shock sound around me. Mortmain makes to speak, but the guards silence him.

King François rises, frowning, from his chair. 'It is true that I received a message from your father shortly before he died. He said he had urgent business he wished to discuss with me on his return to court, though sadly he never got the chance. But these are grave accusations you level at this man, *ma fille*. To say he was the one who took your father's life . . .'

Loose your arrow, Hirondelle . . . Now!

I pull back my shoulders and fix my eyes on Mortmain's glowering face again. 'But I can prove it, Majesty. I was there in the forest the day my father was shot. I didn't see the face of the man who killed him, but I found this torn kerchief not far from where *Papa* fell.' I pull the piece of cloth from my pouch and hold it up so that everyone can see. 'I showed it to Mortmain in the tavern yesterday. He as good as admitted it belonged to him.'

Mortmain starts at the sight of the kerchief, then looks back at me, his eye widening in sudden, shocked recognition. 'The butter-fingered tavern-maid . . . ?'

'Yes.' I fold my arms across my chest. *'And* the boy on the ship that you forced overboard after he stole your precious document.'

The scar on Mortmain's cheek twitches. 'What? But . . . but you drowned. I saw you go under myself.'

A chorus of disapproval echoes around the room.

But I haven't finished yet. 'Most of all, I am Isabelle Boncoeur, daughter of Jacques Boncoeur of the Château de Beauregard – my brave *papa* and the man you shot down in cold blood.' I glare at Mortmain, daring him to speak.

He twists free of the guards and bows down on one knee. 'Majesties, surely you cannot believe the bare-faced lies of this rascal boy, or kitchen-maid – or whoever she is pretending to be now?' He shoots me a look of pure, blood-freezing hatred.

'Enough!' King Henry springs down from the platform and seizes the kerchief from me. As he catches sight of the knotted pattern embroidered into it, his eyes flicker with sudden recognition and his face turns from pale pink to an angry red. Thrusting the kerchief at the cardinal, he strides across to Mortmain, juts his hands on his hips and fixes him with an ice-cold stare. 'The only honest words I have heard spoken are the ones uttered by these brave children. An English maid, and a *jeune fille française*. Thanks to them we have more than enough evidence to satisfy us of your guilt – on both counts.' He slides the battered square of parchment from his coat-sleeve and brandishes it in Mortmain's face.

Mortmain's eye widens. He takes a step back and looks desperately about him, but he's hemmed in by the guards and there's nowhere to go.

The King flashes him a look of cold contempt, then stands back and addresses the room.

'A foul and most treasonous plot to destroy the new peace between our two great nations has, this day, been thwarted.' He exchanges nods with King François and turns to face the room again. 'These two traitors hoped to profit from our deaths. Instead they shall receive the justice they deserve, but only after they have helped us to discover the whole sorry truth. For we have it on good authority' – he tosses me a knowing look – 'that there is more to this villainous business than meets the eye.'

The King motions to the guards and watches on grimly as they march Mortmain and Gobbo away. Then, to the sound of loud cheers and hurrahs, he turns and offers his hand to Queen Katherine. Smiling, she takes hold of it and steps down from the platform to stand at his side. King François and Queen Claude follow, nodding and bowing as they go.

I wrap my arms tight around me and give a shuddering sigh.

I did it, *Papa*. *We* did it.

A cool hand touches my arm. I blink and look up into the blue, shining eyes of Queen Claude.

'*Venez*. The King wishes to speak with you.' She steers me towards where King François is standing a little apart.

'Majesty.' I clutch the hem of my torn tunic and drop into a deep curtsey.

King François puts out a hand and raises me to my feet. 'I see you are blessed with your father's brave heart.' He speaks the words in our own tongue.

My eyes fill with fresh tears. 'But . . . but I'm not brave, Majesty. If I was I would have stopped that man from doing what he did and *Papa* would still be here.'

'Hush, child!' The King nods to Queen Claude who offers me her lace kerchief. 'You are too harsh on yourself. It was a dreadful thing to witness and I am sure that you must have been terribly afraid. But being afraid does not mean you are not brave, as you have so clearly shown. Tell me though, how did you know it was an Englishman who did the deed?'

'I didn't. I thought he was a poacher at first. But the next day *Papa*'s stable-hand, Pierre, told me he'd heard talk of a stranger with an English accent who had taken a room at a nearby inn the night before

Papa was killed. The man kept his face hidden beneath a hood and said little to the innkeeper except that he would be returning to London after some business he had to attend to.' I shiver as I say the words.

Queen Claude takes my hand in hers. 'But did you not tell your mother, child?'

'No.' I gulp back another sob. 'She was overcome with grief and refused to leave her room. I went to the local constable, but he wouldn't listen to me, so . . . so I decided I would have to get justice for *Papa* myself.'

'Well, you have achieved that, there is no doubting it. And I have no doubt either that your father would be very proud of you, Isabelle Boncoeur.' King François flashes me an approving smile, though his eyes are tinged with sadness too. 'When you have made your peace with your mother, you must come and visit us at court. And be sure to bring your best bow with you too.'

I bite my lip. 'I . . . I believe King Henry's guards may have it, Majesty.'

'Is that so?' His brown eyes twinkle back at me. 'Then if we cannot retrieve it for you, I will order my bow-master to make you another. But now we must say our farewells to our hosts and take our leave. Come, my Queen.' Dipping his head, he takes Queen Claude by the arm and steers her back to join the English King and Queen.

A loud *chee-chee* sounds behind me. My heart swoops up. I twist round to see Cat and Meg standing there, their arms wrapped about each other's waists, Pépin dancing at their feet. Before I can say anything, Cat scoops him up and pushes him on to my shoulder, then grabs hold of my hand. 'Can we all go home now, Jack-Bon?'

I smile and lace my fingers through hers. 'Yes, Cat. I think we can.'

· CHAPTER 34 ·

Some weeks later . . .

Cat

I t is pipey-loud in here. The birds are flit-flutter-
ing about, all peeping and cheeping with their
feathers spinning and whirling like snow in the
wind. I skitter-scat the grain on the ground and call to
Pippo, but he is too busy crunching on a nut to listen.

I look round-and-about. I want to let the birds fly
off out of this bird-house and up into the sky, but
then I would be in trouble with The-Lady-Mary's
chief lady-who-waits, so I get on with the scattering
instead.

Then voices sound from over the top of the
garden wall. I peer through the shiny bars and
listen out for who it is, but the birds are too loud in
my ears to hear. I put down the bucket and pick up
Pippo, then I go through the metal door and close it
soft-as-soft behind. When I get closer to the door in
the wall, there's a pitter-pattering of feet and Meg's
voice comes flying over.

'Cat! Cat! There is someone here to see you.'

I frown my face. Is it The King and Queen Catty? No. They come to see The-Lady-Mary, not me. And it isn't Mistress Bristles because Queen Catty sent her away when she found out about her whippy-stick. So I don't know who, but I will soon because here they are, coming in through the door behind Meg.

It is a tall girl in an 'A is for Apple' green gown with soft pink cheeks and brown curled hair. I blink and stop-stare with my heart thud-bumping. Pippo gives a loud chirrup. He bounces down to the ground and runs off towards her.

The girl laughs and gasps and swings him on to her shoulder. 'At least *you* remember me, *mon petit* Pépin!'

And then I really know too.

'Jack-Bon!' I lift my skirts and stumble-run – past the tinkling water-fountain; past the bushes of 'L is for Lavender' and 'R is for Rosemary'; past the stone boy with the bow-and-arrow in his hand. When I get there, I stop and stare again. Jack-Bon stops and stares too. Then she gives another laugh and throws out her arms and hugs me tight-as-tight. After a bit, she holds me back and strokes her fingers over my head.

'So, they have let you grow your beautiful red hair again?'

'Yes. Queen Catty says it is better like that.'

I touch the brown curls hanging down round her face.

Jack-Bon shines me a smile. '*Mais oui*, it is true. Mine is growing back as well. How do you like me?' She lets Pippo down and spins about so her green skirts swish and fly.

'You look belle-and-bootfull. Are . . . are you Isabelle now?'

Jack-Bon's eyes fill with sparkles. 'Yes, but I am still Jack-Bon too.'

I nod my head and hold my arms around me.

Meg shakes me by the sleeve. 'We have another visitor, Cat.'

I turn round and my heart goes even more squeezy-tight, because now Nonny Sweet-Bee is standing there looking back.

After more hugging and telling her and Jack-Bon about how me and Meggy-Peg are staying here with The-Lady-Mary and looking after the birds, we go for a long walk all together in between the flowers and trees. Then Nonny Sweet-Bee tells all about what happened with her and the other nonnies when I went off to find Meg. How Holy Mother Sharp-Tongue went away in the middle of the night without saying anything; how they sent Stewer Boneyface to look for her but he couldn't find her, and then how they made Nonny Sweet-Bee into the Holy Mother instead.

After that, Jack-Bon and Meg tell Nonny

Sweet-Bee all the rest that has happened. They talk about Mort-mane. How he has been made to tell the truth about the Lord Bucket wanting to ass-assinate The King and Queen Catty and blame it on King Franswah, and how Mort-mane was going to kill Gobble with his sword-stick after to keep him quiet and how both of them are now in a deep and dark dunjun and waiting to die. Also how the Lord Bucket is busy keeping out of The King's way, but it won't be long before he is caught and put in a dunjun too.

Jack-Bon stops and frowns her face. 'But there is one thing I still do not understand, Meg. Why did Buckingham believe you were of royal blood?'

Nonny Sweet-Bee gives a small cough. 'He was wrong about Meg. But there is another . . .' She nods her head to me and Pippo.

Jack-Bon's eyebrows go high-as-high.

Meg's do too. 'But . . . but I thought Cat was my sis—?'

Nonny-Sweet Bee does a mouse-quiet sign with her finger, then she holds on to Meg's hand. 'I am sorry, Meg, but for our little bird's protection, Holy Mother Hildegard thought it was safest to pretend you both came from the same family.' She looks across to me again with her eyes all frowny-sad.

I puff a sigh and pull Pippo up on my shoulder. I don't know what they are chit-chattering about, but I am getting hungry after all this talking and walking. I am going to say it, but then Nonny Sweet-Bee starts off again.

'As events have proved, the Holy Mother was right to be fearful of revealing the truth, but I think it is time now to share it with you.' She darts her eyes round-and-about and carries on. 'Before the King came to the throne and was married to Queen Katherine, he became very fond of a young woman. But she was of a lower station in life, and although they were very much in love, as our future king, he would never have been permitted to marry her. When they parted she was with child, though Henry never knew it. The child – a baby girl – was born in secret in our nunnery, but the mother died of a fever soon after childbirth, and Holy Mother Hildegard took the girl in as an orphan.'

Jack-Bon's eyes have gone all owly-wide. 'What was the baby's mother called?'

'Lady Alys Godwin.'

Jack-Bon makes a gasping noise. 'Godwin? But that was one of the names on the parchment I took from Mortmain.'

Nonny Sweet-Bee nods. 'So I understand.'

'But how—'

'One of the King's men paid me a visit to ask about it. Though it was badly damaged, it was clear that Holy Mother Hildegard's signature was a forgery. The man told me Mortmain had confessed to it being a faked version of Lady Alys's will which claimed she and the King – though he was still a prince then – were married in secret a few days before their child was born. A lie of course, but if the Duke of Buckingham had produced it after the King and Queen's death—'

'Then the girl born in the nunnery, and not the Lady Mary, would be first in line to the throne?'

'Hush! Not so loud.' Nonny Sweet-Bee looks round-and-about again.

'But what then?'

'With the help of his friends at court, the duke was going to crown himself King, and marry the girl – King Henry's "true" heir – when she came of age.'

Meg goes all shivery-pale. 'But Buckingham has a wife already! And . . . and what about the poor Lady Mary?'

Nonny Sweet-Bee shakes her head. 'I fear the duke would soon have arranged for the little Princess to meet with some sort of accident. While she was still living, there was too great a danger that Cardinal Wolsey and Buckingham's other enemies at court would have opposed him and tried to claim the throne on the Lady Mary's behalf. And no doubt the duke would have used Mortmain's services to be rid of his wife, the Duchess, too.' She gives a shudder. 'Of course, if you brave girls had not managed to stop the assassination attempt, everyone would also have believed it was the French and not Buckingham who was to blame for their majesties' deaths.'

Jack-Bon's face frowns. 'But how did Buckingham know about Lady Alys and the baby?'

'Holy Mother Hildegard kept it a closely guarded secret, even from King Henry himself. It was only on her deathbed she told Sister Agnes and I about it – and the truth about Cat's real parents. We vowed to her we would keep it secret too. But then, on becoming the new Holy Mother, Sister Agnes turned her face from God and broke that vow . . . '

'Why?'

'As a young woman, she had lived for a while in the duke's household. All I can think is that she gave in to temptation and told the duke in the hope the information might be of use to him and he would offer her a reward.'

'But I do not understand. Why did Mortmain take Meg?'

'Because Meg took her sister's place, isn't that right, Meg?'

Meg flickers me and Pippo a look and nods. 'Holy Mother Agnes sent one of the nuns to fetch "the Sparrow maid" from the herb garden. It is where Cat worked, helping Sister Beatrice tend to the plants and the chickens. But that morning . . . ' she bites on her lip and does a quick shiver, 'I was there too, collecting eggs for the kitchen. The Holy

Mother had a harsh tongue and was always picking on Cat, blaming her for things she didn't do. So I went to see her in Cat's place, hoping to protect her. And then, when I learnt she was going to send Cat away to be a servant, I asked to go instead.' Her eyes go all watery and she puffs a sigh. 'I . . . I couldn't bear to think of Cat all alone in a strange house, with no one to look out for her. But even if I'd known the truth, it wouldn't have made any difference.' She comes and stands side-by-side with me. 'Because we'll always be sisters – and we'll always take care of each other too, won't we, Catty?' She flutters me a smile and squeezes my hand in hers.

I nod my head. I don't know truly what they have all been saying, but Meg is my sister and I won't let anyone take her, ever again.

Nonny Sweet-Bee puffs a sigh too. 'It was very brave of you to do what you did, Meg. If only we'd known the real reason behind Mortmain's visit. But all Holy Mother Agnes would say was that you had gone to work in the household of a great lord in London. Though she knew you were the "wrong" girl, I suspect, understanding what sort of a man Buckingham was, she agreed it would be better for you to go than Cat. Then, perhaps fearful of what might come to pass, she must have decided to disappear with her reward. If the plot had succeeded, I am sure Buckingham would have had her swear the document was genuine and the baby girl born to the King and Lady Alys was the legitimate heir to the throne. Though now . . .' Nonny Sweet-Bee's face goes all shivery-pale, 'if he finds Sister Agnes, he will surely want to silence her, before the King catches up with him.' She does a Holy-Cross sign and sends a prayer-to-God.

Jack-Bon stares back at her. 'So . . . so we are the only ones who know the real story?'

'Yes, and I think it is better that way, don't you?' Nonny Sweet-Bee's eyes dart to me and go all bright and watery.

I push in beside her. 'Don't be sad, Nonny Sweet-Bee?'

'I am not sad, Cat. I am happy.' Nonny Sweet-Bee reaches down with her fingers and strokes me on my cheek.

I am happy too because they have all stopped hubbubbing on about 'true airs' and 'guarding secrets' and other things I do not know about. I pull my new birdy-flute out – the one Queen Catty gave me when we came back to England. I don't need to rattle this one so I blow my blackbird wake-up call loud-as-loud.

Nonny Sweet-Bee wipes at her eyes and beams me a small smile. 'Cat, how would you and Meg like to come back with me to the nunnery and look after my herb garden?'

I tip my head to one side. 'Can Jack-Bon and Pippo come too?'

Jack-Bon swishes down in front of me with her face all crinkled and sad. 'I cannot, Cat. I have to go back to France to help *Maman* look after our lands. But Pépin can, if Holy Mother Beatrice will let him?'

Nonny Sweet-Bee tickles Pippo's chin. He gives a *chee-chee*, but he doesn't bite.

'I think we can find a home for him. Though you had best keep him out of the way of Steward Boniface and his stores.'

Jack-Bon squeezes both my hands in hers. 'And I will come and visit you soon.'

'You will?'

'I promise.' She does a criss-cross sign over her heart. 'And now, I must go or *Maman* will think I have got lost in these grand gardens. *Au revoir*, my dear friends.' She shines Meg a smile and presses her cheek on Pippo's fur. Then she bends in and kisses me soft-as-soft. When she goes back up, her eyes are all watery like Nonny Sweet-Bee's, but I don't say anything, because mine are too.

Nonny Sweet-Bee hugs me tight and says she will go and range-things with The-Lady-Mary's chief lady-who-waits. Then they turn round and walk off, back through the flowers and trees, back past the stone boy and the tinkling fountain, and away into the outside.

When they have gone, I feel in my bag and pull

the thing out that made the rattle inside my old birdy-flute.

'What have you got there?' Meg asks.

I undo my fingers.

She gasps a breath. 'Where did you get it from?'

I peer at the tiny red-and-gold rose which is sparkling and shining fit-to-burst. 'It came out after my birdy-flute got all broken in bits.'

She nods and strokes a finger over it. 'It belonged to your ma, Cat. You must treasure it and keep it safe.' She folds my hand back round it. 'Come on. Let's go back inside.'

When we get close to the bird-house, my stomach does a flit-flutter. 'I want to tell them goodbye.'

'All right, but be quick. We don't want to keep Nonny Sweet-Bee waiting.'

I give her Pippo, then I take out my new birdy-flute again and I open the door and step inside. When I start to blow, the birds swoop round-and-about. They spin and sing, then they whoosh past me, through the wide-open door and off into the outside. I run after and watch them fly up and away into the shiny-bright sky.

Feet pitter-patter and Meg comes hurrying back, her eyes all owly-wide, with Pippo running after. I jump up and down and blow another tune on my flute.

'They are free, Meggy. I have made them all free!'

She stands and looks after for a bit, then she puts

her arms round me and squeezes me tighter-than-tight.

'I love you, my little Catty Sparrow.'

My heart fills so brimmy-full it makes me want to sing and sing.

'I love you too,' I say.

ABOUT THE BOOK

I loved learning about the Tudors when I was at school – especially King Henry VIII and his six wives – and it's been brilliant to be able to revisit the colourful and intrigue-filled world of the Tudor court in telling the story of *The Queen's Fool*.

The book is set just over ten years into King Henry's reign, while he was still happily married to Queen Katherine of Aragon and before he had turned into the cruel, head-chopping tyrant we all know so well. The inspiration for it came from two famous paintings hanging in the magnificent royal palace of Hampton Court near London.

The Field of Cloth of Gold

The first painting shows scenes from one of the great events of King Henry's reign – the so-called 'Field of Cloth of Gold' in the summer of 1520. This was a great meeting between two dashing and athletic young kings, Henry, and the equally charismatic, François I of France, which took place near the town of Calais in what is now northern France between 7th and 24th June. Arranged by Cardinal Wolsey, its object was to celebrate the recently re-negotiated peace and alliance between England and France. In reality, it was also the chance for the kings to demonstrate their power and show off the wealth and magnificence of their courts whilst fostering a sense of mutual respect and friendship between two nations which had been traditional enemies for many years.

The painting, made more than two decades after the event as a piece of royal propaganda, is the artist's impression of what happened during the two-and-a-half-week-long celebration which took place at the site of two purpose-built encampments of tents and pavilions – one French and one English – in the Val Doré or Golden Valley, between the English-owned town of Guînes and the French-owned town of Ardres. Besides the meeting of the two kings in a grand pavilion of richly embroidered cloth of gold – an expensive fabric woven of silk and gold thread – it also featured several days of jousting, tilting and other trials of strength, along with plenty of feasting, music and other entertainments. Both kings were accompanied by their queens – Queen Katherine and Queen Claude – and an estimated retinue of around 6,000 people each. They also brought with them thousands of horses and vast quantities of food, drink and other supplies, including live sheep, cows and birds which were slaughtered, cooked and served at a series of grand banquets.

As it turned out, due to wider tensions in Europe, the peace was short-lived and the two countries were at war again by 1522. But as a piece of political theatre, designed to showcase the power and might of two great Renaissance princes and their nations, it was an undoubted success.

With the grand temporary palace of canvas and glass built to house King Henry and Queen Katherine (called by some the 'Palace of Illusions' and by others the 'Crystal Palace'), the artificial Tree of Honour at the tiltyard entrance, and the great cloth 'town', bigger than many real ones of the day, the unreal, almost make-believe nature of the Field seemed a perfect strange new world in which to plunge my two main characters, Cat Sparrow and 'Jacques Bonhomme'.

Rivals, enemies and intrigues

What the painting of the Field of Cloth of Gold can't portray is the overriding sense of suspicion and paranoia that existed between the English and the French at the time of the meeting. This partly stemmed from the great political and personal rivalry between the two kings. Henry and François were an equal match for each other, both being young, tall, athletic, well-educated and accomplished in music-making and dancing. But it also sprang from the old enmity which existed between England and France. The two countries had been at war for over a hundred years, on and off, between the middle of the fourteenth and fifteenth centuries, and just seven years before Henry had led an army into France and won a victory at the so-called 'Battle of the Spurs'.

Everything at the Field was therefore organized to a strict protocol to ensure absolute equality and to avoid putting either king in a vulnerable position. It was also why the entire event took place in what was considered neutral territory between France and England. Nevertheless, both sides were still fearful of attack and even of a possible royal assassination. While there is no record of such a thing happening, I had fun exploring the idea that it might have, though from a more unexpected source.

The book is set not long after a period of great political turbulence in England, known now as the Wars of the Roses, at a time when the Tudors' future hold on the throne still felt uncertain. Henry and Katherine had a daughter – the Princess Mary – but no son. The King was growing increasingly anxious about the lack of a male heir and was fearful a potential rival with an equally strong claim to the throne might try and overthrow him.

One such man was Edward Stafford, the Duke of Buckingham and Lord High Constable of England. Related by blood to the King, it was widely believed he would succeed him if Henry died without a male heir. Buckingham was a powerful member of the old aristocracy and had great wealth which he wasn't afraid to show off, often to the annoyance of Henry. He owned several large properties and loved to dress in priceless silks, velvets and furs sewn with the family badges, including the Stafford knot. He and the King's chief adviser, Cardinal Thomas Wolsey, Lord Chancellor and Archbishop of York, had a mutual loathing for each other, and Buckingham was opposed to the alliance negotiated by the cardinal with France. He also complained bitterly about the Field of Cloth of Gold – Wolsey's brainchild – and the cost involved in attending it with his large retinue.

While historians believe it is extremely unlikely Buckingham would ever have seriously thought of killing the King and taking the crown, there were rumours that a monk – the duke's religious confessor – had prophesied that Henry would die without sons and Buckingham would become King of England. This is the 'destiny' Buckingham speaks of to his loyal but ruthless retainer and spy, Mortmain, in my story. There were other rumours too, including that the duke had predicted something bad might happen to Henry in France and that he had spoken of kneeling before the King and stabbing him. These came out when Buckingham was arrested and tried for high treason in 1521, a year after the Field of Cloth of Gold, and then executed soon after. However, they are regarded today as part of a conspiracy led by Wolsey to find Buckingham guilty and provide a 'great traitor' to bolster the King's sense of security and demonstrate his determination to reinforce his authority.

Though my own fictional portrait of Buckingham taps into these rumours, in reality historians believe the duke's only likely 'crime' was to speak of a day when he might inherit the throne if the King died young and without a suitable heir.

Fools, maids and monkeys

The second painting that inspired my story is of King Henry, his third wife, Queen Jane Seymour, who gave him his much longed-for son, and his three children – Princess Mary, Princess Elizabeth and Prince Edward – each of whom ruled in their turn after his death. But there are two other people in the portrait too, shown standing in two archways on either side of the royal group. One is believed to be Will Somers, the King's favourite jester or 'fool'. The other shows a young girl believed to be 'Jane the Fool'. Records show that she lived in the households of Henry's second wife, Queen Anne Boleyn, and his sixth and last wife, Queen Katherine Parr, and with Princess Mary too. It is on Jane I have loosely based my own heroine, Cat Sparrow.

So-called 'fools' at court were often 'artificial fools' – clowns who mimicked foolishness. However, there were also people known as 'natural fools' or 'innocents' who were regarded as having some form of deficiency or lack of reason or judgement. Historians have suggested they were probably people with learning difficulties – though that term was not used or recognized then. Jane the Fool is thought to have been such an individual and this is part of Cat's identity too.

Traditionally, so-called 'natural fools' were often objects of fun, ridicule and even fear in wider society. This is something I reflect in the unkind way Cat is treated by certain people. But there was an alternative school of thought, popular at the Tudor court, that such individuals were full of goodness, simplicity and divine wisdom, showing itself in their perceived 'foolishness', which people should take note of.

Besides being appreciated for their talent to help create mirth – a blend of laughter, good cheer, music-making and good company being considered vital for a person's well-being – because their innocence was believed to be a link with God's wisdom, they were also valued for their ability to speak the truth. This meant they were able to say things to their royal patrons that others would never dare to and might even, on occasion, be able to change their minds – something reflected in the role of the fool in many of Shakespeare's plays. Speaking the truth is an important theme in my book and this, plus a natural talent for wordplay and puns – another quality such 'natural fools' were appreciated for at court – is also reflected in my portrayal of Cat.

I have also chosen to depict Cat as being in the care of a 'keeper' – Mistress Bristles as Cat calls her – and shown how, though she was provided with board, lodgings and fine clothes, she also had to wear her head shaved as a mark of her station. Again, this is drawn from the real-life experience of 'fools' at the Tudor court.

In telling Cat's story, I wanted to shine a light on a character in history whose story is not so well known. But I also wanted to celebrate the fact that though her different qualities and skills – her acute sense of hearing and musicality, her joy in birdsong and making friends, and her different way of seeing the world and its truths – might make her more vulnerable in the dark, dangerous world of the court, they are also what make her unique and enable her to achieve things others cannot.

Of course, in addition to her own particular attributes and personality, Cat is a girl, or a 'maid' as girls were called in those days. And maids then had much less freedom than they do today. This is another theme I explore, both in Cat and Meg's sheltered upbringing as poor 'orphlings' in the nunnery and also through my French character, 'Jack-Bon'/Isabelle Boncoeur. Girls like Isabelle were usually married off as young teenagers to seal alliances between noble houses. And if a suitable match couldn't be found, they often ended up going into a convent to live the life of a Holy Sister, or nun. But Isabelle is a little different from her real-life counterparts – something which becomes clear as the story unfolds.

Her companion, Pépin – or Pippo – is special too. Monkeys were a rare sight in Europe at the time my story is set and were usually only found as pets in wealthy households. King Henry brought two monkeys with him to the Field of Cloth of Gold and King François liked them so much he insisted they attend every banquet. There is also a monkey pictured on the shoulder of Will Somer, the King's jester, in the painting at Hampton Court.

After I had imagined Pépin, I was thrilled to come across a monkey in a portrait of Katherine of Aragon too. I like to think he might have been the artist's original inspiration.

A word on knots, badges and emblems
Heraldic signs and symbols on clothes, buildings and other items, were used at both the English and French courts to reinforce ownership and communicate meaning about individuals and their status. I have used these in different ways throughout my story.

They include:

The Tudor Rose – the traditional heraldic emblem of England, which the Tudors used to show the unification of the warring houses of Lancaster (the red rose) and York (the white rose) after the Wars of the Roses. Henry VIII claimed descent from both houses and used it to help reinforce a sense of his heritage and right to rule.

The Pomegranate – Queen Katherine's personal heraldic symbol came from the Spanish house of Aragon. It symbolized fertility and regeneration and the hope of many children for the new King and Queen, though sadly this was not to be.

The Stafford Knot – one of the emblems of Edward Stafford, Duke of Buckingham. This plays a key part in unveiling the identity of the man who killed Isabelle's father.

The Salamander and *Fleur-de-lis* – the Salamander – a lizard-like amphibian – was the personal emblem of King François. The *fleur-de-lis* is the emblem of the French monarchy. They are both linked to the story behind the dagger which Mortmain supplies to Gobbo for use when he makes his attempt on the King and Queen's lives.

The Dragon – the symbol of the Tudors, which appears in the story on King Henry's temporary palace at the Field of Cloth of Gold, and also in the form of the flying monster kite.

The Queen's Fool is set in a real time and place and, where I can, I have tried to make it as authentic as possible. The descriptions of Greenwich Palace, the sea voyage from Dover to Calais and the camp at the Field of Cloth of Gold are as accurate as I can make them based on written and visual evidence. Many events in my fictional account of the meeting of the two kings did actually take place. For example the storm and the strange and unexpected appearance of the great dragon kite-firework near the end of the festivities.

But my main intention has been to tell as dramatic and exciting a story as possible. So I have also taken a few liberties – especially with timings, the actions of real-life personalities and some of the actual events. For example, in the book, the scenes at the Field take place over a couple of days rather than the much longer period of more than a fortnight which the real event lasted for. In addition, the kings did not say their farewells at a final grand meeting at King Henry's cloth-and-glass palace, but rather at the tiltyard. It is most likely too that Henry and François would have spoken French to each other rather than English. And of course, the interruption of the joust by a certain young maid and her monkey and the attempted assassination scene are also my inventions.

Finally, though it is well-known Henry had a number of illegitimate children, including a son called Henry Fitzroy, the secret relationship with Lady Alys Godwin is the product of my novelist's imagination – until any evidence is found to prove it otherwise!

More information

View the paintings that inspired the story:
The Family of Henry VIII (c. 1545)
rct.uk/collection/search#/15/collection/
405796/the-family-of-henry-viii
The Field of Cloth of Gold (c. 1545)
rct.uk/collection/search#/1/collection/
405794/the-field-of-the-cloth-of-gold

Also:
The Embarkation of Henry VIII at Dover (c.1520-40)
rct.uk/collection/search#/1/collection/405793/
the-embarkation-of-henry-viii-at-dover

Read:
allthekingsfools.co.uk – an excellent website covering a project at Hampton Court Palace to stage a performance about the lives of jesters with learning difficulties, or 'natural fools', at the court of King Henry VIII. Written and performed by a company of actors with learning difficulties called The Misfits.

Henry VIII: 500 Facts by Suzannah Lipscomb, Brett Dolman, Lee Prosser, David Souden and Lucy Worsley. Edited by Sarah Kilby (Historic Royal Palaces, 2009).

Life in Tudor England by Peter Brimacombe (Pitkin Publishing, 2002) – a good, brief, introductory guide to life at the time my story is set.

The Field of Cloth of Gold by Glenn Richardson (Yale University Press, 2013) – a comprehensive account of the event and its wider significance.

The Last White Rose: The Secret Wars of the Tudors by Desmond Seward (Constable, 2010) – includes a fascinating portrayal of Henry VIII's relationship with the Duke of Buckingham and how the duke came to be executed for high treason.

Places to visit:

Hampton Court Palace, Hampton Court, Surrey – Tudor royal palace built by Cardinal Thomas Wolsey and later owned by King Henry VIII. It gives a good impression of what Henry's royal palace at Greenwich – the remains of which lie beneath the Old Royal Naval College – would have looked like.

hrp.org.uk/hampton-court-palace

Information about **Greenwich Palace** is available from:

rmg.co.uk/discover/explore/greenwich-and-tudors

The Mary Rose – The preserved remains of the wreck of King Henry VIII's royal flagship discovered in the Solent off the southern coast of England in 1982. The fascinating museum at Portsmouth Historic Dockyard gives a vivid sense of life on board a Tudor ship.

maryrose.org

There are plenty of other historic Tudor properties open to the public, many, though not all, owned by **English Heritage**
english-heritage.org.uk
and **The National Trust**
nationaltrust.org.uk

ACKNOWLEDGEMENTS

A book starts life a bit like a small, precious egg. The author has the original idea and then does their best to keep it warm with plenty of imagination, research and determination so the chick inside has a chance to develop, hatch and fly the nest. But like every author, I am also very fortunate to have had the help of a whole skyful of bright and beautiful birds in the hatching of my story.

Nicola Grove, retired speech and language therapist and founder of Openstorytellers (www.open storytellers.org.uk) supplied me with much wise counsel when I was starting out on my journey to explore the voice of my heroine, Cat Sparrow. I'd also like to thank her for reading a later version of the manuscript and for providing invaluable observations and advice both on Cat's use of language and elements of the wider story. Thank you too to my friend and fellow writer, Lizzie Bryant, for introducing us.

If Cat lived in our time she would likely be regarded as a person with learning difficulties. But in Tudor times, when literacy levels were very low (most people couldn't read and write) and medical and social understanding of such issues was so different from today, such a term would not have been used or recognized. Instead, as I mention in the notes about the book, Cat is more likely to have been regarded as an 'innocent' or 'holy fool'. To breathe life into her, I took my early inspiration from the suggestion in an interview on the National Geographic website from American journalist and author, Jennifer Latson that so-called 'fools' at medieval courts – valued for their storytelling skills, their wordplay ability and their humour – share similar traits to people with the rare genetic condition known today as Williams syndrome (WS). Besides distinctive physical characteristics and a number of health-related concerns and developmental delays, people with WS also display a range of learning difficulties and a very strong desire to connect with others. Other common attributes include a heightened sensitivity to noise and a strong affinity to music. Following on from the interview, I read Latson's *The boy who loved too much*, a fascinating account of her friendship with a young boy with WS and his mother, to help me in laying the foundations for Cat's character.

In addition, I accessed many inspirational and extremely useful interviews (both written and filmed) with individuals with WS on both the Williams Syndrome Foundation (UK) (williams-syndrome. org.uk) and the Williams Syndrome Association (US) (williams-syndrome.org) websites.

There are degrees of disability with WS just as there are with so many other conditions, and no two people with WS, like anyone else, are the same. And there is a balance that needs to be struck too, when writing a book for young people, between providing a fully fledged representation of a character with a learning disabled voice and the readability and accessibility of the story. It is in this spirit that I have created Cat – a person I hope readers will understand and empathize with as someone with her own unique talents, skills and vulnerabilities which enable her and the others she loves to find their voices and fly.

From an historical perspective, I gleaned invaluable learning about the role of 'innocents' from the brilliant Wellcome Trust-funded research project and collaboration between historian, Professor Suzannah Lipscomb, Hampton Court Palace, Past Pleasures, The Misfits Theatre Company and others on the *All the King's Fools* project (allthekingsfools.co.uk) which showcases the lives of jesters with learning difficulties at the court of Henry VIII.

To build the world my characters inhabit, besides referring to the portraits which provided the original inspiration for *The Queen's Fool* (mentioned in the 'About the Book' section), I also drew on a number of eye-witness accounts of the Field of Cloth of Gold and more recent studies by historians of life at the Tudor Court. As the book is a work of historical fiction, I hope I will be forgiven for taking certain liberties in the interests of telling a good story, and of course, all errors and inaccuracies are my own.

My heartfelt thanks are also due to Barry Cunningham and everyone at the wonderful story-incubator extraordinaire that is Chicken House. Over the past twenty years since its founding, the team in 'the Coop' has hatched brood after brood of brilliant children's books. It was thanks to an early conversation with Barry, Kesia Lupo and Rachel Leyshon, after I'd submitted a first outline for the story to them, that I was inspired to stretch my own wings and set off in a slightly different direction with my interpretation of Cat's character.

I also feel very blessed to have Kesia as my editor again. Her insights and clear-eyed vision have been invaluable in helping grow and shape my story to realize its full potential. Grateful thanks are also due to Esther Waller and Sue Cook for their keen eyes and ears during the copy-edit stage, and to Rachel Hickman, Jazz Bartlett Love, Elinor Bagenal and Laura Smythe for their hard work and flair in giving Cat and co. the best possible launching pad. The cover, by Georgie McAusland, is gorgeous and I'm so grateful to her, to Rachel H. and to Helen Crawford-White for the work they've done to capture so perfectly the colour and feel of my story. And thank you to Charlotte Norman for saving my blushes and correcting my French where it was needed.

A massive thank you as well to all my friends (you know who you are) and to my family who have been so supportive of this new story from the off.

My biggest champion of all has been my lovely husband, Steve, who listened to my first peepings and cheepings about Cat and friends all that time ago and came up with a number of brilliant suggestions for where I might take them – including to France. And he has been there every step of the way since, providing encouragement and advice in abundance, plus the all-important sanity checks when I've needed them too. Thank you! You are my safe harbour and my best friend.

And finally to you, dear reader. Thank you for buying, or borrowing, this book. I hope you have enjoyed reading my tale of finding your voice and taking flight as much as I have enjoyed writing it.

BLACK POWDER by ALLY SHERRICK

England, 1605

Twelve-year-old Tom is in a terrifying race against time to save his father from the hangman's noose. In desperation, he makes a deal with a fearsome scarred stranger, known only as the Falcon. But what's really at stake in this murky world of plotting and gunpowder? Tom must rely on his wits and courage, as his loyalty is put to the ultimate test . . .

> This historical tale is steeped in intrigue, mystery and danger.
> BOOKTRUST

> . . . a wonderfully explosive adventure . . . I loved reading about (and rooting for) Tom, though I have to admit developing a rival soft spot for his mouse.
> JULIA GOLDING

Paperback, ISBN 978-1-910655-26-9, £6.99 • ebook, ISBN 978-1-910655-65-8, £6.99

THE BURIED CROWN by ALLY SHERRICK

He Who Has The Crown Has The Kingdom

It's World War II and Britain is on the brink of invasion. Londoner George has been sent to live in the countryside, but he's very far from safe. A priceless Anglo–Saxon crown has been unearthed, and George is plunged into danger. It seems it's up to him – and Kitty, the granddaughter of a Jewish archaeologist – to protect the crown from Nazi invaders before it's too late . . .

. . . a stunning historical story, embroiled in magic, myth and legend.
THE PHOENIX

This fast-paced adventure zips along, with chapters that often end on exciting cliffhangers.
BOOKTRUST

Paperback, ISBN 978-1-910655-32-0, £6.99 • ebook, ISBN 978-1-911077-61-9, £6.99

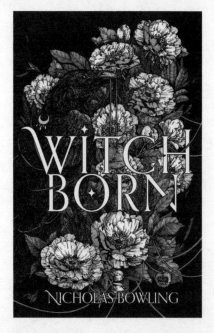

WITCHBORN by NICHOLAS BOWLING

Alyce is in Bedlam asylum – mad, they say. Her mother has been executed for witchcraft, her home destroyed and her spirit crushed ... so maybe it's true.

Or maybe she isn't as broken as she seems.

A visit from two masked strangers provides an opportunity to escape – and Alyce takes it. Now she must navigate the dark streets of London where there's a secret waiting to be unravelled. In an England divided by rival queens, it seems Alyce has a part to play – if only she can master the rising power within her ...

. . . [a] beautifully written Elizabethan fantasy that crackles with scholarship . . . Nicholas Bowling is a thrilling writer, who keeps the reader permanently on edge..
THE TELEGRAPH

Paperback, ISBN 978-1-911077-25-1, £6.99 • ebook, ISBN 978-1-911077-26-8, £6.99